The making o
Texas to Kansas, ught a legacy
of vengeance.

## SUDDEN westerns by Oliver Strange

Sudden—Outlawed
Sudden
The Marshal of Lawless
Sudden—Goldseeker
Sudden Rides Again
Sudden Takes the Trail
Sudden Makes War
Sudden Plays a Hand
The Range Robbers
The Law o' the Lariat

## Publisher's Note

Hachette India is delighted to bring back into print the original Sudden series by Oliver Strange as part of its revival of popular fiction.

The first Sudden books were first published in the 1930s and were hugely popular because of the period details and the rather iconic character of the eponymous hero. So much so that, like other hugely popular series of the day (P.G. Wodehouse or the 'yellowbacks' in the crime-thriller genre), the books were written to a formula. These books about cowboys but written by British writers were called Piccadilly Westerns. The plots have repetitive elements and the characters too have a formulaic sameness, but the fast-paced storytelling, the Western landscape, the laconic one-liners and the 'lightning draw' gunfight sequences combine to create addictive page-turners.

The books have been reprinted as is, with no bowdlerizing for political correctness. As one critic points out, 'The language used is a product of the times and if there is any message to Sudden it is one of anti-racism. The character is respectful to Indians; indeed was brought up by one. In fact the books portray racism on the part of any character as bad and undesirable.'

We've numbered the series in keeping with the plot chronology, but *The Range Robbers* was actually the first book written, and the rest of the novels were back-story adventures. The series was so successful that after Strange's death, they were continued by acclaimed Western writer Fred Nolan (creator of the Angel series), writing as Frederick H. Christian. Christian wrote five more books.

Oliver Strange

# Sudden Outlawed

hachette
INDIA

Originally published in 1935 by George Newnes Ltd.
This edition published in 2013 by Hachette India
(Registered name: Hachette Book Publishing India Pvt. Ltd)
An Hachette UK company
www.hachetteindia.com

1



ISBN 978-93-5009-676-5

Hachette Book Publishing India Pvt. Ltd
4th & 5th Floors, Corporate Centre,
Plot No. 94, Sector 44, Gurgaon - 122003, India

Typeset in Bembo 11/13.75 pt
by Innov Technologies, Chennai

Printed and bound in India by
Bhavish Graphics, Chennai

TO

MY BROTHER

THE LATE LT.-COL. E. F. STRANGE, C.B.E.

# Chapter 1

"I'm pretty near down to my last chip, son, an' before I get outa the game there's somethin' I wanta say."

The voice was weak, little more than a whisper, and the breath came with difficulty from the speaker's labouring lungs. Out of the gaunt, angular face, deeply graven with lines of suffering, hard eyes rested approvingly upon the youth who, with downcast head, stood beside the bed. Tall, slim, and supple, wide-shouldered and narrow-hipped, strength showed in every line of him. In his eyes lay a deep-seated misery.

"I've allus had the name for a square shooter, but I ain't done right by yu, Jim," the sick man went on. "There won't be nothin' for yu—but a debt to two men."

"Yu've been mighty good to me," the boy muttered, and despite his iron effort for control there was a quaver in his voice.

The other was silent awhile, fighting for breath, and then. "Peterson stole my li'l gal an' broke my heart," he said slowly. "An' when yu was East, gettin' some larnin', that houn' Webb stripped me." His voice was harsh, pregnant with passion; hatred gave him a last spasm of strength. "Yo're the fastest fella with a gun I ever see, an' I've knowed some o' the best; I'm leavin' them two skunks to yu."

The younger man's bronzed face remained impassive as a redskin's, save that the muscles of the square jaw firmed up and the grey-blue eyes became icy.

"I'll get 'em," he promised, and this time there was no tremor in the low vibrant voice.

A gleam of fierce satisfaction flitted over the pallid features of the dying man and then his head sagged sideways. The boy just caught the whispered words, "S'long—Jim."

For a moment he stood dazed, hardly realizing that all was over. Death he had seen before, but not in this guise. Now, as he looked down upon the stark form of the man who had been his only friend, a convulsive sob tore at his throat. Gently he drew up the sheet to cover the glazed expressionless eyes, and went out.

Seated on a bench in front of the ranch-house, he mechanically rolled and lighted a cigarette, his mind delving into the past. He saw himself, a half-starved, lanky lad, parentless, nameless, friendless, practically the property of an old Piute brave, travelling the country with a band of ponies. How he had come to be with them he had never learned, but he knew that he was white—the Indian woman had once told him as much, after a successful sale when her lord and master became drunk before the fire-water was finished, an unusual occurrence of which she promptly took advantage. The nomad life toughened the boy, gave him selfreliance, and the ability to stay on the back of anything that wore hair. He was not unhappy, for the Indian couple were kind enough when sober. And he loved the horses.

With the advent of Bill Evesham had come a complete change, for the kindly-faced, lonely rancher took a fancy to the boy and bought him, together with a string of ponies, from the Indian horse-trader. So Jim—Evesham called him that—had come to the ranch at Crawling Creek. The ensuing years were happy ones. He acquired some rudiments of knowledge at a school fifteen miles distant, and learned the cattle business. Then Evesham sent him East to complete his education and for nearly two years he paid only flying visits to the ranch. He had returned finally a few months ago to find his benefactor ailing and broken, a glum, dispirited man who remained obstinately silent respecting his troubles.

"Things ain't gone none too well, Jim, an' I've had to sell stock," was his grudging explanation when the young man remarked on the depleted herds.

"Yu should 'a' fetched me back—I've been spendin' coin yu couldn't afford," Jim had protested.

"Shucks! Had to give yu yore chance. We'll make the grade," the rancher had replied.

But although Jim had applied himself whole-heartedly to work on the range, matters did not improve, and the cattleman's failing health proved a heavy handicap. One by one the few remaining riders had drifted until only Limpy, a disabled cowboy who acted as cook, and Jim, were left. And now.... A halting step on the porch aroused him.

"Jim, he's—gone," Limpy announced in a shocked voice.

The boy nodded miserably. The older man put a hand on his shoulder.

"I'm powerful sorry," he said. "Bill was a good fella—one o' the best I ever knowed. 'S'pose the place'll be yores now?"

Jim shook his head. "Reckon not, Limpy," he replied. "I figure the ranch is pretty well hawg-tied. I expect I'll be ridin'."

* * *

The following afternoon found Jim again on the porch seat, brooding, restless, his eyes on the blue mountains which rimmed the horizon and hemmed in the broad undulating stretches of sunscorched grass. Though he had seen Evesham buried that morning, he still found it difficult to believe that the man who had been all the father he had ever known was gone.

Presently a tiny blot appeared on the trail to town, gradually growing in size until it became a rider, jog-trotting leisurely towards the ranch. The visitor proved to be a short, stout man of more than middle age, dressed in rusty black, and obviously ill at ease in the saddle. He got down clumsily, tied his mount to the hitch-rail, and mopped his moist face.

"Damn hosses anyway," he complained. "Why didn't the A'mighty give us wings?"

Despite his sadness, a glint of a smile wrinkled the corners of the young man's mouth as he tried to vision the stumpy form of the speaker flapping its way through the air.

"Yu'll get 'em in the next world, Pyke—mebbe," he said, sardonically, adding, "There's liquor inside."

Pyke shook his head. "On'y makes yu hotter," he said, and plumped himself down on the bench.

Neither spoke for a while. The visitor filled and lighted a pipe and the other constructed a cigarette. Pyke did not seem in a hurry to open the conversation, and Jim sensed the reason. He had seen him at the little cemetery in the morning and had noticed his constraint.

"Well, o'-timer, spill the beans," he said quietly. "Come to tell me to pull my freight, huh?"

Pyke looked still more uncomfortable. "Hell, no, Jim," he protested. "Stay as long as yu've a mind to, but——" He paused awkwardly and then went on with a rush. "Pore ol' Bill owed a lot o' coin an' thisyer ranch is all there is to show for it. Won't cover the debt nohow; he didn't own more'n a section o' the land, an' if what I've heard is correct, he's been losin' cattle, so ..."

"There'll be no pickin's for me," the young man helped him out. "I knowed that a'ready."

"Yu see, Jim, I ain't alone in this," Pyke said hastily. "Two—three of us chipped in to tide Bill over. If it was just me I'd be willin' to let the debt run, but——"

The other smiled sombrely. "Yu don't have to tell me," he replied. "What's come o' Webb?"

"Ain't a notion," was the answer. "He faded 'bout the time yu was due to get back. Never liked the fella m'self but Bill trusted him—too much, I reckon."

Jim nodded a gloomy acquiescence. He had seen the man on the last of his brief visits from the East, and recalled him as big-built, red-headed, and something of a blustering bully. Evesham had made him foreman, and with increasing ill-health, had left things largely in his hands.

"I didn't oughta gone away," he muttered, voicing an everpresent regret.

"He was dead sot on yore goin'," the elder man consoled. "What yu aimin' to do, Jim?"

"I've got a job," came the instant reply, rasped out through clenched teeth.

Pyke's mild gaze noted the set, out-thrust jaw, the frosty gleam in the grey-blue eyes, and shook his head as he guessed the boy's intention.

"She's a large country," he offered. "Now, I was thinkin' we'll want someone here to run the ranch...."

Jim stood up. "It's mighty kind o' yu, Pyke but..." He looked at the familiar scene. "No, I couldn't stand it—without—him," he said. "I reckon I'll scratch gravel."

"Well, chew it over—there's no hurry," Pyke told him, as he climbed into his saddle.

The young man's smile was tight-lipped. "I'll be away early in the mornin'," he said. "Mebbe I'll be back—some day "

There was a finality in his tone which conveyed that further argument would be futile. Pyke had no more to say; the West held that "a man must skin his own meat," and advice, unless plainly asked for, was seldom offered. So, with a nod of farewell, he rode away.

Jim watched the visitor dwindle to a mere speck and vanish where the trail dipped into a hollow, but he was not thinking of Pyke; his mind was milling over the last few days. For the first time he had had the bitter experience of standing helplessly by while a dear one passed over the Big Divide, and now—as at the time—the thought of his impotence filled him with a blind, unreasoning rage, the rebellion of youth and strength against the immutable law of Nature. There was nothing he could have done then, but there was something he could do—now.

"Peterson and Webb."

He murmured the names, his face a grim threat; his hands flashed to his hips, the black-handled guns leapt out, a staccato stream of crashes shattered the stillness, and a tall weed, twenty paces distant on the edge of the trail, dissolved into fragments before a hail of lead. From inside the ranch-house came a scurry of clumsy footsteps and Limpy appeared in the doorway carrying a rifle.

"What th' blazes, Jim ?" he began. His darting eyes took in the lounging figure on the bench, the smoking guns, and the stricken target. "Thought it was Injuns, or some o' them Mex raiders."

"Just me, lettin' off steam," the other explained. "Wanted to see if I'd got rusty, but I reckon if that'd been a man...." He nodded at the weed.

"He'd shore be hittin' the high spots for hell," the cook said, and then, curiously, "Did yu have a particular fella in mind, Jim?"

The answer took the form of a question. "Any idea where that chap Webb went?"

The lame man's eyes narrowed. "Wish I had, the buzzard," he growled. "But for him, Bill wouldn't have ..." He paused as the significance of the query dawned upon him. "Yu ain't stayin' then?"

"I hit the trail in the mornin'," was the reply.

"Good huntin'," was all Limpy said, and went in to prepare the evening meal.

Jim reloaded his empty weapons and thrust them back into the holsters. His spate of anger was past, leaving only a cold determination. He had to find two men, only one of whom he had seen, and such is the optimism of youth, the magnitude of the task did not daunt him. Even had he known of the years which were to elapse ere he would fulfil his promise to the dead man it would have made no difference; his early life had endowed him with much of the redskin's patience and relentlessness. This strange quest, which set him drifting in a wild, lawless land, flung him headlong into many perilous adventures, with one of which this story deals.

# Chapter 2

The rider was talking to his horse.

"We gotta have a label, Nig—Evesham won't do nohow."

He looked meditatively at the broad rolling prairie which stretched away on each side of the rough trail he was following, a monstrous expanse of sun-baked, brown grass.

"Green is a good name, kind o' refreshin', nothin' fancy nor outstandin'. Jim Green o'Texas shore listens well, huh?"

The big black, pacing demurely along, tossed its head as though in agreement and his master patted the sleek neck.

"Good," he said. "Settles me, but yu ain't got no brand a-tall, an' that'll mean trouble with a large T."

He got down, trailed the reins, and stroked the satiny muzzle thrust inquiringly towards a pocket. He produced a biscuit, which the horse daintily accepted.

"Now be a good fella," the rider admonished. "This ain't goin' to hurt like an iron."

With a knife-blade held against his thumb he plucked the hair from the skin on the animal's rump, and, in time, produced a creditable J G brand. Surveying his work, he decided that it would serve, though an expert would not be deceived. He resumed his journey.

"Looks like we might be gettin' some place," he remarked presently.

The trail was broadening out, and as they topped a billow in the surface of the plain a huddle of black blotches, from a few of which spirals of smoke twisted into the clear sky, came into view.

"Must be what that joker we met called the 'pop'lar an' progressive township o' Fourways," the traveller soliloquized. "She don't appear to have progressed very far."

The criticism was justified. Two irregular rows of habitations formed some sort of a street, the surface of which was a hoofscored, wheel-rutted desert of dust. The better of the buildings, the stores and saloons, were constructed of timber or 'dobe; the dwelling-places, for the most part, were mere shacks with earthcovered roofs. Save for a few citizens lolling beneath the board awning of the largest saloon, the place appeared to be deserted. The newcomer deciphered the weather-scarred sign, and surveyed the lounging group with a fleeting smile.

"The Early Bird," he murmured. "An' some o' the worms waitin' to be catched."

Dropping from his saddle he stepped into the saloon. After the fierce glare without, it was comparatively cool and dark inside. As he advanced, a short figure rose from behind the bar, stretched lazily, and rubbed half-open eyes.

" 'Lo, Jud. Back again?" Then, as the stranger neared him, he added, "Sorry. Took yu for another fella."

"I shorely hope he's good-lookin'," the customer grinned, and spun a coin on the counter.

"Well, that's as maybe, but no woman ain't grabbed him yet," the saloon-keeper laughed.

He pushed forward a bottle and glass, accepted an invitation to help himself, and deftly tossed a three-finger dose of spirit down his capacious throat.

"Town seems quiet," the visitor offered.

"Too blamed hot," the other explained. "Come back in a coupla hours, if yo're aimin' to stay, an' yu'll see some action."

The remark was as much of a question as politeness permitted; the stranger answered it in part only.

"I'm huntin' a meal an' a bed," he said.

"Yu'll find both at the hotel a piece along," he was told.

The customer nodded his thanks. "Reckon I'll go chase that chuck right now," he smiled. "My belly an' my backbone is shore gettin' acquainted. See yu later—I expect."

The saloon-keeper's gaze followed him speculatively, noting the long, easy stride and the swing of the wide shoulders.

"Two guns an' wears 'em low," he commented. "I'd say they ain't just ornaments neither."

Jim found the "hotel"—a shrivelled log and shake edifice which had the distinction of possessing the only second storey in the town. Having put his mount in the corral, he carried his saddle into the building. A slatternly woman showed to one of the bedrooms and went to prepare food.

Two hours later, having fed and "slicked himself up," he was again in the Early Bird. As its proprietor had predicted, the scene was very different. The harsh light of large kerosene lamps shone down upon about a score of men, some lined up at the bar, others gambling at the tables which occupied part of the space in front of it. Every few moments the door swung back to admit additions to the company. The rattle of poker chips and dice, strange oaths, and occasional raucous laughter punctuated the incessant hum of voices.

Squinting through the blue haze of tobacco smoke the man from Crawling Creek studied the company. Apart from casual glances, no one took any notice of him—strangers were hardly a novelty in Fourways, and curiosity a dangerous commodity, liable to be resented. One man only looked him over keenly and turned away, apparently satisfied. This was a dumpy, bulbous-faced fellow with a big paunch and a strut suggestive of an over-fed turkey. From the somewhat ironic deference accorded him and the fact that he paid for no liquor, Jim deduced that he held a post of importance, and this was soon confirmed.

"Where's Jud ?" the fat man asked.

"Ain't a notion, sheriff," the saloon-keeper replied. "Should 'a bin back hours ago. He warn't——"

He stopped, mouth and eyes opening as the swing-door jerked wide and a man staggered in, flung his arms out, and pitched forward on the sanded floor. Mallick, the sheriff, hurried to the prone figure.

"By God, it's Jud hisself!" he cried. "What the hell ...?"

Others sprang to help and the senseless man was lifted to a chair. One of them looked at his hand in surprise; it was smeared with blood. He snatched aside the open vest, disclosing an ominous patch of red on the coarse woollen shirt front.

"He's bin drilled!" he cried.

Astonishment, expressed in lurid language, greeted the statement, and the excited onlookers, eager to get a sight of the wounded man, crowded in and threatened to engulf him. The sheriff, feeling for a fluttering pulse, looked up and cursed them savagely.

"Satan burn yu," he snapped. "Stand back an' give him a chanct, he ain't cashed yet. Gimme some liquor."

The circled widened and the saloon-keeper brought a glass of whisky. Mallick tilted back the hurt man's head and administered a stiff dose. The fiery spirit took effect. Jim, who had helped with the lifting, saw the pale lips move and caught the whispered words:

"Bushwhacked me—one man—waitin' in th' chaparral." He paused, and then, "On'y 'nother—mile—bronc. Guess—we can—make it."

His mind was wandering, living over again those terrible hours during which, hurt to death, he had clung to the back of his horse and paced the long, long miles which lay between him and help. Then out of the pain-drawn face, sickly grey under the tan, a gleam of recognition flashed from the heavy-lidded eyes as they met those of Jim.

"I saw—that fella—on the trail. He ..." The voice faded out and the speaker's head fell forward.

"He's gone," someone said.

"He ain't. Carry him to the hotel an' fetch the doc," Mallick replied. "I got suthin' to see to."

Four men picked up the chair and its burden, while another held open the door. When they had gone the sheriff turned abruptly to Jim, an ugly look in his eyes. For a moment there was silence, and then:

"Yu heard him," the officer rasped, jerking a thumb in the direction of the door. "What yu gotta say?"

"I met that hombre this afternoon, 'bout twelve miles out on my way here," Jim explained. "I asked him if I was on the right road for Fourways, an' mentioned that I aimed to spend the night there. He took a shine to my hoss an' wanted to trade, but I told him there was nothin' doin'. He said he was comin' back hisself in a coupla hours an' he'd talk to me again this evenin'. That's all I know."

The sheriff's sneer deepened. "He didn't say he was goin' to collect two thousand bucks for cattle he'd sold, huh ?"

"No. Would he be likely to tell a stranger his business ?"

"Mebbe. Jud was allus a trustful kind o' cuss. I'm sayin' he did, an' that yu laid for him, an' helped yoreself."

The accused man shrugged his shoulders. "If yu can find that amount o' coin on me ..."

"I ain't expectin' to," Mallick cut in. "Yu wouldn't be such a damn fool as to tote it round with yu."

'An' I wouldn't be such a damn fool as to come here a-tall," the young man retorted hotly.

"Shucks, yu figured him cashed, an' that trail ain't used much," the other countered. He turned as the door swung back to admit a tall, cadaverous man whose bent shoulders were encased in a long, shabby black coat. "How's yore patient, doc?"

"He's powerful bad," replied the man of medicine,

grabbing the glass the saloon-keeper pushed out. "I'm afraid Jud is peekin' through the pearly gates right now."

A growl of anger from those present greeted the news and the sheriff's mean eyes shifted to the stranger.

"That settles it, young fella," he said. "I'm holdin' yu, an' if Jud ain't able to clear yu in the mornin'..." The unfinished sentence was charged with menace. "Take his hardware," he added.

Jim's glance swept swiftly over the company and read the grim faces. If Jud died—and he was not too sure they would even wait for that—he was doomed to a shameful end. The odds were impossible, but if he must die, it should be fighting. He had a shrewd suspicion that the sheriff did not care whether he was guilty—he wanted a victim. Well, he would get one, but not easily.

In obedience to Mallick's order, two of the bystanders stepped forward and reached for the weapons. Instantly the motionless figure came to life, the hanging fists shot out right and left, and the unsuspecting men went down as though struck by lightning. With a bellow of rage the sheriff snatched out his gun, only to drop it and clutch his right wrist in agony as a bullet smashed it. For though no man saw how it came about, both the stranger's Colts were out and spitting lead. Through the swirling smoke they got a glimpse of him, his young face tense and savage, his guns held at a hip level.

"Come on, yu curs," he taunted, and sent a shot crashing into one of the lamps.

The invitation was unnecessary; they meant to have him and he knew it. To shoot him down would have been easy, but that was not what they wanted. With a sudden surge they drove forward. Three times he fired, aiming low—he had no desire to kill any of them—and then one of the men he had felled clutched him round the knees. Thrown violently backwards, Jim had to drop his guns and grab a nearby chair to keep his feet. He kicked himself free, felt his boot-heel impact on flesh and bone, and they were upon him. Swinging the chair above his head he flailed the leaders with it. Two went down groaning, and of the weapon only the back remained in his grasp. With this and his fist he continued the unequal contest until a blow from behind brought him to his knees and the human avalanche submerged him.

For a few hectic moments the cowboy struck or kicked whenever he could free a limb but at last the writhing tangle broke up to disclose a battered, unconscious form on the floor. The sheriff regarded it with savage satisfaction.

"Tie an' chuck him in the calaboose," he ordered. "He'll pay for this, even if Jud comes through."

When the prisoner had been carried away, willing hands helped to straighten up the battlefield, rearranging overturned tables and chairs and removing fragments of others. The saloon-keeper's expression was one of deep disgust.

"Many customers like him an' this business would be plain hell," he remarked. "Allasame, he put up the purtiest scrap agin odds I ever see, an' warn't he *sudden*?"

"Sudden?" ejaculated the man who had received the first blow, tenderly touching a swollen jaw. "I reckon yu said it, Teddy. 'Sudden' describes him from hair to toe-nails; we'll have to christen him that. Set 'em up, ol' hoss."

The idea appealed to their sense of humour, and with

jesting comments, they drank to the new name of the man they had fought with, and whom they would just as cheerfully help to hang. The sheriff, cursing as the doctor bandaged his damaged wrist, contributed a grim witticism:

"Mister Sudden'll come to a sudden end in the mornin'."

"An' that'll be a pity," the medico smiled, as he surveyed the group of patients awaiting his services. "He'd make my fortune if he settled here."

At which even some of the sufferers grinned. After all, though about a dozen had been more or less crippled, no one had been killed, a fact to which the saloon-keeper drew attention:

"I'm bettin'—if he'd wanted to—he could 'a' turned three or four o' yu into cold meat," was how he put it. "I was watchin' an' them guns 'peared to leap into his paws. Yu can gamble he can use 'em; yore head is a bigger mark than yore wrist, sheriff."

Mallick turned a malignant eye upon him. "Why not make a gory hero out'n this murderin' thief an' be done with it?" he sneered. "Jud'll be pleased."

"Sheriff's right, Teddy," another chimed in, whose unpleasing countenance a pair of blackening eyes did not improve. "The fella's a bad actor. I ain't shore we oughtn't to stretch him right away."

"He'll keep," Mallick said darkly.

* * *

The Fourways gaol was a small, one-roomed hut built of stout logs, the iron-barred window a foot square, and the sole furniture a rough bench along the back. It was on the hard-packed earthen floor of this place that the man from Crawling Creek came back to consciousness, his bemused mind groping for an explanation. His hands were tied, his head throbbed, and when he attempted to move, his body appeared to be one big bruise. The pain stirred his sluggish memory and his swollen lips twisted in a lop-sided grin.

" 'Pears like they got me," he muttered. "She was shorely a great little battle—while she lasted."

For a while he lay there, supine, content to remain just still, idly speculating upon what was to come.

"Wonder how Jud is makin' it? If he passes out..." The reflection was not conductive to comfort. The wounded man was his only hope, a poor one at that, after the happenings in the saloon.

"Mebbe I'd oughta give in," he told himself, and then, "Shucks, that sheriff was set on swingin' me anyways."

It was very dark and no sound came from the town; he judged that the night must be well advanced. Despite his bound wrists, he managed to find the "makings" and construct a cigarette. He had but just lighted it when a faint chink of metal against metal and a muttered oath came from outside. His first thought was that some of the citizens had grown impatient, but the lack of noise argued against that; lynchers would be in force and would care little if they were heard. A slight creak followed, and the darkness was less deep where the door had been. A shadow slipped into the hut, paused on the threshold, and chuckled as the prisoner became dimly visible.

"Yo're a nervy cuss," the visitor said gruffly, "but I guess yu ain't anxious to figure in a necktie-party?"

"Yu don't need to guess again," was the reply. "It's an interestin' sight but lookin' at it through the loop of a rope don't improve it any."

"My sentiments exactly," the unknown agreed. He cut the captive's bonds. "Here's yore guns—the sheriff thinks he's got 'em." He laughed quietly. "Yore hoss is outside—saddled; yu'd better stretch him. I'm tellin' yu plenty serious this burg has on'y one use for yu."

In the faint grey light outside, Jim studied his liberator but could make little of him. A square, stocky figure of medium height, dressed in range rig, with hat-brim pulled down and a bandana covering the lower part of his face. His low, husky voice had a curious metallic timbre.

"I like to pay my debts, an' I shorely owe yu a lot," the young man said.

"Nothin' to that," came the quick reply. "I'm payin' one my own self—yu done me a good turn to-night. Mebbe we'll meet again."

It was plain that he wished to remain unknown, and Jim swung into the saddle. "If we do yu can count on me to the limit," he said simply.

"Get agoin'," the stranger replied. "Adios—Sudden," and the chuckle was once more in evidence.

At a walking pace the fugitive passed through the silent town, the deep dust of the street muffling the horse's footsteps. Once clear of the buildings, he patted the sleek neck and Nigger settled down to a steady lope which would devour distance and leave the animal still fresh.

The rider, greedily drinking in the cool air, was conscious of a fierce elation in his freedom. For Jim knew that he had escaped an ignominious death only by the good offices of a stranger. Who was this man, and why had he intervened ? What was the "good turn" to which he referred ?

"Mebbe he was thankin' me for cripplin' the sheriff," Jim reflected. "I'd say Mallick ain't liked overmuch."

It came into his mind that his deliverer had called him "Sudden," and the mystery seemed to be solved.

"Took me for some other fella, shore enough," he concluded. "Wonder who this 'Sudden' person is, anyways?"

He was to learn, ere many days, and get no joy of the knowledge.

# Chapter 3

Several days of wandering in the wilds—for he had avoided the regular trails—brought the man from Crawling Creek to San Antonio, at that time the Mecca of the cattleman, and the happy-hunting ground of the gambler and desperado. Though Jim still mourned the loss of his only friend, change of scene had dulled the ache. A young and vigorous man, with a good horse between his knees, and all his life before him, cannot long remain a prey to melancholy. But his determination to find and punish Evesham's enemies had not lessened.

Since his hurried departure from Fourways he had not seen a human being, sleeping with his saddle for a pillow, and living upon the game his gun had procured. His first thought now was for a square meal for himself and his mount. These were soon found, and leaving the animal in the livery stable, he set out to "take in the town."

Though there were many people about, most of whom seemed to have something to do, no one hurried. Huge wagons, drawn by sleepy-eyed oxen, plodded through the street, the great creaking wheels revolving slowly; the caballeros, picturesquely attired and mounted on magnificent steeds, paced by to dismount gracefully but without exertion at a store or saloon. The *manana* spirit of Old Mexico was all-pervading.

About to enter the Buckhorn Saloon, that famous rendezvous, the Texan paused abruptly, his eye caught by a single word on a square of paper affixed to the wall.

"Sudden!"

The crudely printed bill offered a reward of five hundred dollars for the apprehension of one "Sudden," wanted for robbery and murder. A description was given: "Young, dark hair and moustache, grey-blue eyes, dressed as a cowboy, wears two guns, and rides a black horse with a white blaze on face and white stocking on off fore-leg." The notice bore the name of the sheriff of Fourways.

For a moment the young man stared at it in blank amazement, and then, as the full significance came home, anger surged within him. Not only was he to be hounded down for a crime of which he knew nothing, but he had been given a name which would follow him wherever he went. In a word, he was outlawed; the hand of every man would be against him, and he was liable to be shot like a mad dog. Impulsively he made a gesture to tear away the placard.

"I wouldn't," a warning voice said. "If yo're honin' for one as a sooveneer there's others in less prominent places; the town is fair spotted with 'em."

He turned and found the speaker at his elbow, a tall,

spare fellow in the thirties, with a lean, angular face, close-set eyes, and thin lips wearing a smile intended to be friendly but which only succeeded in being malicious.

"If yore hoss tallies, that description would fit yu pretty good," the stranger went on.

Jim's jaw hardened. "If yu had a black hoss an' moustache yu might qualify yore own self," he retorted.

"But I don't have neither o' them things," the other grinned.

"Both of 'em can be got rid of," Jim pointed out. "See here, I'll match a dollar with yu to settle which of us takes the other in an' claims the cash."

The stranger laughed outright. "Yo're a cool card," he said.

"No, sir, they might glom on to the pair of us. I got a better proposition. I know a fella who'd be glad to meet yu."

"If he's wearin' a star..."

"He ain't, an' he's got no use for them as do," the unknown replied. "Hook up with him an' yu needn't let that"—he spat contemptuously at the notice—"scare yu."

"Did I mention I was scared?" Jim asked frostily. "Allasame, I ain't huntin' trouble."

The man nodded. "Ever hear o' Rogue's Riders?" he asked.

Jim had. Under the leadership of a man named Roger, but more generally known as "Rogue", they were perhaps the most notorious of the bands of desperadoes who raided and robbed over a wide area of south-west Texas.

"Please to meet yu, Mister Rogue," he said dryly.

"Oh, I ain't Rogue," the stranger laughed. "He's the fella I was speakin' of, an' I can fetch yu to him."

"Much obliged, but I figure I can take care o' li'l Mister Me," the cowboy grinned.

"Well, she's a free country. If yu should find yoreself crowded, head west till yu come to the Split Rock—yu can't mistake her—foller the left trail an' yu'll be looked after. Sabe?"

Jim nodded his thanks and turned away in the direction of the livery stable. Though he had displayed indifference to the man who had warned him, he had no illusions regarding the danger of his position and knew that he must get away from San Antonio without delay. At any moment he might be linked up with that damning description. The gaze of the man he had left followed him for a moment, a sneer of chagrin on his slit of a mouth.

"Can take care o' yoreself, huh? Well, that wouldn't surprise me," he muttered. "But when the deck is stacked, my friend ...."

He lifted his shoulders. "Rogue wants yu, an' a fella as won't be persuaded must be drove."

Striding down the street, he pushed open the door of one of the smaller saloons and peeped in. Apparently what he saw satisfied him, for he entered. It was a mere dive, dark, dirty, and ill-kept. Three men sitting at a battered table with empty glasses before them, and the Mexican lolling behind the bar, comprised the company. The newcomer called for a drink and remarked aloud, with seeming irrelevance:

"Shore is a sorry sight."

One of the trio at the table, a craggy-faced fellow with greedy little eyes, looked up hopefully. "Yu said it, friend," he grunted. "But when gents is down to bed-rock ...."

The stranger laughed. "Oh, that's soon remedied," he said, and signed to the bartender.

While the glasses were being replenished he studied the thirsty ones with an appraising expression of disdain. He did not know them, but he knew their kind. Though they were drinking to him now, he was well aware that they would rob him if opportunity offered.

"Yu got me wrong," he explained. "What I was referrin' to was the sight o' five hundred wheels gettin' ready to ride outa this town, to say nothin' of a fine black hoss with a white blaze, an' a saddle the present owner shouldn't have much further use for."

Craggy Face looked up. "Yu tellin' us that jasper Sudden is around?" he asked.

"Just that," the other returned. "Saw him readin' the bill outside the Buckthorn; he was mighty interested too, an' then he streaks for Juan's livery stable. What do yu guess ?"

"If yo're shore, why didn't you hold him up an'——" Craggy Face began.

"Collect the mazuma, huh?" the stranger finished. "Well, for one thing, he knows me, an' there's another reason to that why I can't take any part in the affair."

He stressed the last six words and the listeners smirked understandingly; he was wanted himself, this hombre, and the chance of gaining five hundred dollars would not offset the likely loss of his liberty. Craggy Face again was the spokesman:

"Amounts to this: we take all the risk, an'..."

"All the reward—I don't want none of it," he was told. "I disremember if that notice said 'dead or alive.'"

"It did not, an' I'm bettin' that Fourways fella ain't buyin' corpses."

Craggy Face emptied his glass and stood up, the other two following suit. Their informant added a word:

"I guess he'll take the western trail."

The ruffians nodded and went out. The stranger waited to absorb another drink and then did likewise, keeping well behind. Presently he saw the man he had betrayed jog-trotting listlessly along the street, heading—as he had surmised—for the western exit from the town. Callous as he was, he could not but admire the young fellow's nerve.

"He's the right stuff, shore as shootin'," he soliloquized. "Kind o' hombre Rogue can use. If them rats ain't weakened, they gotta do it here; he'll be in the open soon."

As the black horse approached, he slid round the corner of a Shack, from whence he could watch unobserved. Save that his hat was slouched over his face, the wanted rider appeared to be indifferent to his danger. But beneath the brim, his keen eyes scanned each passer-by, alert for the least sign of undue interest in himself, every sense taut and ready for action. So that he was not taken by surprise when three men, strolling aimlessly along the board sidewalk, abruptly swerved into the road in front of him, pulled their guns, and shouted:

"Han's up, Sudden!"

Jim did not hesitate—made no attempt to parley. The revelation of his identity—an astute move on the part of his attackers—would bring them immediate aid. Dropping the reins—already knotted for just such an emergency—over the saddlehorn, his hands went up, but with a gun in each. As they rose he fired both weapons, once, and his opponents on the right and left went down. Then, with a pressure of his knees, Jim jumped Nigger full at the man in the middle—Craggy Face. With an oath of dismay, the fellow saw the black thunderbolt hurling itself upon him and tried to leap aside. He nearly succeeded, but the massive shoulder caught and drove him into the dust.

The whole affair had occupied but a few seconds, and by the time the almost petrified pedestrians had realized the facts, the fugitive was two hundred yards away. Ineffectual shots were fired and then he was no more than a diminishing dot on the trail. The man behind the shack smiled felinely and did not join the group round the discomfited reward-hunters.

For some miles Jim rode hard, without looking back. When at length he did so he saw no sign of pursuit and eased his mount He reloaded his pistols, thrust them back into the holsters, and swore with savage anger at the thought of the price he had had to pay for his freedom. This second exploit had put him definitely outside the pale of the law. Despite the sparse population, the story of it would travel quickly in a land where topics for conversation were few and news of any kind eagerly retailed.

Head hanging, he puzzled over the problem of what to do. Southern Texas was closed to him—entering any settlement would probably result in having to shoot his way out of it, thus. only adding to his unwanted reputation. The nearest border was hundreds of miles distant and he was without supplies. The dull beat of hammering hooves apprised him that he had been careless. Turning, he saw a compact group of about a dozen riders pounding across the plain. San Antonio was not minded to let a noted desperado escape without making an effort.

The posse was less than half a mile behind and the members of it were doubtless congratulating themselves upon an easy capture when they saw the black horse quicken its stride and begin to draw away. Spurring and quirting their mounts they decreased the gap again, several pulling out their rifles and firing in the hope of a lucky shot. The cowboy felt the wind of a bullet on his cheek, others zipped through the grass beneath the flying feet of his horse, and a cold fury flamed in him.

"That's a game two can play at," he grated.

Dropping the reins, he drew his rifle from the sheath under the fender, twisted round in the saddle and flung four shots at the bunched-up party of pursuers. Two of the ponies went down, throwing their riders heavily, a man reeled, clutched at the air, and pitched sideways to the ground. The posse, disorganized by this disaster, pulled up, and the quarry, with a wave of defiance, vanished over a fold in the surface of the plain. His own kind had made him an outlaw, had hunted and fired on him as though he were a dangerous animal. Well, he would accept the verdict.

"Nothin' else for it, Nig," he told his horse. "We gotta find Mister Rogue; he's our best bet."

It was a small salve to his conscience to reflect that among the desperate class of men he was now being driven to mix with, he was more likely to find those of whom he was in search. From the top of a slight rise he looked for the posse, but it was not in sight.

"Kind o' lost their enthusiasm, mebbe," he said grimly, and rode on.

Gradually the character of the country changed, the open plain being broken by small, flat-topped mesas, shallow gullies, and occasional miniature forests of post-oak and mesquite, the latter sometimes of tree size. He halted at last before a great chunk of rock, with a curious V-shaped crack dividing it as from a giant axe-blow. The main trail—wagon-rutted—here turned sharply to the north, but westward there were hoofprints leading down into what appeared to be a welter of canyons.

"Split Rock," the traveller decided. "Well, ol' hoss, this is where we say good-bye to a law abidin' life."

With a mirthless, sardonic smile, he sent his mount loping to the left, following the faint trail which plunged into the broken country, and came at length to the narrow mouth of a gorge, the rocky walls of which almost met. Half-way up, on a ledge about thirty yards distant, the rider's questing eye caught a flash of steel.

"Stick 'em up, stranger; I got yu covered," boomed a voice, and a man with a levelled rifle rose into view.

Jim guessed this must be one of the bandits' sentinels. He had already decided on his own line of action, and though he halted, he did not obey the command to put up his hands. Instead he laughed satirically.

"I've had yu fixed for the last two minutes," he said. "Yu oughta get that gun-barrel dulled some—I saw it away back. Got any ideas?"

"Ony' this," the man replied, tapping his rifle.

Jim laughed unpleasantly. "Shucks, yu'd miss an' I wouldn't.

Well, if it'll relieve yore mind any, I'm lookin' for a fella called Rogue."

"I take it yo're Sudden then."

"An' yu might be right at that," Jim smiled. "What about it?"

"I've had word to pass yu along," the guard admitted, "but yu'll have to leave yore hardware with me—I'll fetch 'em in later."

"Like hell yu will," the visitor retorted. "No, sir, me an' the li'l hoss have had a long ride, but we're plenty strong enough to tote my guns, yu betcha."

"It's the rule," the bandit grumbled.

"There's allus an exception—I'm it," Jim told him lightly, and then, dropping his bantering tone. "Cut the cackle; either I go on or back, an' I don't give a damn which it is."

Sullenly the fellow motioned him on. "Go ahead," he said. "See yu later—mebbee."

Jim sensed the sinister implication and laughed. "Yu will, if nothin' don't happen to yu meantime."

The man appeared to have an afterthought. "Anybody follerin' yu?" he asked.

"Yo're a reg'lar question mark, ain't yu?" was the sarcastic reply. "Did I seem to be hurryin'?"

Half a mile father on he rounded a bend and saw that the perpendicular sides of the gorge closed in; apparently there was no outlet. He had pulled up, and was studying the grey, weatherstained walls when a man stepped abruptly from behind a big boulder and strolled nonchalantly towards him. He was carrying a rifle, and though he did not raise the weapon, his finger was on the trigger.

He was young, about his own age, Jim figured—though he had never known precisely what that was; his hair and moustache were very red, his blue eyes very pale, and the grin on his good-looking face very impudent. In a land where little attention was paid to such matters, the cleanliness and neatness of his attire drew the eye. He was obviously surprised to find the visitor armed.

"Meet a gent called Ropey back there ?" he asked bluntly, pointing to the entrance of the gorge.

"I guess, but he didn't mention his name," Jim replied.

"An' he let yu pass with that ars'nal?" the young man went on. "Yu musta showed him a good reason."

"I'm showin' yu the same," was the grim reply.

The youth looked at the levelled Colt which, having somehow got into its owner's hand, was now covering him, and laughed with affected dismay.

"Put her back in her li'l bed," he said. "I ain't arguin' with yu none whatever. Do we have to plant Ropey?"

"I reckon it would be premature—he was a healthy corpse when I left him," the visitor replied gravely, but there was a twinkle in his eyes, and the menacing gun had vanished.

"Glad yu didn't hurt Ropey, I hate diggin'," red-head remarked. "I figure yo're here to see our revered chief an' that yore name is mebbe—Sudden?"

"I've been called that," Jim admitted.

"Good enough," the other said, and pointed to the end of the gorge. "There's an opening under the cliff, an' on the other side yu'll see the select but not pop'lar hamlet o' Rogueville, consistin' of a few undesirable villas tenanted by still more undesirable villains, of whom I am one. The man yu wanta see ain't the biggest rogue but he has the name an' the say-so. Savvy?"

Having delivered this satirical address, he leaned his rifle against a rock and began to fashion a cigarette.

"Ain't s'posed to smoke on this job but I never could obey orders, which explains me," he grinned. "See yu again, I hope."

The visitor expressed the same desire and went on his way. He found the opening—cleverly concealed by an out-flung buttress of rock—and rode through. Before him lay a beautiful little ovalshaped basin, the grass-covered floor of which sloped up on every side to an enclosing rampart of rock. In the centre, a tiny circular lake, fringed with willows, gleamed amid the surrounding green like a huge silver coin. Cattle and horses were grazing near and on the far side of the valley were several log shacks.

By the time he reached them some half-dozen men had appeared; there had been no one in sight when he entered the valley. A brief glance told the visitor that red-head had probably described them correctly.

"An' what th' hell might yu be wantin'?" asked one, a coarsefaced, broken-nosed fellow.

"Civility first, from yu," Jim snapped. "An' then—to see yore boss."

The reply produced a scowl and a sneer. "We don't go much on bosses here. If yu want Rogue, he's there."

Following the direction of the jerked thumb, Jim walked his horse to a shack some twenty yards away, in the doorway of which a man was standing watching the proceedings without apparent interest. The bandit leader did not look formidable. Over forty, shortish but heavily built, with greying hair and beard, he might have passed for a prosperous rancher. He greeted his guest with a grin.

"Light an' rest yore saddle," he said, and the low, husky voice seemed familiar.

Jim got down and trailed the reins. "Best tell yore men to leave this hoss alone—he don't like strangers," he warned.

"They won't interfere with him," Rogue replied. His gaze dwelt on the animal. "Shore is a beauty, an' yu trained him right. Like a woman, a hoss any man can handle ain't no good."

They entered the shack. It consisted of one room only, furnished with a pallet-bed on which blankets were spread, a rough, homemade table, and chairs with rawhide seats. Pegs driven into the log walls supported guns, bridles, ropes and other paraphernalia of the range. Rogue pointed to a chair and produced a bottle and glasses.

"Well, yu got here—Sudden," he said.

This time there could be no mistake. "So it was yu?" Jim said, and smiled. "I guess that sheriff man was peeved."

"Peeved?" repeated the other. "He was madder'n a teased rattler an' twice as poisonous. He'd 'a' stretched yu."

"So Judson—died?"

"Yeah, durin' the night; never opened an eye again."

There was silence for a few moments and then Jim said, "I'm still wonderin' why yu—interfered?"

Rogue laughed. "I don't like sheriffs nohow an' yu put up a pretty fight," he explained. " 'Sides, yu done me a service."

"I'm still in the dark," the visitor persisted.

The outlaw hesitated for a space, his hard grey eyes studying the boy before him; but he learned nothing.

"I'm playin' straight with yu, Sudden," he said, and the husky voice had a harsh note in it. "If yu hadn't been there they'd have picked on me an' I had Judson's money-belt round my middle."

Jim sat up. "Yu did it ?" he cried, jolted out of his impassivity.

"Yeah, but I didn't wanta kill the fool," Rogue said. "I got the drop on him an' I'm steppin' in to take his gun when he jumps his hoss at me. I try to wing him but he's movin' yu see, an'..." He shrugged his shoulders. There was no regret in his voice; rather there was blame for a murdered man who had not played the game properly, and paid the penalty. "I was a plain fool to come into town but I figured him finished. I had to have the coin; things have been quiet lately an' the boys was gettin' restive."

The latter remark sounded like an excuse, but Jim knew it was not so intended; Rogue was simply giving him all the facts. To Jim, the important point was that, this man who had coolly confessed to the crime had not been content to let another suffer for it, and he, Jim, owed his life to him; he could not condemn, and in his present rebellious attitude to his own kind, had no wish to.

"What made yu think I'd come here?" he asked.

"I saw them bills an' knew Mallick would close the towns to yu," Rogue explained. "Reckoned yu'd make for San Antonio an' sent one o' my men to watch for yu. Didn't he find yu ?"

"Shore, but it wasn't him sent me," Jim Said, and told of the attempted arrest and chase.

If the outlaw smiled it was behind his beard; he guessed the part his envoy had played. His comment contained more than a touch of admiration:

"Three fellas, with their guns out, an' then yu busted up the posse! Yu ain't losin' any time justifyin' yore label. Sudden."

"My name's Jim—I'd prefer yu called me that."

"Mine's Roger, but everybody calls me Rogue an' I dunno as I care. Allasame, Jim goes with me. Now, yu better stick around awhile, yo're safe here. Later on, yu can decide 'boutstayin'; I'm hopin' yu will; I want a fella I can trust."

"I'm obliged to yu," the visitor said.

"Yu can double up with Sandy, an' we all feed together in the big cabin. Now, there's another thing: yore face wouldn't look no worse without hair on it."

He rummaged on a shelf and produced a bottle. "This dye'll wipe out them markin's. I'll show yu yore quarters."

He led the way to a little hut standing rather apart from the others, built of unbarked logs, clinked with clay. As they approached a cheerful but unmelodious voice within announced that it was "his night to howl."

"An' he's shorely doin' it," Rogue said, with a saturnine smile. "Hey, Sandy, I've brung yu a bunkie."

The young man who emerged proved to be the second sentinel of the gorge and his face opened in a wide grin when he saw the new-comer.

"Yu can put him wise an' make him known to the boys."

"Pleased to," Sandy said, shaking hands.

When the outlaw leader had gone, with a word that he would see them at supper, Sandy turned to the visitor.

"I'm lucky to get yu," he said. "Last fella I bunked with musta been bit by a mad dawg some time, the sight o' water gave him the fantods."

Together they inspected the quarters. Two beds—mere frames with strips of rawhide nailed across them, a couple of up-ended boxes for seats, a cracked mirror, and a few pegs comprised the furniture. The previous sole owner of all this magnificence waited covertly for comment, but when the stranger spoke it was about something entirely different.

"Yu ain't been with this crowd very long," he said.

Sandy stared at him and retorted quizzically, "Tell me somethin' about my future, Mister Medicine Man."

"Shore," Sudden smiled. "I'm sayin' yu won't be with 'em a great while, neither."

Sandy grinned. "Now I'll do a bit o' wizardin'," he said. "Listen, yo're a nifty poker player, an' yu an' me is goin' to be good friends."

They shook hands on that, and then, having brought in his saddle, blankets, and war-bag, the visitor proceeded to shave off his moustache. Sandy watched the operation in silence and then laughed slyly.

"I grow one an' yu get shut o' yores—funny, ain't it?" he remarked, and, inspecting the result critically, "It certainly makes a difference. What yu goin' to do with the bottle?"

"Rogue thinks my hoss would look better all black, an' I'm inclined t`o agree with him," Sudden explained, his eyes twinkling.

The removal of the tell-tale marks did not take long and when the horse had been turned loose to graze, Sandy suggested that it was getting near grub-time. On the way, Sudden put a question.

"Rogue ain't a bad ol' scout but difficult to figure," was the reply. "There's times he's near human an' others when he can be a devil from hell, gotta be, I reckon, with the team he has to handle; there ain't a tougher crowd between Kansas an' the Rio Grande."

Sudden's own observations during the meal supported this description. Sandy alone seemed to be of a different type; somehow he did not "belong." Rogue's remark about a "man he could trust" no longer astonished him.

They fed at a long table in the largest building, which served as a general living-room for the community. Rogue sat at one end, and at the other was a man who immediately attracted the attention of the new-comer. In the thirties, of medium height, slim and supple, he had the face of a demon. The acquiline nose, high cheek-bones, cruel mouth and lank, black hair proclaimed a mixed origin, despite his yellowish-white skin, and Sudden was not surprised to hear him addressed as "Navajo." His dark eyes, flashing from beneath lowered lids, and sinuous movements, were reptilian. He was, Sandy whispered, a sort of second in command of the band. Rogue's presentation was perfunctory:

"Boys, this is Jim," he said. "He's stayin' with us a while."

Nods and a muttered "Howdy" here and there came in response, and the men went on with the business of filling their bellies. The food was good and plentiful. Not until their voracious appetites were appeased and pipes or cigarettes lighted did the company take much notice of the guest. Then he came in for a good deal of furtive scrutiny.

Presently, when most of the men were playing or watching a card game, he slipped away, and from a bench outside, sat gazing over the valley. It was a restful sight: the green expanse, with its verdure-ringed pool and grazing beasts, the rock-rimmed walls where the gathering shadows heralded the approaching night, and to the west, a lingering golden glory in the sky.

"Looks peaceful, don't it ?" Sandy said, squatting beside his new chum.

"Shore does."

Sandy did not pursue the subject. He sensed the bitterness in the tone, guessed what the speaker might be thinking, but knew he must not ask. Though they felt a mutual kinship, these two, they had exchanged no confidences.

# Chapter 4

Rogue was absent from the breakfast table on the following morning, but there was a new arrival in the person of the man Sudden had seen in San Antonio. He grinned cheerfully at the cowboy and, when the meal was over, beckoned him outside.

"So yu changed yore mind ?" was how he opened the conversation.

"Yu might call it that," was the sardonic reply.

"Aimin' to throw in with Rogue?"

Sudden did not reply at once. Despite the man's apparent friendliness, he did not like him; there was a lurking malignancy which suggested that he enjoyed the misfortunes of others.

"I ain't decided," he said, adding savagely, "What else is there for me to do ?"

"Come a-swimmin'—that's what."

It was Sandy who had answered the question, and he smiled as he waved a hand to the pool, glittering in the bright sunshine like a jewel in a green setting. Sligh—so the outlaw was called—shrugged disdainful shoulders.

"Yu did oughta remember them critters has to drink that water," he said.

"Which is why yu don't go in, huh?" Sandy retorted.

The water looked cool and inviting and Sandy hurriedly divested himself of his clothing. Sudden followed his example but more leisurely. He watched the boy step lightly towards a jutting bit of bank which afforded a good place for a plunge and then snatched a gun from the belt he had just discarded and fired. Sandy whirled instantly.

"What the hell…?" he cried, and then, as he saw the bulletshattered flat venomous head and greenish-grey body thrashing about in the long grass only a yard from where he stood, his face paled. "A cotton-mouth!" he gasped. (The moccasin snake, when angry, appears to have its jaws stuffed with cotton-wool.) "Jim, I'm not forgettin' this—ever."

"Shucks," was the reply. "Saw him just in time."

"Yu shore did—'nother step an' I'd 'a' trod on him," Sandy agreed, with a shiver.

A careful search of the bank revealed no more reptiles and they had their swim, but much of the enjoyment had gone. As they lay on the warm turf drying themselves in the sun, Sudden asked a question.

"There's a way out at the other end o' the valley," Sandy said. "Goin' ridin'?"

"Thought I'd look around; don't seem to be much to do."

"We'll be busy to-morrow—the boys'll fetch in a bunch

o' cattle —there's plenty mavericks in the brush. I'd go with yu but I gotta relieve Ropey, durn it."

Dried and dressed again they made their way to the bunkhouse, which they found empty, save for the cook.

Having fed, they got their horses and separated, Sandy turning east to set free a man who was eagerly awaiting him, and Sudden heading in the opposite direction.

The exit was easily found, a tunnel-like crack in the rim-rock just wide enough to permit the passage of a mounted man. There was little light, for the cliff overhead appeared to be unbroken and the far end of the opening was masked by a mass of dense scrub. The few tracks showed that this means of entering or leaving the valley was seldom used.

"Takin' a herd o' cattle through would be apt to keep a fella's tongue busy," the cowboy ruminated. "She'd be a useful bolt-hole though."

Sandy had already told him that the nearest settlement on this side of the valley was some thirty miles distant, and that the only habitation of importance was the S E ranch.

"Got a big range, has Sam Eden," the boy had said. "They say he owns a lot o' the land too. Dessay our valley belongs to him, but up to now he ain't served no writ of ejectment."

It was a wild bit of country into which Sudden emerged, a jumble of scrub-choked gullies, flat-topped mesas, ridges of bare rock, and forested slopes hemming in grass-covered savannahs. Every now and then, a fierce-eyed steer would break from a thicket, glare at the rider, and crash back into the brush. Some of these bore the S E brand but more were unmarked.

"Sandy was right," Sudden reflected. "Either Eden's outfit is damn careless or he ain't had a proper round-up in years. He can't holler if someone takes care o' them mavericks."

A little later, as he was riding the rim of a shallow ravine, he heard a startled cry, followed by the beat of galloping hooves. It was a woman's voice and he judged it came from just ahead. A whispered word quickened the speed of the big black and rounding a bend, the rider swore in angry surprise:

"Damnation!"

Along the bottom of the ravine, and only a few hundred yards away, a girl was desperately spurring her pony. A short distance behind, two mounted Indians were racing to overtake her. Sudden pulled up, swung his horse round, headed it for the inclined wall of the gully, and leaned back in the saddle. Nigger knew what was required; bunching his feet together he slithered down the slope, and took up the chase. The long leaping stride of the black soon began to overhaul the poorer animals in front, but Sudden saw he had not time to waste; already the foremost Indian had grabbed the bridle of the girl's pony and was endeavouring to drag her from the saddle.

She was resisting, striking at the savage with the butt of her quirt, and fearing that the fellow would do her an injury, he uttered a shout. Instantly the second redskin whirled, dropped his lance, his right hand flashing to the quiver behind his shoulder, and Sudden felt a searing pain at the side of his neck. With incredible speed, the Indian notched a second arrow but ere he could despatch it the white man's revolver roared and the redskin pitched to the ground. His companion, seeing what had happened, abandoned the girl, flogged his pony savagely up the steep bank of the ravine—which climbed like a cat—and, with a whoop of defiance, vanished over the edge. The cowboy followed, but by the time he reached the top the fugitive was half a mile distant on an open plain. When Sudden returned the girl rode to meet him, a grateful smile on her firm lips.

"Thank you," she said, holding out a slim, gauntleted hand. Then, as her frank brown eyes studied this stranger who had so providentially come to her rescue, she saw blood on the collar of his shirt. "But you are hurt," she cried.

"On'y a scratch—mebbe," he smiled.

"We'll wash and tie up that *scratch*," she said, and though he protested, had her way.

When the job was done to her satisfaction and they were in the saddle again, she turned to him with a smile.

"I am Carol Eden," she told him. "The S E ranchhouse is only about eight miles from here and my father will want to thank you."

"Why, there ain't no need——" he began, but she cut the protest short.

"He will think there is, and I agree with him. Besides, there may be other Indians about."

This was an unanswerable argument and again Sudden had to give in; he was beginning to realize that here was a young woman who usually got what she wanted. Riding side by side along the ravine he had an opportunity to study her more closely. She rode astride, cowboy fashion, and was clearly at home in the saddle, her slender form swaying in rhythm with the movements of her mount. Her neat shirt-waist, divided skirt, and riding-boots with tiny silver spurs provided a costume which showed her youthful figure to advantage. From beneath the broad-brimmed felt hat peeped rebellious brown curls which the sunlight turned to copper. He noted the wide-spaced brown eyes, the straight little nose, the firm but rounded chin, and spoke his thought:

"Yu didn't oughta be ridin' alone so far from home." For a moment he feared she would resent the remark as an impertinence, and then she smiled. "I know it. Dad warned me, but I thought the Indians were quiet now. You see, I have been East, at college, for some time."

"Injuns is never quiet till they're like—him," the young man said grimly, with a jerk of his thumb backwards. "I'd oughta got that other; I've a hunch I'll be seein' him again."

"I hope I don't," the girl said fervently. "I'll never forget that hideous painted face. If you hadn't come..."

To take her away from the subject he mentioned that he too had recently returned from the East, and she looked at him with a new interest.

"Would you care to live there?" she asked.

He shook his head and smiled. "I couldn't stand it," he confessed

"This is my country; a man can breathe without feelin' he's robbin' another fella of air; there's room for all."

"Except the Indian," she said, a little sadly.

"Why, yo're right," he agreed. "An' it's shorely an odd

thought that the time is comin' when, in this vast land, there won't be a place for the men who once owned it all. When the buffalo an' the game have gone, the redskin will follow. He ain't adaptable; educate him all yu please an' he's still a savage at heart."

"A case of the survival of the fittest?" she suggested.

"No, ma'am," her companion replied. "The Injun will lie, steal, an' murder, but if yo're his friend he'll die for yu. Some o' the white men who are wipin' him out will do all them things an' sell their own kin for a few dollars. On top o' that, the red man is a healthy hater."

"You rate that a virtue?" she said surprisedly.

He nodded, his face—which when he smiled was that of a boy—hard and grim as granite. The look warned her that she bad plumbed hidden depths and aroused her woman's curiosity; in the hope that he would respond in kind, she went on to speak of herself. He learned that she was not really an Eden, the rancher having adopted her some years earlier, when the death of her father—his old friend—left her unprotected.

"He has been very, very good to me," she finished softly.

Her innocent little ruse proved unsuccessful. He told her his name and that was all. When she ventured a half-question, she received—as she had feared—only a half-answer:

"I'm just takin' a look at the country," he said.

"I'm glad you chose this bit of it to-day," Carol smiled. "We are near the ranch; I must prepare for a tongue-lashing from Dad."

"He needn't to know," Sudden pointed out. "Yo're safe now; I can fade——"

"No, I'll take my medicine," she told him, and in mock reproach, "I shall begin to think you don't like your company."

The cowboy's eyes crinkled at the corners. "I could bear to be with yu a whole lot, ma'am," he said gravely.

# Chapter 5

The S E ranch-house was not beautiful but was eminently adapted to the purpose for which it had been erected. It stood in the middle of a small, level plain which afforded no cover whatever for an attacking force, and the walls, constructed of squared logs, were loop-holed on all sides. Of one storey only, it comprised a large living-room, bedrooms, and a kitchen. Immediately behind was an sample coral, and to the left, a bunkhouse for the outfit, a barn and smithy.

On the broad, covered porch which extended along the front of the building two men were sitting. The elder, short, big-shouldered, dressed in range rig, was Sam Eden, owner of the ranch. Though he was past fifty, only his iron-grey hair betrayed the fact; the keen blue eyes, firm lips beneath a clipped moustache, and pugnacious jaw all spoke of virility; the deep cleft between the bushy brows told of temper.

The other man was of a different type. Tall, not yet forty, his fleshy, clean-shaven face appeared unusually pale in that land of bronzed skins. It was not an attractive face—the flattish nose, rather prominent eyes, and thick lips had a negroid character, and in fact, Jethro Baudry had sometimes been described as a "white nigger." His attire formed a striking contrast to that of his host: a "boiled" shirt, neatly-tied cravat, and long black Prince Albert coat. His hands were carefully tended: they had to be, for Baudry was by profession a gambler, though he was now sitting in a bigger game. His expressionless gaze studied the man before him.

"So you are going to take the chance, Sam?" he said.

"Shore I am—nothin' else for it," the rancher replied. "Yu see, Jethro, I want things clear for Carol—case anythin' happens to me. Sabe?"

"You don't think I'd press her, do you?" Baudry asked.

"No; but yo're mortal too, an' gamblin' aint the safest callin'," Eden replied bluntly.

"I can take care of myself," Baudry said with a thin smile. "Still, there's the chance. Setting that aside, you know I'm willing to wait?"

"Shore, yu've been mighty good lettin' me have the coin, Jethro," the rancher said warmly. "But think of it, man; a hundred thousand acres that, in a few years' time, may be worth as many dollars as I've paid cents for 'em. Wouldn't yu wanta feel it really belonged to yu?"

Actually the gambler was feeling just that, but his bland features expressed nothing of the greed which possessed him.

"Natural enough; but these big drives are risky they tell me," he rejoined. "You may lose your herd."

"I'm losin' 'em anyway," the cattleman said bitterly; and reading the question in the other's eyes, "Yeah, rustlers, o' course. It's an easy play; the beasts is scattered in the brush an' a lot must be unbranded; our round-ups ain't been too thorough the last year or so—I couldn't afford a large outfit—an' what was the use when all yu could get for a steer was a few dollars for the hide an' taller? An' for that yu gotta drive 'em to a coast-town, which cut the profit to near nothin' a-tall.

"Now, they tell me, it's different; the East needs beef; the Gov'ment wants it to feed the Injuns on the reservations—when they can git the war-whoops to stay on 'em; the northern ranchers have discovered that the buffalo grass on their big plains will fatten cows, an' they're lookin' for stock. There's a shippin' point at Abilene, Kansas, an' beasts worth little more'n nothin' here will fetch as much as fifteen dollars or more apiece."

"Certainly sounds good," the younger man said. "If you can make it."

"I gotta make it, or bust," Eden said grimly. "Anyways, yo're sittin' pretty, Jethro; if I win through, yu get yore dinero; if I don't, the ranch is yores; yu needn't to worry."

"I don't intend to," Baudry assured him; and again a fleeting smile swept over his pale face. Then he asked casually, "Any news of that son of yours ?"

The rancher's brows met in a heavy frown. "I've no son," he said harshly. "When he went from here he stepped outa my life; I'll be glad if yu'll remember that, Jethro." And, after a pause, "No, I ain't heard nothin'."

The other made no comment, but in his eyes there was a gleam of satisfaction.

"When do you expect to start north?"

"Soon as we can gather an' road-brand a sizable herd. Hello, who's that with Carol?"

The girl and her companion, having left their mounts at the corral, had suddenly appeared round the end of the ranch-house. Baudry rose and bowed to the lady, whose expression did not convey too warm a welcome. Murmuring a formal greeting, she turned to the cattleman.

"Dad, this is Mister Green, and I've brought him, much against his wish"—she smiled at the culprit—"because I knew you would want to thank him."

In a few words she told the story of her adventure and Sam Eden's face paled beneath its tan as he comprehended the terrible fate she had so narrowly escaped. Impulsively his hand went out.

"Young fella," he said, "if there's anythin' I've got an' yu want, name it. Yu couldn't 'a' done me a greater service."

Sudden gripped the proffered fist. "It don't need speakin' of, seh," he said. "I happened to be handy, an'..." He bogged down and looked thoroughly uncomfortable.

The rancher realized his feelings; he knew the breed—they would rather be blamed than thanked. He turned to the girl.

"As for yu, miss, didn't I tell yu——" he began sternly.

Before he could say any more her arm was through his and her cheek against his shoulder.

"Now don't be an old bear; I'll 'fess up," she smiled. "Of course you warned me, and I was wrong to go so far, but I didn't think of Indians."

"It ain't on'y them pesky critters," the old man growled

"Yu might 'a' met up with some o' Rogue's Riders—his hideout is somewhere around." He looked at the cowboy quizzically, "Yu don't happen to belong to that gang, do yu?"

Sudden shook his head, grinned, and repeated the reply he had given the girl. "I'm from the south; havin' a look at the country."

The explanation satisfied the cattleman; he was aware that the range rider was a restless animal, liable to fork his horse and set out, at short notice or none at all, in search of fresh fields. He liked the look of this loose-limbed, competent-appearing stranger.

At the meal to which they sat down later, Eden reverted to the momentous steps he was contemplating, asking the cowboy if he had any experience of trail-driving?

"On'y short distances," Sudden told him. "Never been north; but I hear it ain't no picnic."

The rancher nodded grimly. "Others have done it, an' I'm goin' to," he said. "Like to come along? I can do with a couple more men." He saw the hesitation, and added, "Think it over—we won't be ready yet awhile."

Sudden promised he would do so, and asked the probable size of the herd.

"I'm hopin' for three thousand head," Eden said. "Take some handlin' but I got a good outfit. The pay is thirty a month an' every man gets a share when we sell the cattle."

The cowboy nodded. He liked the rancher, recognized him as a good specimen of the bluff, straightforward frontiersmen who, penetrating and settling in the wildest parts of the country, were preparing the way for the civilization which would inevitably follow. Baudry he did not take to, instinct telling him that under the smooth exterior lurked passions by no means in keeping with it. Once or twice he caught him looking at the girl, plain desire in his eyes.

"Miss Carol, of course, will remain here," the gambler said.

"Miss Carol, of course, will—not," the lady promptly stated.

Her father looked at her in astonishment. "Don't talk foolish, girl," he said. "There's no place for a lone woman on a trail drive."

Carol's reply appeared to be irrelevant. "Aren't you taking Peg-leg?"

"Shore I am; we'd do fine without a cook, wouldn't we?"

"Then you'll have to take his wife—Judy won't let him go without her—so I shan't be a' lone woman,' you see." The rancher's face was clouding up, but she did not wait for the storm to burst. "Can't I ride, rope, and drive cattle as well as the boys?" she asked, and when he nodded a grudging assent, she added triumphantly, "Well then, you get a top-hand for nothing, and you grumble. But of course, you were only teasing; you meant I should go all the time. I must tell Judy."

She jumped up, blew him a kiss, and danced away. Her parent opened his lips to call her back, but was too late. He turned to his guests with a droll expression of hopelessness.

"I can handle the savagest steer or woolliest cowboy that ever forked a pony, but when it comes to what some funny fella called the 'weaker sex,' I'm beat," he confessed. "That bit o' impudence does what she likes with me."

Sudden left soon after the meal, returning the way he had come. The body of the dead Indian had vanished; his companion must have returned. The circumstance was to bear a significance later, but now he gave it no thought. His brain was busy with the offer he had just received. It seemed to present a means of getting out of the mire into which chance had so unceremoniously thrown him; and moreover, the very enterprise itself appealed to his adventurous nature. The task of shepherding three thousand wild cattle through eight or nine hundred miles of fierce, untamed country seemed worthy of a man, and there was the added incentive that, in the lawless cow-towns of the north, he might find the fellows he was seeking. But he would not decide yet, for though, when necessity demanded, he could think and act with lightning speed, he was a deliberate person. And because of that, he would not mention his afternoon's experience—even to Sandy.

"I'm bettin' he's straight," he told himself. "But our friendship is some recent."

When he reached the valley he found the men loafing outside the large cabin, smoking and yarning. Having disposed of his horse, he joined them. Rogue had apparently not yet returned. They watched him curiously as he seated himself on a bench next to Sandy, who was looking uneasy.

"Supper's through," that young man remarked, and then, in a whisper, "Suthin's up, dunno what, but watch out."

"I've fed," Sudden replied.

He had already sensed the air of expectancy with which his arrival had been greeted, and guessed that some attempt to "try him out" might be made.

Navajo and Ropey, standing six or seven yards away, were engaged in an argument, their voices rising. Sudden noticed that the other men were watching them. Presently Ropey, who was rolling a cigarette, snapped out an oath, and cried:

"Texas ? I can tell yu what I think of it right now. When a Texan dies an' goes to hell—as they all do—he shore figures he's in heaven."

He had turned as he spoke and his narrowed eyes were glaring at the visitor. It was a direct challenge, as all knew, and the chatter ceased. Sudden, lounging on the bench, took no notice, and Ropey, with a grin of contempt, struck a match. Ere he could apply it to the cigarette between his lips, a gun flamed from the lounger's hip and the light was extinguished.

"What th' hell!" the man gasped.

"I'm from Texas," Sudden quietly stated, and waited.

But Ropey had nothing to say; the fragment of wood remaining in his fingers appeared to hypnotize him. Sudden addressed himself to the others generally:

"Any fella is free to damn Texas," he said, "but if he looks at me while he's doin' it, I take it as personal."

Ropey made a desperate attempt to save his face. "I was on'y joshin'," he expostulated.

"Same here," Sudden told him, with a cold smile. "If I hadn't been, I could 'a put yore light out pretty permanent."

This raised a laugh, in which, however, neither Navajo nor the victim of the "joke" joined. Later on, when the visitor and Sandy had retired, the incident was again discussed. It was Navajo who brought it up.

"Didn't think yu'd be scared by a bit o' trick-shootin',

Ropey," he sneered. "Anybody knows it's the wind o' the bullet puts the flame out."

"Trick-shootin' my eye," Ropey retorted. "That match-stick was cut clean in half, a left-hand shot, an' him sittin' down. He's a born gunfighter, that fella; he'd have to try—to miss."

And because the speaker was deemed only second to Navajo in that gang of expert gunmen his word carried weight. One only still expressed scornful doubt, and Ropey did not let it pass.

"Take him on yoreself, Navajo," he challenged. "He's all yores —hide, horns, an' taller—an' I'm bettin' two to one agin yu."

The half-breed shrugged impatiently. "Kid's talk," he said. "C'mon, boys; time to hit the hay; we got a stiff job in the morning'."

Meanwhile, in the little cabin they were to share, Sudden and Sandy also referred to the incident; the latter was full of admiration for his new friend's marksmanship.

"My Gawd, I never seen anythin' like it," he remarked. "I ain't a mite surprised they named yu 'Sudden'."

"My friends call me 'Jim'," came the meaning reminder.

"Shore, whatever yu say goes with me—Jim," was the ready reply. "Ropey didn't think o' that play—though he might be feelin' sore over yore bluffin' him when yu came in. Navajo put him up to it—he don't like yu—much."

"I got the edge on him there—I don't like him a-tall."

"See many folks on yore ride ?" Sandy asked presently.

"Well, I wouldn't say the country was thickly-populated," was the smiling reply. "What's doin' to-morrow?"

"Like I told yu, brandin', damn it. They fetched in 'bout three score mavericks this afternoon an' we gotta put the 8 B iron on 'em."

"Who owns that brand?"

"Couldn't say. There ain't no 8 B ranch around here that I know of, but Rogue gets four dollars a head for all he can turn over."

Sudden was surprised; this was legitimate enterprise, for in those days of free range, unbranded cattle were the property of the finder unless the real owner could prove a claim.

The explanation was to come in the morning, when the valley presented a scene of animation. A few hundred yards from the pool, a fire had been lighted, and to this each steer had to be dragged or driven, thrown and tied, while the hot iron was applied. This was no easy task, for the cattle were scattered and full of fight. Sudden found that he had been assigned the ticklish job of hog-tying the victims. As he had not yet joined the band, he might have declined to share the work, but the idea never occurred to him; he was there, and it was the natural thing to help. He had tied the first brute before he noticed the branded letters, S E.

"Hey, this critter's got a label a'ready," he said to Ropey, who came up swinging a long iron with a curved, red-hot end.

That individual grinned maliciously. "Well, well, fancy that," he said. "Say, Navajo, the boys brought in one o' Sam Eden's cows yestiddy; what we goin' to do about it?"

The half-breed slouched over. "S'pose we oughta take her back an' 'pologize, but I guess we won't," he replied, and grabbing the iron he added a few deft touches to the old brand, joining the ends of the S and the horizontal strokes of the E. "There, she's an honest-to-Gawd 8 B now, an' as cows can't talk, nobody'll know different." He gave Sudden an ugly grin. "Mistakes will happen, an' I wouldn't be s'prised if there's a few more."

The tie-man knew he was being chaffed, but he was not foolish enough to show resentment. Instead, he returned the grin.

"Eden oughta make his brand bigger—he's got all the side o' the animal," he said.

They laughed at this, but he fancied he could detect disappointment in their expressions. The arrival of another steer, hauled by the ropes of two perspiring, blasphemous riders, ended the incident. From then on the man from Crawling Creek was kept busy, and, as he now expected, four out of every five of the beasts he handled bore the S E brand. So it was plain rustling. Nevertheless, he did his work with a thoroughness which earned reluctant approval even from Navajo.

"That hombre knows his job," he admitted to Ropey.

"Shore does," that worthy agreed. "Never seed anyone tie 'em so slick."

"Mebbe; but I don't like him," Navajo said.

"I'm plumb astonished," was Ropey's unveracious retort.

# Chapter 6

The outlaw leader returned that same evening, and from his cheerful mood, it was evident that his errand had been successful. After supper, he called Sudden aside.

"Been helpin' the boys brand?" he asked casually.

"Been helpin' 'em blot brands," Sudden corrected.

Rogue's brows ridged in a little frown. "Yu didn't think this was a Methodis' community when yu come here, did yu?" he asked acidly, and then, "Shucks, what's a few cows anyway? I got a big thing on now, Jim, one that'll give yu a chance o' gettin' away for a time. Savvy?"

Sudden nodded, and the other went on exultantly, "Here's the lay-out: Eden is takin' a hefty herd—three thousand head—north, an' a fella I know is hopin' it won't get there." He smiled felinely. "In fact, he's hopin' so hard that he's willin' to pay pretty handsomely if it don't, an' buy—at a fair price—all the S E cows offered him."

"Failure to make the drive would bust Eden wide open, huh?"

"Yeah, it's his last hope, I reckon; he's been buyin' land an' got in deep. But that don't concern me; a fella has to take care of hisself. Now, he'll want riders an' I'm proposin' that yu an' Sandy get took on—can't use the other boys, their faces is known. Yu can see how it would help me to have a coupla men on the inside. We'll be on the heels o' the herd an' can keep in touch with yu. Far as yo're concerned, it gives yu a trail outa present trouble an' a tidy wad into the bargain. What d'yu say?"

"I'll drop in at the S E in the morning'," Sudden told him. "Where d'yu aim to break the drive?"

"That'll depend on how things pan out, but not till they've got too far to come back an' gather another herd," the outlaw said. "Glad yo're comin' in, Jim; yu can wise up Sandy." He hesitated a moment. "Hear yu had trouble with Ropey."

Sudden laughed. "I just had to let the fellas know that I'm growed up. I'd say it was Navajo's play."

"Like enough," Rogue agreed, and his face grew dark. "One day I'll have to argue with that hombre."

The cowboy came away from the interview with mixed feelings, certain only of one thing—he would join the S E, but whether as friend or foe he had not decided; the deliberate part of his nature was in charge at the moment. He found Sandy loafing outside their habitation and prefaced his message from Rogue by relating his adventure of the previous afternoon.

"Well, if yu ain't the lucky one!" the young man ejaculated. "Here's me been ridin' round for weeks an' never had no chance to deliver a distressed damsel. Bet she's hatchet-faced, squint-eyed, an' bellers like a sick cow."

"Yu musta seen the lady," Sudden smiled.

"I ain't—never knowed there was any female women in this neck o' the woods," was the reply. "Who is she?" For Sudden had not told all the story.

"Sam Eden's daughter."

"She was stringin' yu—he ain't got any."

"Adopted daughter, I oughta said—orphaned kid of an old friend," Sudden explained, adding inconsequently, "Eden offered me a job."

"Goin' to take it?"

"We are," replied the other, and went on to tell of the outlaw leader's designs, and the part they were to play. Sandy listened with wooden features.

"Sounds good," he commented. "I'd shore like to be in on that drive; but Rogue's wrong in one thing—I ain't such a stranger around here." He thought awhile and then slapped his knee. "Got it!" he exclaimed.

"What, a mosquito ?" Sudden asked.

"No, an idea—don't yu never have none?"

"Yeah. Why, *both* my knees are sore right now."

The youth ignored the gentle raillery. "Where's that stuff yu used on yore hoss?" he inquired.

"On the shelf inside," Sudden replied. "Goin' to black yore face an' play nigger?"

Sandy's retort was neither polite nor printable.

* * *

Sunrise found a grumbling cook giving the man early breakfast; but his curiosity regarding Sandy's black hair, eyebrows, and moustache remained unsatisfied.

"Ask Rogue about it," the boy told him with a grin, knowing perfectly well that he would do no such thing.

For the first few miles the pair rode in silence. Sudden was trying to convince himself that the affairs of the S E owner were no concern of his, and not succeeding very well. His companion was also deep in thought, riding head down.

The morning air had an invigorating keenness which would presently change to a blistering heat. Around them, Nature was awaking; birds whistled, rabbits scuttled across their path, and once they saw the long grey form of a big wolf slink into the brush at their approach. It was Sandy who made the first remark:

"Odd I ain't heard o' this gal at the S E."

"She's recently arrived from the East—educated there, I gathered," Sudden explained.

Sandy snorted. "I get yu," he said. "One o' them high-toned dames, with a forehead bulging out like a cliff, who thinks pore ignorant cowboys is doormats to wipe their number eights on."

Sudden chuckled silently. "Now I know yu've met her," he said.

"Yo're wrong, but I savvy the breed," the boy went on. "Thinlipped, an' that sot in their ideas they'd argue with a charge o' giant-powder."

"She looked liable to get her own way most times," Sudden admitted. "She had the ol' man roped."

"There yu are," Sandy cried triumphantly. "An' let me tell yu, a mule is an easy-goin' critter alongside Sam Eden. Why, it's told of him that once, when he was gettin' the worst of an argument, he finished it by sayin', "Well, I wouldn't believe it if I knowed it was true.' What can yu do with a fella like that, huh?"

Sudden laughed, partly at the story, but more at the reflection that his friend was due to receive a severe shock when he met the girl he had condemned unseen. Sandy's next remark changed the subject.

"I wouldn't be so terrible distressed if Rogue fell down on this drive-bustin'," he mused. "I don't owe him nothin' an' I shore would like to see them northern cowtowns."

Sudden did not reply at once; he was wondering if the words had any hidden significance.

"I've a hankerin' thataway my own self," he confessed.

They reached the S E ranch-house to find it apparently deserted; the morning meal was over and the men had gone to their work. A hail brought Eden himself to the porch. At the sight of Sudden he called a hearty greeting:

"Hello, young fella, I'm main pleased to see yu. Hope yu aim to stay this time."

"Shore do, Mister Eden, if yu'll have me," Sudden replied. He pointed to his companion. "This is Dick Sands—he's huntin' a job too."

The rancher studied the second of the visitors closely for a moment. "Any friend o' yores is welcome, Green, an' I can certainly use another man," he said, but the warmth had gone out of his voice.

Before another word could be said, Carol emerged from the house, her face lighting up when she recognized the rider who had come to her rescue. Sudden stole a look at his chum and had hard work to restrain his merriment. Sandy had snatched his hat off and was staring goggle-eyed at the girl who had, so far, hardly looked at him. Sudden mentioned his name again and Carol gave the young man a smile of welcome which completed his discomfiture.

"Well, boys, what's the word?" Eden asked.

"We'll go yu," Sandy blurted out eagerly.

"Good," the rancher replied. "Leave yore war-bags in the bunkhouse. There's plenty hosses in the corral—that mount o' yores, Green, is too good for hazin' longhorns out'n the brush." He pointed to a cloud of dust some miles away on the plain. "The herd is there."

He climbed briskly into his saddle, the girl followed, and they galloped away. Sandy watched till they vanished over a swell in the ground, and then turned to find his companion doubled up over his saddle-horn. He looked at him suspiciously.

"Got a misery in yore stumick?" he asked.

"Yeah, these hatchet-faced, squint-eyed dames allus give me a pain," Sudden chortled, ashake with mirth.

Sandy swore. "Damn funny, ain't it? Look here, yu misfit, breathe a word o' that to her an' I'll trample the gut's out'n yu."

"Get her to do it with them number eights," Sudden advised, and then his hand went up. "Awright, I'll be good. Come an' grab them hosses; I'll bet there's some work a-waitin'."

They soon reached the spot the rancher had indicated. Already about a thousand head had been assembled, and, kept bunched by a couple of riders, were grazing contentedly on the short grama grass which covered the plain. The herd was a mixed one; evidently everything in the shape of a cow was being rounded up, and the bellowing of the bulls mingled with the bleating of the calves as they staggered weakly after their mothers. At the moment Sudden and his partner approached, an addition of thirty animals arrived, convoyed by two riders who presented a striking contrast, one of them being tall and abnormally thin while the other was short and fat. As Sudden learned later, the pair were great friends, and quarrelled perpetually.

"Well, boys, yu shore have been busy," Eden greeted them.

"Ain't all our'n," the tall man explained. "Met Pebbles an' the Infant, an' took over their gather."

"Here's a couple o' fresh helpers, Jed. Yu better take Green, an' Dumpy can put Sandy wise."

As the four men rode away, Jed cast a quizzical glance at his late partner and remarked audibly, "Now I got me a real side-kick 'stead o' that dollop o' drippin' we'll git some cows."

The fat man rose to the bait instantly. "G'wan, yu graveyard relic," he retorted. "Yu watch out, stranger; he'll let yu do all the work; that fella wouldn't breathe if he could git anybody to do it for him."

Jed replied with an impolite gesture, and wheeling his horse to the left, motioned Sudden to follow.

"We've pretty well cleaned up around here—have to go further afield," he said.

A short ride brought them to where the plain slid off into a spread of country which looked as though it had been the scene of an earthquake. Out of this the longhorns, wild, fierce-eyed, had to be driven, and the task proved to be a trying one to both man and horse. Crashing into the underbrush the riders unearthed a couple of steers and drove them into the open. Then, in turn, each guarded the "catch" while the other searched for additions. Both jobs demanded alertness and patience, for the cattle made repeated efforts to break away. The approach of evening found them with a collection of near two score.

"Pardner, we done noble," Jed said. "Reckon when we git 'em to the main herd we can call it a day."

"Suits me," Sudden grinned, and smacked the nose of a straying steer with his rope. "I certainly hope yu got a good cook; my belt's damn near slippin' off'n me."

"Peg-leg's the finest cook in Texas—he says so hisself," Jed laughed. "An' he shore can talk to mules in the language they understand."

In their search for cattle they had drifted some distance from the plain, and dark was creeping up by the time they reached the herd. The sight of a big fire and the near-by chuck-wagon brought a doleful expression on Jed's face.

"Gotta sleep on our saddles to-night, seemin'ly," he said.

"Yu'll be some lucky if yu sleep a-tall," a new voice put in.

Another rider had caught them up—a wispy little man, nearing fifty, from whose brown face, wrinkled like a walnut, small blue eyes peered at the pair amusedly.

"'Lo, Jeff." Jed greeted, and turning to his partner, added, "This is our foreman—a pretty ornery fella, as yu can see, Green."

The little man chuckled and shoved out a paw. "Heard o' yu from the ol' Man," he said. "We can use yu." He waved towards the grazing cattle. "The bunch is gettin' big an' wants watchin', which is why we're campin' alongside. Also, Sam is on the rampage, I reckon we gotta start *workin'* to-morrow."

"Sufferin' cats!" wailed the cowboy. "C'mon, Green, let's join the other loafers an' load up before this slavedriver makes it to-day."

Having unsaddled and turned their mounts loose—the beasts were too tired to stray far—they joined the group squatting round the fire.

"Hey, Jed, how many yu fetch in?" Dumpy inquired.

"Coupla score, if it's any o' yore damned business," Jed said.

"An' mighty good goin'," commented another.

"Aw, Jed knows the easy places," the fat man gibed.

"Then I wish he'd picked on 'em," Sudden said ruefully. "I'll never see a pincushion again without feelin' sorry for it."

There was a general laugh at this, for all the men were scratched and torn, despite the stout leather "leggin's" they wore.

Sudden had a word with Sandy.

"We joined this outfit too soon," he said whimsically. "We'd oughta waited till they was ready to drive."

"I wish we hadn't joined a-tall," his friend replied. "No, that ain't so neither, but—hell, what's the use?"

With which cryptic remark he rolled his blanket round him and went to sleep. Sudden, too tired even to wonder about this attitude, followed his example. Slumber must be made the most of; if anything disturbed the cattle, there would be no more for any of them that night.

# Chapter 7

Soon after dawn the men were astir and crowding round the fire, for the early air was keen. Breakfast over, Jeff divided his forces, half were to begin the branding while the others continued to build up the herd. Sudden and Sandy, as not knowing the range, were allotted to the second task, a decision which—to the former's surprise, met with his friend's satisfaction.

"We're shorely outa luck," he remarked tentatively.

"Suits me," Sandy replied gaily. "We'll show these hombres how to label long-horns." He straightened his neckerchief, slapped the dust from his clothes, and fingered his chin uneasily. "Say, Jim, yu got a razor?" He saw the dawning grin of comprehension on the other's face, and added hastily, "These whiskers o' mine'll come out the wrong colour, yu know."

"Mine's at the bunkhouse," Sudden said. "I saw the cook scrapin' his jaw a piece ago."

Peg-leg obliged with a razor and a cracked mirror.

"Which if yo're goin' to this trouble on account o' Miss Carol, yu needn't," he advised. "She'll be too busy to look at yu."

"I ain't," Sandy stated, with a flash which contradicted the assertion. "Can't stand a scrubby chin, that's all."

The cook's grimace was one of disbelief—he had seen other newcomers suffering from the same affliction, but he said no more; he was a man of few words but, as was once remarked, those few were frequently "damn near as strong as his caw-fee."

The branding promised to be a big job. Chutes were unknown in the south-west of that day, and each animal had to be dealt with separately. Sandy found he was to work with his friend. Sudden was waiting for him, a bundle of short tie-ropes (piggin strings) in his hand.

"Hey, yu lady-slayer," he called. "Yank some o' them bawlin' brutes over here an' don't keep me waitin'."

"They'll come so quick yu'll get dizzy," the young man promised. "I'll make yu think it's rainin' cows."

Sudden smiled at the boyish boast. While his was the more dangerous and tricky task, he fancied he could keep ahead of Sandy. But that optimist had helpers and soon the tie-man had his hands full. The rays of the rising sun quickly drove the chill from the air, and growing in intensity, added to the discomfort of the workers. Perspiration drenched their faces but failed to remove the grime from the ever-rising clouds of dust. Sweat caked on the flanks of galloping mustangs. Cows bellowed and frightened calves blatted as they were hauled willy-nilly to the fire. The shouts and rough banter of the riders merged with the rattle of horns in the milling herd. Sudden looking up in a moment of respite, found Eden watching him.

"Good work, Green," he said, and as Sandy with a whoop, rushed up another unwilling victim, roped and threw it, he added: "Yore friend seems to know his job too."

He rode off without waiting for a reply, and Sudden was glad; the praise worried him. He stole a glance at Sandy—who was freeing his rope from the helpless steer—and was surprised to see that the boy's face was redder than even the fierce sun and his exertions warranted. He too had heard what the cattleman had said.

"Yu boys have certainly made a hit with Sam," the foreman commented.

Sudden grunted an agreement. He liked the outfit and its owner, and he was there to help ruin him. He tried to tell himself that the world, having made him an outlaw, was to blame for any consequences, but he could not make the argument convincing. Fortunately, he had little time for reflection; the cutters were doing their work well.

"Told yu I'd make yu hustle, didn't I ?" Sandy said, a little later.

" 'Pears to me some other fella fetches along a steer now an' then," Sudden replied, as he mopped his dirt-streaked features. "Say, I got an idea. Yu swap jobs with me tomorrow an' yu won't have to worry 'bout shavin'."

"Nothin' doin'. Wouldn't change places with yu for a blue stack."

Sudden detected his involuntary glance over the plain to where Miss Carol was busy bunching the branded cattle into a separate herd, and his eyes twinkled understandingly. Sandy's work took him near that trim little figure.

"Shucks, I've done told Jeff yu can tie 'em two at a lick," he said teasingly.

"I'm goin' to tell him that as a liar yu got Ananias beat a mile before he opens his mouth," Sandy retorted, and to his horse, "G'wan, yu son o' sin, we'll give this fella suthin' else to think about."

He shot off towards the herd and had almost reached it when he saw something which made him swerve suddenly: a newly-branded steer, mad with rage and pain, was rushing full at Carol Eden, who, intent on her charges, did not see it. With a yell of warning, Sandy raced and swung his rope. The loop dropped over the brute's horns and with a flip, he sent the slack over the rump and spurred his mount to the left, jerking the hind legs from under the steer. As it crashed down, the girl became aware of her danger and jumped her pony away. The fall had taken the fight out of the steer; as soon as the rope was removed it scrambled to its feet and lumbered off. Carol's face was pale.

"Thank you," she smiled. "I'm afraid you'll think I'm a tenderfoot to be caught like that."

Sandy's customary assurance had deserted him; he was the picture of confusion. Also, he was finding breathing difficult, for it had indeed been a near thing; had he missed his throw....He shuddered at what might have been; the pony ripped up, the rider on the ground, at the mercy of those sweeping, sharp-pointed horns. Hat in hand, he stammered some commonplace, cursing himself inwardly for a tongue-tied fool. Her eyes rested on him kindly.

"You are Mister Green's friend, aren't you?" she asked. "He came to my assistance too, so I'm now obliged to both of you. I ought to be glad you joined the outfit."

"I'm hopin' yu will be," Sandy managed to say, and, as he saw his employer approaching, "Gosh, I'm forgettin' I got a job."

As he dragged a complaining calf on the end of his rope to the branding fire he communed with himself:

"What come over yu, yu lunkhead, to let a bit of a gal like that scare yu all up ? She musta thought yu was dumb."

But his eyes were shining when he handed over his prisoner, and his sweaty, grimed face wore such an expression of content that Sudden could not help but notice it.

"Yu look like yu was all lit up from inside," he said. "Havin' a good time, huh?"

"Never had a better," came the sober reply.

"It would do Rogue's heart good to see that bunch over there," Sudden said meaningly, nodding in the direction of the gathered cattle.

"Yeah," Sandy snarled, whirled his pony, and was gone, leaving his friend in a thoughtful frame of mind.

* * *

Days passed, days made up of long hours filled with incessant, monotonous toil in the blistering heat, and steadily the herd increased. The weather remained fine, feed was plentiful on the plain, and the branded cattle gave no trouble.

"For which, thank the Lawd," Jeff said fervently. "If them critters took it into their fool heads to stampede, it'd be just merry hell."

Even when the herd was complete, much remained to be done. The big covered wagon, with its team of six mules, had to be overhauled and loaded with provisions, flour, bacon, coffee, New Orleans molasses—familiarly known as "blackstrap"—pickles, and a limited supply of dried fruits. The remuda had to be selected —five horses for each man—weapons and ammunition prepared.

Twelve men, including the rancher and the cook, were to accompany the herd, two older members of the outfit remaining behind to "hold down the ranch." These preparations entailed constant effort, for Eden was eager to start.

Sudden had little chance of converse with his friend during these days of stress, for the brief hours of rest were too precious to be wasted, but he got more or less acquainted with the other members of the outfit and decided that Sam Eden was a good judge of a man. Rough, reckless, and shabby-looking, they were nevertheless capable. Only one he did not approve of—a newcomer like himself —a big, dark, bewhiskered fellow named Lasker, who was in charge of the remuda, a position which was poorly-regarded in a cow-camp. He knew nothing against the man but instinctively distrusted him.

"He's got mean eyes," he explained to Sandy.

"Well, I dessay the hosses won't mind," was the indifferent reply.

Sudden looked at him thoughtfully. The boy had changed since they had joined the S E; his gay impudence had gone, to be replaced by a moody irritability. "He's pretty near played out, like the rest of us," was his unspoken reflection, but he knew it was not a satisfactory solution, for bone-weary as all the men were, enthusiasm prevailed, whereas Sandy appeared disgruntled, sick of the whole business.

"Jeff tells me we're all set for an early start tomorrow," Sudden offered.

"It'll be a relief to get away from this blasted plain," was all Sandy had to say.

When the rancher and his daughter made their appearance in the morning they were accompanied by Baudry. Together they inspected the herd.

"They look good to me, but surely you have some oldish stuff amongst them," the gambler commented.

"Oh, I reckon they'll pass with the rest," Eden said. "Yu remember what the foreman o' one o' the early drives told the buyer who made the same complaint? 'Stranger,' he says, 'if yu'd bin through half what them critters has, yu'd look twice yore age.'"

Baudry laughed. "Well, you know your business, Sam, and I wish you all the luck there is," he rejoined. "I'll be coming north myself and shall expect to see you. Hear of the killing at Littleton?"

This was a settlement some thirty miles distant, and the ranch having had no visitors was without news. Eden said as much.

"Coolest thing ever," Baudry went on. "A stranger steps into Gregg's Saloon just after dusk, shoots the dealer at the monte table, collects all the cash in sight and backs out. When the company comes to life again, he's clean away."

"Another o' Rogue's capers, I s'pose?" the rancher said.

"They say not, unless he's got a new hand," Baudry replied.

"From his looks, and a remark he made, he was Sudden, the Fourways and San Antonio killer." A rider on a big black horse, waiting to assist in starting the herd, caught his eye. "Why, that might be the fellow, by the description," he finished.

"What, Green?" the cattleman grinned. "He's been tied to this camp pretty tight the last two-three weeks. No, Jethro, there ain't no murderers in his outfit; Jim's all right."

The young man heard the words, but they brought him no satisfaction; the gambler's harsh voice had also carried to where he sat and the bitterness he had been trying to blot out of his life had overwhelmed him again. Another crime had been unjustly placed to his discredit. The world was determined that he should be an outlaw. Very well, since there was no other way...

He came out of his dark musing to find that the word had been given and the herd was already on the move, the point riders leading the way, the swing and flank men stringing the cattle out into a long line. Two men looked after the "drag," and behind came the remuda, in charge of the horse-wrangler, and the wagon. The Great Adventure had begun.

Under the blazing sun the herd tramped steadily on. No great difficulty was anticipated until they crossed the Colorado River, the country south of that being familiar to most of the men. Nightfall found them camped near a little creek. From where the cattle were settling down came a somewhat cracked voice wailing the interminable verses of "The Cowboy's Lament" and one of the men squatting at the fireside laughed.

"Lucky cows ain't got no ear for music," he said. "The Infant's screech would start a stampede."

For Sudden, riding moodily round the herd, watching first one and then another sink down to sleep, the night brought only the opportunity to brood over his own troubles. Little more than half a mile away he could see the gleam of the campfire; if the men sitting round it knew who he was, they would hang him before dawn. And for this he had to thank Rogue, whom he was there to serve. Idly he wondered what the outlaw was doing, or about to do, and then swore savagely that he did not care. Which was not the truth.

* * *

Having watched the herd depart and waved an ironical farewell, Baudry turned his horse's head towards San Antonio. Five miles along the trail, squatting with his back against a spreading cedar, a man was waiting. Baudry got down, glad to avail himself of the shade.

"Well, Navajo, the S E drive has started," he said. "What are Rogue's plans?"

The half-breed grinned unpleasantly. "Yu better ask him," he retorted. "His word was that he'd do the job—his own way."

The gambler's face reddened but he summoned a smile. "Suits me, so long as it's done," he replied. "Sam seems pretty confident."

"He ain't got a chanct," the other stated.

"I think he has," Baudry said coolly. "In fact, I have so strong a belief in my friend Eden's courage and determination that I'd be willing to wager that he'll take his cattle through and return safely to his ranch."

The ruffian laughed evilly. "Shore yu would," he sneered. "How much?"

"One thousand dollars."

"I'm takin' yore bet. Give it me in writin'—I got a shockin' memory." The jeer in the man's voice was insulting but Baudry chose to ignore it.

"You needn't worry, I always pay my debts," he said.

Nevertheless, he wrote a few words in a notebook, tore out the page and passed it to the other. Navajo grinned as he tucked it away in a pocket.

"Money from home," he chuckled. "This ain't nothin' to do with Rogue, yu savvy? So long."

The gambler stood watching his receding form, his thick lips set in grim threat.

"There's more than one way of paying a debt, you scum," he snarled. "When you've served your purpose..."

# Chapter 8

The Colorado River had been reached without any untoward incident, and the S E drive was camped on the south bank waiting for daylight to make the crossing. So far, everything had gone well, and, with perfect weather, the herd had made good time. Supper was over, and the foreman, Sudden, and several others were smoking beside the fire, for, though the days were hot, the evenings were chill. There was a thicket to the right of the camp—the first timber they had seen for days—and the cook was busy chopping wood and loading it into the rawhide slung beneath the wagon, for his store of buffalo "chips"—the only fuel to be found on the plains—was getting low.

"Well, trail-drivin' suits me. Why, it won't be no trick a-tall to push the bunch into Kansas."

This from the gangling youth known as "Infant." The foreman surveyed him sardonically.

"Bein' a kid I s'pose yu gotta talk like one," he said. "If yu think it's all going' to be like this yu got another guess comin'. An' that kind o' yap is shore unlucky. Ol' Man Trouble allus camps on the tail of a trail-herd, an' we'll hear from him soon enough without askin' for it."

"That's so," agreed another, who, being reputed to be the biggest liar in Texas, was called "Truthful." "I remember once——"

"Forget it twice," Jeff snapped. "What's come o' Sands? He ain't with the herd."

No one seemed to know. He had eaten with the rest of them and then slipped away. Sudden had seen him go and smothered an impulse to follow because he had a feeling that the boy had avoided him of late. He glanced round the camp, but there was no sign of the missing man. Against the dark background of the trees the little tent used by the women gleamed whitely. A few yards away from it, Sam Eden leaned on the wagon-tongue and chatted with the cook. Then, out of a thick tangle of bushes some forty paces from the wagon came a spurt of flame, followed by the vicious crack of a gun, and the sturdy figure of the rancher staggered and fell.

"Hell's bells!" Jeff cried, and ran to the stricken man.

The others followed, all save Sudden, who raced for the spot whence the shot had come. Noiselessly he searched, peering into the gloomy depths of the brush, listening for the snap of a breaking twig which would tell of a stealthy retreat, but he saw and heard nothing. Then came a careless footstep, a slouching figure swung into view and halted at Sudden's curt command.

"Lo, Jim. What's the bright idea, stickin' up yore friends?" asked a familiar voice.

It was Sandy, and despite himself, a note of suspicion crept into Sudden's question, "What are yu doin' here?"

"Goin' back to camp; what yu reckon?"

"Where yu been?"

"Pickin' flowers," came the ironic reply.

"Quit foolin'," Sudden said sternly. "Sam Eden was shot from bout here less'n a quarter of an hour back."

"Sam—Eden—shot?" Sandy repeated. "God! An' yo're guessin' I did it?"

"I ain't doin' any guessin'," Sudden told him. "I came to catch the skunk an' bump into yu. Come clean."

"Is he hurt bad?"

"I didn't wait to see; Jeff an' some o' the boys is there. Yu ain't answered my question."

"I had nothin' to do with it, Jim," the boy said hoarsely, "but it's likely I saw the fella. Mebbe ten minutes or so ago, a mere shadow, slippin' through the bush. I didn't give it much attention—reckoned it was Lasker, goin' after his hosses—but it may not have been him a-tall. Hell! it'll break his gal's heart." Sudden's silence told him there was more to say. "Yu hear an owl hootin' while we fed ?" he asked.

"Yeah, an' judged he was a pretty early bird," Sudden said.

The other nodded. "Overlookin' details like that'll land Rogue's neck in a noose some day," he remarked. "Yeah, I saw him."

Sudden's eyes narrowed. "When did he leave yu?"

"Pretty near half an hour back—I didn't hurry."

"Then he mighta done the shootin'?"

"Could have—he had time, but it don't fit with his plans."

"We better get back—it won't look too good for us to be absent, an' together," Sudden suggested. "We'll have a pow-wow later."

They had almost reached the camp when Lasker pounded up with a string of night-horses. He stopped on seeing them.

"Heard about the ol' Man bein' bushwhacked, Lasker?" Sudden asked.

The man's surprise seemed genuine. "Hell, no; who done it?"

"Yore guess is as good as mine," was the reply.

"With him cashed the drive ends, I s'pose," the wrangler offered.

"Who told yu he's dead?" Sudden asked quietly, and then, "Well, mebbe he is; we'll soon know."

The camp was very still. The other men had sought their blankets but the foreman sat near the fire, rifle beside him, and his face a mask of worry. He looked up as the two friends approached; the horse-wrangler was seeing to his charges.

"This is a turr'ble business, Jim," he said, and sensing the question uppermost in their minds, "No, Eden ain't cashed—yet. We got him bedded down in the wagon, an' I've tended, the wound—it ain't the first time I've played doctor by a-many. The slug went clean through an' 'pears to have missed the vital parts. Plenty desperate, but it might be wuss; he's got a fightin' chance."

"Then he'll make it," Sudden said confidently. "He's the fightin' sort."

"Beats me who the murderin' houn' could be?" Jeff pondered.

"I went to see if I could catch him but didn't have no luck," Sudden explained. "Sandy saw someone hot-footin' through the brush an' figured it was Laskar."

"Laskar, huh?" the foreman muttered. "Well, he's a new hand, but there ain't no reason. Yu boys better turn in—I'll be needin' yu presently; gotta have four men watchin' the herd to-night."

It was two hours later when Jeff's low voice awakened them—in those dangerous days it was unwise to arouse a sleeper by touching him. They approached the slumbering herd slowly, exchanged a few words with the men they had come to relieve, and separated.

Sudden was riding Nigger, for the night-horse has to be the surest-footed, clearest-sighted, most intelligent of the cowboy's string of mounts. Knowing that the black would give instant warning of anything wrong, the rider allowed himself to think. The cold-blooded attempt to remove Eden had brought him definitely to the parting of ways. He had little doubt but the outlaw chief had been concerned in it, and the thought of working with men capable of such a deed sickened him. The world had given him the name, but not the stomach, of a desperado.

Another point which worried him was the attitude of Sandy. "The girl has him spell-bound, an' yet he's runnin' with Rogue," he mused.

The two things did not seem to jibe and he resolved to clear the situation at the earliest opportunity. This came when, relieved in their turn, they were riding slowly back to camp.

"I'm puttin' a plain question," Sudden said. "Are yu workin' for Rogue, or ain't yu?"

"I'm givin' yu a plain answer," Sandy replied. "To hell with Rogue, an' yu can tell him I said so. Yu may be in his debt but I ain't. Sabe?"

Sudden's laugh was bitter. "I'll tell yu what I owe him," he said slowly.

Pacing side by side in the starlight, he could not see the listener's face, but the muttered exclamations the story evoked showed his. interest. When it was ended, Sandy drew a deep breath.

"My Gawd, yu have shorely had a tough break, Jim," he said. "I reckon all that's due Rogue from yu is a slug o' lead."

"Well, he got me in a jam unmeanin' an' he certainly took a risk to get me out again—which some wouldn't," Sudden replied. "Anyways, it's past mendin'; even if I could prove I didn't kill Judson, the San Antonio affair an' this other, would hang me. Yo're ridin' with a shore-enough outlaw, Sandy."

"An' damn glad to be," the boy said impulsively, thrusting out a fist. "I'm with yu to the finish, Jim, whatever it may be."

Sudden gripped the hand; it did him good to feel that he had a friend who, knowing all, trusted him.

"I'm obliged," he said simply. "When I joined this outfit my mind was all twisty-ways an' I didn't know what I was goin' to do. Now, I've got things straightened out; I'm on Sam Eden's payroll."

"That goes for me too," Sandy rejoined. "We'll beat that gang o'chaparral thieves yet."

Immediately after breakfast, the foreman called a meeting of all the men in camp to discuss what should be done. Lasker was the first to speak:

"Nothin' for it but to turn back, fur as I c'n see."

"Then yore eyesight ain't what it oughta be," Sudden put in. "I'm for goin' on; the ol' Man'll want that, I'm bettin'."

Other opinions, for and against, were expressed and in the middle of the argument a hail from the cook appraised Jeff that his employer wanted him. From his bed in the wagon the rancher glared at his foreman.

"What's all the chatter about?" he asked in a weak but angry voice. "Why ain't yu startin' the herd?"

"We was sorta settlin' which way to go," the foreman excused.

"There's on'y one, yu ol' fool—north'ards," Eden snapped, and then, as comprehension came to him, "Yu wasn't thinkin' o' goin' *back*?"

Jeff looked uneasy. "Well, yu see, Sam, we figured yu oughta have proper medical attention," he explained.

The patient's pale face grew red with rage. "Medical attention, huh?" he sneered. "Yu talk like a perfessor, an' a damn silly one at that. D'yu reckon I've never been shot afore? Pretty fine outfit I got if yo're goin' to turn tail an' run at the first bit o' trouble."

"That's not fair, Dad," Carol reproved. "They are thinking of you."

"You're right, honey," Eden said. "I didn't mean that, Jeff, but yu can cut out the doctor-talk—I don't need no help to die. An' let me hear no more o' goin' back; we'll take this herd through come hell or high water. Now, git them cows movin', or I'll be up an' see to it my own self."

"An', by Christmas, he'd 'a' tried it," Jeff said, when he reported the conversation to the others. "Stubborn as two mules, ol' Sam is, an' tough as rawhide. They say he once rode fifty miles with a busted leg—tied hisself to the saddle, knowin' if he fell off he'd never git on again."

The only man who did not seem pleased was Lasker. "It's a fool play," he said sullenly. "He'll never make the trip—we'll have to plant him."

"Awright, we won't ask yu to dig the hole," Jeff retorted. "Take care o' yore hosses—we're shorely goin' to need 'em."

Sudden had a small investigation to make. In a patch of bare earth in the brush from whence the shot had come he found clear prints of a pair of moccasins, and scorched, shrivelled leaves showed where the weapon had been fired through the foliage. With a strip of rawhide he measured the marks, making knots to indicate the width and length. His search for further footprints proved fruitless.

"Either made his getaway over grass or wanted them tracks to be seen," was his muttered conclusion.

Dismissing the matter for the moment he rode to the river, where preparations for crossing were in full swing. Conditions were favourable, shelving banks, and not much current. Already the cattle, grazed and watered, were being strung out and headed for the stream. Jeff, bawling orders right and left, was watching the operation.

The riders who had to guide the herd across the stream had stripped to the middle, also removing boots and saddles, and were shivering in the keen morning air. One of them had already made the trip, returning with the tidings that the bed of the river seemed fairly firm and the deep water not too extensive.

"Don't rush 'em, boys," the foreman instructed. "Haze 'em along gradual-like but keep 'em movin'. We want to be over before the sun gits too high, an' these damn streams is liable to rise mighty sudden."

There was little trouble; the leading steers, when they felt the cold water sweeping beneath their bellies, tried to retreat, but the watchful riders, with quirts and the ends of their ropes kept them from turning and soon they took the plunge and swam steadily for the opposite bank.

The crossing took time but went without a hitch, and Jeff breathed a sigh of relief when the last steers climbed the far bank, shook themselves, and went to peacefully grazing. The remuda followed, and then the wagon came lumbering up, a sizable, trimmed tree-trunk lashed along each side. Drawn, by its full team of six mules, it rocked and slithered down the slope to the stream. The leaders baulked at the water but the biting lash of the long whip stung their flanks and threw them into the collars again.

With a couple of riders on either side steadying it with their ropes, the wagon proceeded slowly but majestically across, to be greeted with a cheer when the dripping team hauled it safely up the bank.

The foreman, who had followed the vehicle over, poked his head through the flaps at the back. "How'd she go, Sam?" he asked anxiously.

"Fine—never jarred me none," the invalid lied stoutly. "Get agoin' soon as yu like; it does me good to feel we're movin'."

Jeff was not deceived; he knew quite well that the crossing must have caused intense pain to the wounded man, but he also knew Sam Eden. As he turned away, Carol jumped down lightly from the wagon.

"Jeff, you're a dear," she said impulsively. "Of course it hurt him terribly although we did all we could to spare him the jolts, but he bore it without a murmur. We must push on; he'll fret himself into a fever if we delay."

The foreman made unintelligible noises in his throat and was obviously glad when Sandy rode up leading Carol's pony.

"Thought yu'd mebbe like a ride after the boat-trip, ma'am." he grinned.

She thanked him, swung into the saddle, and loped along the trail. The cowboy's eyes followed her, until a slight cough from his companion recalled his wandering thoughts.

"She shore can ride," he remarked hastily, and then, "How's the Ol' Man makin' it?"

"Pretty good, considerin'," the foreman told him, "an' liable to raise Cain if that wagon ain't on the move pronto."

Sandy took the hint and found himself a job.

# Chapter 9

The long straggling line of men and beasts moved like a sluggish stream over the apparently unending area of brown, sun-dried earth, cracked and fissured by the fierce heat, and covered, for the most part, by short curly grass which, the colour of hay, needed only rain to transform it into a carpet of brilliant green. No tree, save an occasional thicket of stunted mesquite or live-oak, was to be seen.

Uneventful days had slid by since they crossed the Colorado, and the outfit was making the most of an easy time. Lolling in their saddles, the riders had little to do save check the ambition of any steer who seemed disposed to stray too far. Even the foreman's lined, leathery countenance wore an unwonted smile as he rode to Sudden's side and nodded at the surrounding scene.

"All like this an' it'd be easy, but it ain't goin' to be," he remarked. "We got most of our troubles ahead of us."

"Yu can say that any time, any place," the cowboy grinned. "How's the Ol' Man?"

"He's a flamin' merricle," the foreman replied. "It's a wonder that bullet didn't bounce off'n him." Then his voice sobered. "I'd like to know who done it. Got any ideas?"

Sudden told of the moccasin marks and mentioned the Indian who had escaped when he rescued Carol. Jeff shook his head.

"Might be, o' course, redskins is vindictive devils, but I don't think it an' neither do yu," he said shrewdly.

To this the other made no reply. He was studying the broad, trampled track they were following.

"Yu figure this is Chisholm's trail?" he asked.

"I'm hopin' so. Anyways, she's good goin' an' pointin' north, which is all we want," Jeff told him. His gaze travelled forward along the line of cattle to where Sandy and Carol were riding together, and his eyes twinkled. "Yore friend is cuttin' yu out."

Sudden looked at him amusedly. "That was a mighty poor throw, ol'-timer," he said. "I've got somethin' to do before I think o' wedded bliss. Ever hear o' fellas called Webb an' Peterson?"

"No, but names ain't nothin' in these parts," Jeff replied. "Yu wantin' 'em special, Jim?"

"I'm hopin' to run across 'em," Sudden said, and though there was no threat in the words, the cold, passionless tone sent a chill down even the hardened spine of the foreman.

That evening, before supper, Sudden drew Sandy apart.

"If yu can get yore mind off that lean, hatchet-faced female yu been ridin' with all day——" he commenced.

"Jim, she's an—angel," Sandy interrupted.

"Shore she is," his friend agreed dryly. "Likewise, she's the daughter of a big rancher, an' yo're just an—outlaw."

"D'yu think I need remindin' o' that?" the boy asked, so bitterly that Sudden's heart smote him.

"After all, what's the odds?" he consoled. "I'll bet her dad blotted a few brands in the early days—most o' the old settlers was afflicted with defective eyesight when they happened on a cow what looked lonely."

This did not have the effect he intended; Sandy flared up instantly. "Don't yu dare say it," he cried. "Sam Eden never stole a cent's worth in his life."

Sudden saw that he was really angry, his face flushed, and fists clenched. "Shucks," he said placatingly. "I ain't sayin' he did; they usen't to call it stealin'. Besides"—he smiled disarmingly—"she ain't really his daughter, yu know."

The boy's belligerent attitude vanished. "Sorry, Jim. I'm a plain fool to lose my wool like this," he apologized. "Yu wanted to ask me somethin'?"

"Yeah, what did Rogue tell yu of his plans?"

"Nothin' definite, but I gathered that he aimed to hold up the herd, get what coin he could outa Eden, bust up the drive later on, an' collar the cows. It's a-plenty."

"Shore is," Sudden said soberly, and then his eyes twinkled. "I'm takin' it yu still don't propose to help him in them Projects?"

"Yo're damn right," the boy returned hotly, "an' the sooner he knows it the better."

"That's somethin' we'll let him find out," Sudden decided. "Our hand'll be hard enough to play without showin' it."

Cheerfulness was in evidence at supper that evening; the

easy going and the improving health of the wounded man had put everyone in a good humour. The men chaffed one another, told tall stories, and kept Peg-leg busy.

Early on the following morning the camp had visitors, six mounted men, well-armed, and range-riders by their rig. One, who appeared to be the leader, signed to the others to halt, and rode forward. Peg-leg was busy loading his vehicle for the day's march. Carol, who had just mounted her pony to join the herd, halted at a word from Sudden, the only other man in camp.

"Tell Jeff to fetch in some o' the boys," he told her. "I ain't likin' the look o' these hombres."

The girl nodded and rode away. Sudden waited, his fingers concerned with a cigarette, but his eyes taking in the newcomer. A dark, evil-faced fellow this, with lank black hair and a straggly, ill-kept beard which only accentuated a cruel mouth. His narrowed eyes were arrogant, provocative.

"Mornin'," Sudden said laconically.

The other man returned the greeting, adding brusquely, "Whose outfit is this?"

"Yu got any right to ask?" the S E rider retorted.

The visitor shot a glance at his escort and smiled grimly. "I reckon," he replied. "A 'full house' allus beats a 'pair,'" With a significant look at the other's guns.

Sudden smiled too. "We ain't come to the 'draw' yet," he said. "However, if it'll ease yore mind any, this is the S E from San Antonio way drivin' north, an' I don't like talkin' to a fella on a hoss when I'm afoot."

"Fair enough," the stranger replied, and got down, keeping

his horse between himself and the cowboy—in itself a hostile action. "I wanta see the boss."

"He's sick. I'm speakin' for him. Yu ain't told me who I'm talkin' to yet."

"Name's Dale, foreman o' the Double O; yo're nearly across our range now."

Sudden weighed the answer and found it wanting; they had seen no cattle bearing that brand. Out of the corner of his eyes he saw an approaching dust-cloud and knew that help was on the way.

"What's yore trouble?" he asked.

"Ain't got none, but yore herd musta picked up quite a few of our cows an' we want 'em back. Sabe?"

The S E man did. It would mean a couple of days' delay, to say nothing of the hard work involved. He wondered if this was one of Rogue's moves? He did not know the man before him, and the others were too far off and had their hatbrims pulled down.

"We ain't seen any Double O cows," he demurred.

"The outfit ahead o' yu told us the same an' we found near a hundred when we combed the herd," Dale countered.

In a flurry of flying sand, Jeff and four riders pulled their panting ponies to a stop. The foreman was on the point of riding forward when Sandy put in a word:

"Leave it to Green. I'm bettin' he can handle it—now."

The fact that the sides were no longer unequal brought a change in Sudden's attitude, but he showed no hostility.

"We ain't got time to waste," he said. "Anyways, what yu gotta grumble about? We're drivin' north, where cows—they tell me—is worth four or five times what yu can sell 'em for here. Yu'll be paid what it fetches for every Double O steer we find, an' we won't charge yu nothin' for handlin' 'em neither."

"Mighty generous," sneered the other. "Now I'll make yu a better offer. Call it fifty of our beasts yu got, which is lettin' yu off easy. Well, pay me ten dollars a head for 'em now 'an when yu sell yu git a nice profit. How about it?"

Sudden laughed at him. "Didn't I tell yu we're from the south?" he asked. "Where'd we raise all that coin, d'yu reckon?"

"We'll 'cut' yore herd then," Dale said angrily. "It's that or fight." He glanced at Jeff and his companions. "I've got more men within call."

"Yu'll need 'em," Sudden told him. "But where's the sense in a ruckus which may cripple two outfits? Here's me, an' there's yu; why not state a case for Judge Colt an' settle it between ourselves?"

Through his slitted eye-lids the Double O foreman glared at the young fellow who had so coolly challenged him to single combat, and now stood, teetering on his heels, waiting for an answer. There was a sardonic, almost hopeful gleam in the half-veiled greyblue eyes; the butts of the two guns were shiny with use; the hand that lifted the cigarette to the firm lips was as steady as a rock. Dale had killed several times, was noted for his speed with a six-gun, and nothing would have given him greater pleasure than to shoot down this nonchalant obstacle to his plans, but doubt assailed him, and he evaded the issue.

"Yu talk about sense," he sneered. "Why not show some an' let us take our cows like them fellas in front o' yu?"

"How long was yu cuttin' 'em out?" Sudden asked casually.

"Coupla days," was the answer.

"They were that much ahead of us, an' we ain't been delayed," the S E man said musingly. "Funny we didn't catch 'em up, ain't it?"

Too late Dale saw the trap he had stumbled into. His face flushed as he said savagely:

"Meanin' I'm a liar?"

"Just that," Sudden told him, half-turning as though the interview was ended.

Passion swept the other man's caution to the winds, and he did not stop to think that he had been jockeyed into doing what his opponent had already proposed.

"Why, yu damned young squirt," he rasped, and grabbed at his gun. He got it clear of the holster, but before he could press the trigger there came a flash and a roar from Sudden's side. Dale dropped his weapon and clutched a ripped forearm.

Thrusting his smoking gun into its sheath Sudden stepped forward, and before the ice-cold fury in his face the other man fell back. For the lust to take his life was there and Dale knew that only by a miracle had he escaped the fate for which he had asked. Sudden knew this too. For a few terrible seconds he had been possessed by that cruel craving to slay for the sake of slaying; he had wanted to shoot this man; to see him writhing in the agonies of death at his feet. Then the evil moment passed and though his face was granite-hard, the old satirical note was in his voice.

"Yu ain't hurt much an' yu got another gun. If yo're wishful to try the left hand..."

The Double O man looked at him, stark hatred in every line of his face. He was nearly mad with pain and humiliation, and for an instant, it seemed he might take up this second challenge. The cowboy had an idea.

"I'm advisin' yu not to," he said quietly. "Further south, they call me 'Sudden.'"

The fellow's eyes widened and something very like fear took the place of the ferocity in them. He picked up his pistol, and grabbing the horn of his saddle with his left hand, hauled himself up.

"We'll be meetin' again an' mebbe I'll be lucky," he growled.

"Yu've been lucky this time," Sudden replied. "Keep on thinkin' that. Now, roll yore tail, an' take that bunch o' trail-robbers with yu."

Watching them ride away, he became aware of Jeff at his elbow asking what it was all about. The foreman's face when he heard the particulars was a picture of puzzlement.

"Mebbe we have got some o' their cows," he suggested.

"Shucks, then we can turn over what they fetch," Sudden argued. "Any o' yu boys seen the Double O brand?"

Not one of them had. "Me neither, an' I've been lookin' pretty constant for strays," Sudden went on. "I'd risk a little that there ain't such an iron hereabouts—his hoss warn't wearin' it. No, sir, it was a plain hold-up."

"If they'd combed the herd an' hadn't found any..." the foreman speculated. "Why should they want to hang up our drive?"

"I ain't a wizard, Jeff," Sudden told him.

"I'm not so shore, seein' the way yu got that gun goin'," was the smiling reply.

The shrill voice of Aunt Judy came from the wagon. "Hi, Jeff, yo're wanted."

They found the invalid anxious and irritable. "What's the shootin'?" he barked.

Sudden explained, and Sam Eden's frown deepened. "Yu done right, Jim," he commended. He was silent for a while, thinking deeply. "I was warned o' this," he went on. "There'll be other damn thieves further along the trail, waitin' to try the same game. We've got precious little coin, an' I won't hand over a cow, so that means fightin' our way through."

His fierce eyes carried a question and the little foreman answered it without hesitation:

"We're all willin' to do that, Sam, but there ain't too many of us to handle the herd as it is. What yu think, Jim?"

"Well, these hold-up gents will be watchin' the used trail," the cowboy pointed out. "S'pose we was to bear away to the west for a spell an' then strike north again, nosin' out a road for ourselves; wouldn't that razzle-dazzle 'em?"

"By the Devil's teeth, he's hit it, Jeff," the cattleman swore. "It'll mean a longer an' harder drive, but that'll be better than losin' men scrappin', an' it's possible Chisholm didn't pick the best path after all. Now, go an' get them steers started. Jim, I'm obliged to yu."

Notwithstanding his employer's approval, Sudden did not feel too comfortable. The step he had suggested was dangerous and might well plunge the expedition into all kinds of difficulty. On the other hand, there was the chance that it would dislocate Rogue's designs on the drive, and this had been his main reason. That Dale was one of the outlaw's men he felt sure, and he was relieved by the thought that he had now declared himself.

# Chapter 10

The new plan was not to be put into operation immediately, and dusk found them camped again on the trail they had been following. Straight across the dreary, brown expanse it ran, a road some hundreds of yards in width, carved out of the plain by the sharp hooves of hordes of cattle. Throughout the day no tree broke the monotony of the sky-line.

They had another visitor that evening. The herd had been bedded down, four men left in charge, and the others were grouped around the fire awaiting Peg-leg's intimation that supper was ready, when a figure materialized out of the gloom and came towards them, right hand raised, palm foremost.

"Evenin', folks," greeted a high, reedy voice. "Saw yer fire an' it made me feel kind o' lonesome."

"Step right up, friend," the foreman called out.

The man came on, moving with the easy, tireless stride of a redskin. The firelight showed him to be an oldish fellow, thin but wiry, with long grey hair and beard and bright eyes which seemed never to be still. His tattered doeskin garments, raccoon-skin cap, and moccasins proclaimed that he was a trapper.

"Sit an' eat," the foreman invited.

"Thankee," the stranger replied. "But I pay my footin'."

He lifted the long gun from his shoulder and proffered the carcass of a small deer slung upon it. Jeff protested, but the visitor would not listen.

"Sho, I'm tired o' totin' it," he said. "Mebbe a change for yu fellas, but a hunk o' good beef to me is wuth all the game that ever ran or flew."

"I'm obliged," the cowman said. "We've got a invalid who won't subscribe to them sentiments."

"Sick folk is finicky," the other agreed.

He dumped his pack—the crackling of which suggested dried skins—on the ground, placed his gun upon it, and sat down. When the food arrived, he ate so wolfishly that even in a land of large appetites he knew it must be remarked.

"Yu gotta excuse me, friends," he said, "but yu have one damn fine cook, an' I've bin livin' on straight meat an' water for most a week; run right outa meal, salt, an' coffee."

"I guess we can fix yu up," the foreman said. "Goin' fur?"

"Makin' for the nearest settlement to trade my pelts for supplies," the stranger explained, He sighed contentedly as he finished his fifth mug of coffee. "That's the best feed I've put under my belt for many a day." He produced a battered pipe and regarded it ruefully. "I went shy o' smokin' too." Several hands shot out, and when he had filled, lighted, and taken a long draw, he smiled whimsically at the company.

"I figure yu boys'll be wondering' over me."

They were, but not one of them would have admitted it. He nodded understandingly and went on—as he put it—to explain himself. His name, it appeared, was Tyson, and his story a common one enough in those days. Just a tale of a ravaged cabin, a murdered wife and children, and another blood-debt to the shrieking painted devils who had wrecked his life. He told it quite simply in his high-pitched voice, without passion, but in his eyes smouldered a hatred which only death would quench.

"Since then I've bin a sort o' missionary," he concluded grimly. "Yes, sirs, me an' 'Betsy'"—he patted the stock of the rifle at his back—"has converted quite a few war-whoops."

The cowboys smiled at this. They too held the cynical view that the only "good" Indian was a dead one. Therefore the knowledge that their guest was a "still-hunter"—one who tracked down and slew the redskin on foot—aroused no feeling of repulsion. The foreman questioned him regarding the country for which they were heading, and the chances of getting the herd through.

"Middlin' slim," he said bluntly. "Yu'll have a man-size job to make it. Steers is bringin' real money at the rail-head, an' it's knowed that herds is comin' up from Texas. The Nations is lousy with bad men, hide-hunters, rustlers, outlaws of every sort, an' they ain't likely to overlook a bet o' that kind. Then there's the Kiowas an' Commanches from the headwaters o' the Red River; they're watchin' the trail mighty close."

"S'pose we turned west for a piece an' then cut our own road north?" Sudden queried.

Tyson grinned. "She ain't a bad idea—might diddle 'em," he admitted. "But yu gotta mind yu don't hit the Staked Plain—no water an' as hot as Hell's gridiron—an' if yore cows git tangled up with a herd o' buff'ler yu can wish 'em good-bye. Allasame, I'd say it's yore best bet."

Soon after midnight, Sudden, having done his turn of night-herding, returned to camp and sought his blankets. He had not fallen asleep when he heard the low, musical but melancholy hoot of a dwarf-owl. Since there were no trees or bushes in the vicinity, the presence of the bird was sufficiently remarkable to call for investigation. Slipping from beneath his covering he crawled cautiously in the direction from which the sound had seemed to come. At the side of a small hummock he stood up, drew his gun, coughed slightly, and instantly moved.

"That yu, Sandy?"

"No, it's Green."

A shadow detached itself from the side of the hummock.

"'Lo, Jim, I was wantin' a word with one o' yu," Rogue said, and then, abruptly, "Why for did yu shoot up my man, Dale?"

"How in hell was I to know yu owned the Double O brand?" Sudden retorted.

"I don't," the outlaw chuckled, "but yu mighta guessed how it was. Bad luck he had to bump into yu."

"I'd say he was plumb fortunate," Sudden retorted. "Next time he starts to pull a gun on me he won't get off with just a busted arm."

"It looks like yu mean to double-cross me, Jim," Rogue said harshly.

"Double-cross nothin'," was the reply. "I never joined yu, an' I don't owe yu anythin' but a bad name an' a prospect o' swingin' for a crime yu committed."

The savage intensity of his tone seemed to impress the other and when he spoke again the rasp had gone from his voice:

"That's so. I got yu in bad, but short o' givin' myself up, I did what I could to get yu clear. I liked yu, Jim, an' when yu consented to join the S E I reckoned it meant..."

"That I was ready to be what yu had made me—an outlaw," Sudden finished bitterly. "Well, it mighta been—I was undecided —but when it came to shootin' old men from cover..."

"I had nothin' to do with that, Jim."

"Yu were around when it happened."

"I'd gone. I knew afterwards, but it was no part of my plan."

"Then who did it?"

"I don't know who fired the shot, but Navajo fixed it. I had trouble with him over that—an' other things. He's gettin' uppity."

The cowboy was silent, considering. Somehow he believed Rogue was telling him the truth. Ruthless ruffian he undoubtedly was, yet he possessed a streak of something—bravado, it might be —which made him scorn a lie as the resort of a coward. He had been frank over the killing of Judson, when he need not have been. The husky voice broke in on his thoughts:

"Must be gettin' tired holdin' that gun, Jim; there ain't no manner o' need."

Shame swept over Sudden as he slipped the revolver back into its holster. "Sorry, Rogue," he said. "I warn't noticin'."

"Shucks," the outlaw said, and there was a weariness in his tone. "I don't blame yu for playin' safe, boy. I'm takin' it I can't count on yu an' Sandy?"

"That's correct," Sudden told him. "We ain't neither of us bitin' the hand that feeds us." An impulse stirred him. "Why don't yu cut away from that gang, Rogue? Yo're too good a man..."

The outlaw laughed. "Sorry for me, Jim?" he gibed. "Well, yu needn't to be. I went wrong with my eyes open because the world treated me mean an'—"

"It's done that to me, but I'm goin' to forget it," Sudden cut in.

He could not see the pitying smile on the older man's face. "Yu never will, boy; the faculty o' forgettin' what yu don't want to remember is one o' God's greatest gifts an' few has it," Rogue said bitterly, and then his voice grew harsh again. "I'm gettin' mushy. Bite on this, boy: I've passed my word to bust Eden's drive an' I'm goin' to do it."

"An' I'll fight yu till hell freezes," Sudden smiled, and shoved out a fist. "No hard feelin's, Rogue, but that don't go for yore followin'. Sabe?"

The bandit gripped the hand heartily. So this strange compact between men who were to war, one against the other, was sealed. The intruder melted into the shadowed plain and Sudden crept back to the camp, his mind full of the man he had just left. For the interview had surprised him. He had gone to it expecting reproaches, threats, even attempted violence, and found none of them. He had given his promise to his employer and would do his best to fulfil it. As to whom this might be. Sudden could make no guess; Sam Eden's bluff, outspoken nature and quick temper would earn him enemies enough.

His thoughts veered to the dark, sinister face of Navajo, the man who—according to Rogue—had "fixed" the attempted murder of the cattleman. Was it a misguided effort to help his leader, or was the fellow playing a hand for himself? The stars, paling in the sky, warned him that the night was passing, and he turned over to snatch an hour's sleep before sunrise.

In the morning, the guest, after packing his spare frame with bacon, beans, and coffee, went on his way, rejoicing that—thanks to the generosity of his hosts—he would again be able to "feed like a Christian."

"I figure yu'll be all right till yo're over the Red River," he added. "Then make yore pass west. Adios."

Gun on shoulder and pack on back, he swung off southwards along the trail, moving swiftly but unhurriedly. Several of the men stood watching the gradually diminishing form.

"A queer little cuss," Jeff commented. "One time them devils will catch him an' then—he'll want death a hell of a while before it comes."

"Well, he's sent some to wait for him," Jed remarked. "Did yu notice the nicks on the stock o' that gun? I didn't count 'em, but I'll bet there was mighty near two score."

During the morning, Sudden made an opportunity to tell Sandy of his meeting with Rogue.

"I'm relieved he took it that way," the boy said. "An odd mixture, Rogue. At times, a fiend from the Pit itself, an' yet, he can be real folks. Navajo now, he's bad all through, an' he hates Rogue. I'm glad to be clear o' that crowd, Jim."

Sudden regarded him sardonically. "Yo're tellin' me news."

"Yu know what I mean," Sandy replied.

Sudden did. He had already noted that his companion's gaze was never long away from a certain graceful figure riding ahead. His eyes twinkled with mischief as he said gravely:

"Shore I do, but what's worryin' me is"—he paused, and Sandy looked up expectantly—"does she like *red hair*?"

He was yards away before the boy realized the significance of the question and then it was too late to do anything but swear softly.

"Yu damned pirut," he smiled. "But Gosh! I'm mighty pleased I met up with yu."

# Chapter 11

The days oozed by, days of long, lazy hours in the saddle under a scorching sun, for the fine weather held. Jeff was too good a cowman to hurry the herd but he took care that the animals were healthily tired and ready for sleep when they reached a good average.

They had crossed the Brazos River without much difficulty, being fortunate in finding it low, and, as Tyson had predicted, no "trouble" had materialized. Moreover, the wounded man was progressing favourably, so that the outfit generally was in high good humour. Only the foreman refused to join in any jubilation.

"Everythin' is goin' too slick—it ain't natural," he grumbled, pacing behind the wagon as it bumped its way over the cracked and rutted surface of the plain. "Just when yo're feelin' careless an' contented is the time Lady Luck chooses to give yu a kick in the pants."

The cattleman pulled a wry face. "If yu was lyin' here yu

wouldn't think it was all so hunky, yu ol death's-head," he replied. "How're the new men pannin' out?"

"Green an' Sands is awright but I don't like Lasker," Jeff said bluntly. "Does his work but..." He did not finish. "Wish I knowed who put that pill in yu, Sam."

"Yu ain't thinkin' it was one o' the outfit, are yu?"

"I'm in the dark," the foreman admitted. "Sands or Lasker could 'a' done it—they weren't in camp or with the cows."

"Forget it," Eden said irritably. "I'm here, ain't I? Why should any o' the boys want to crab the drive? I figure it was a war-whoop, the one that got away from Green, likely; Injuns never let up when it's a case of evenin' a score."

"Dessay yo're right, but I'm wonderin'," Jeff insisted.

"Then stop it, yu fool," his employer told him. "All yu gotta worry about is the cows; they're goin' through if we have to carry 'em one at a time. Yu sabe?"

In his excitement he raised both his voice and his body, only to sink back with an oath. Instantly the hard-faced woman on the driver's seat thrust her head through the canvas flaps.

"Yu, Jeff, pull yore freight, pronto," she ordered. "Ain't there critters enough out there to pester but yu gotta come here an' git my patient all het up? If yu didn't wear a hat yu'd have no use for yore head."

The foreman made no reply; he knew better than to engage in verbal warfare with the lady. Sam Eden, however, promptly protested:

"Jeff's doin' his duty, reportin' to me, Judy," he said. "It ain't his fault if I'm restive, lyin' in this damn wagon day after day." He looked at her slyly. "Mebbe, if I could have a smoke..."

"Sam Eden, yo're plumb crazy," she snapped. "Here's yu with yore innards all tore up an' yu want baccy. Where'd yu be if it makes yu cough an' starts a bleedin'?" She looked at Jeff. "Beat it," she added.

The foreman obeyed, leaving them wrangling, but there was a smile on his face. Riding beside the wagon he stopped and peeped through a hole in the cover. The patient had a pipe in his mouth and his nurse was striking a match.

"Pure gold, that woman," Jeff murmured. "But her tongue cuts like a bowie."

Quickening his pace, he rode after the herd. As he passed the remuda, he spoke to Lasker:

"We must be near Injun country now. Best not let yore hosses stray far to-night. Yu can have help if yu want it."

The wrangler nodded sullenly. "I can manage," he said.

"Been this way afore?" Jeff asked.

"Nope, it's new to me," the man replied.

Two or three miles were covered and their eyes were gladdened by the sight of trees in the far distance. For days past they had seen no timber—for the sparse scrub-oak and stunted mesquite could not be so designated—and they knew the line of foliage indicated a river.

"Reckon that'll be the Red," Sudden remarked to Sandy.

"She'll be high," Sandy predicted.

Their fears proved to be well founded, when, a little later, Sudden and the foreman—who had ridden ahead—halted on the bank of the river. Jeff's face fell as he surveyed the swift-moving, eddying torrent, murky with the red sediment which stained the timber and driftwood along the banks and gave the river its name. He shook his head.

"She's all of six hundred yards across an' with the drift that means swimmin' near twice as fur, an' she's carryin' too much sand," he said. "We'll never make it as the cards lie."

"Better play it safe, ol-timer," Sudden agreed. "These streams, I've heard, rise an' fall in a day."

He was studying the ground; there were cattle-tracks in plenty but his experienced eye told him that they had not been recently made.

"S'pose them jaspers in front of us beat the floodwater, but I'm guessin' they didn't cross here," he remarked.

"They may still be this side—further downstream," the foreman suggested. "The trail forked a few miles back. Well, we gotta wait, whether Sam likes it or not."

The wagon was drawn up beneath some tall pines, and the cook was busy with his pots and pans when a horseman rode in from the gloom. Sudden, watching the leaping flames of the big fire, stepped forward.

"This Sam Eden's outfit?" the new arrival queried, and then, peering from his saddle, "but of course it must be, unless you're riding for someone else. Isn't your name Green?"

Sudden did not reply. Directly the rider had come within the circle of firelight he had seen that it was Jethro Baudry, and, for some reason he did not attempt to track down, the aversion he had experienced on first meeting the man returned.

"And where is Sam? Not working while his men warm their hands, I hope?" Baudry went on, with clumsy facetiousness.

"Yu'll find Mister Eden in the wagon, seh," the cowboy said stiffly, and walked away.

The gambler's eyes followed him and their expression was scarcely amiable. "Starchy, eh?" he muttered. "Odd about Sam though."

He rode over to the wagon, got down, and looked in. By the light of a hanging oil-lamp he saw the invalid, pale and haggard, but obviously on the mend.

"Hello, Sam, what's the meaning of this?" he greeted.

"Howdy, Jethro," the cattleman responded. "Come right in an' I'll tell yu."

Squatting on a sack of meal, chewing a black cigar, the visitor listened in silence to the story and then gave his opinion:

"Looks like redskins; who else would want to lay you out?"

"Yu can search me. But how come yu here, Jethro?"

"Meeting a man at Doan's Store—some way down the river. Got news of a herd arriving and suspicioned it might be the S E. You're making good time, Sam."

"Barrin' this," Eden tapped his chest, "we've been lucky. Mebbe all our troubles is to come."

"Likely enough, and that's one reason I wanted to see you, Baudry said. "I've been told there's some pretty tough gangs haunting the trail, waiting for herds, and I thought I'd warn you to be on the lookout."

"Mighty good o' yu, Jethro," the rancher said warmly. "I've had word a'ready to the same effect but"—his eyes twinkled—"if they wait for the S E they're liable to get tired o' the job."

Baudry looked puzzled.

"We're aimin' to turn west and cut our own trail," Eden explained triumphantly.

"You're a sly old fox, Sam," the gambler said. "But isn't

it risky? You may avoid the rustlers but you'll certainly run into the redskins."

"I figure them varmints will be watchin' the trail too," the cattleman argued. "As for bein' risky, the whole damn drive is that. Seen anythin' of another herd this way?"

"Yes, they crossed some miles lower down—just beat the flood. The river's dropping—you'll get over tomorrow, I'd say."

"Hope so. I fair hate hangin' about. Comin' with us, Jethro?"

The gambler shook his head, and rose. "Have to wait for my man," he said. "I'll be seeing you later. Good luck to ye, Sam."

He was about to mount when he saw Carol talking to one of the outfit and walked towards them, leading his horse. The cowboy turned away when he saw the newcomer. The girl asked the inevitable question and got the same explanation her father had received.

"Of course, I had no notion of Sam being hurt," Baudry said. "He's not looking too bad."

"His recovery is wonderful," Carol agreed.

The man's eyes dwelt on her, absorbing the straight slimness of her figure and the healthy freshness of her young beauty. She stirred him, and there was warmth in his usually cold voice when he said:

"He's had a wonderful nurse."

There was a mischievous gleam in Carol's eyes. "He certainly has. If ever you fall sick, Mister Baudry, I can recommend Judy."

The gambler's lips tightened. Was the girl playing with

him? But a man who depends upon cards for a living must learn to mask his emotions and Jethro Baudry was no novice.

"You have some new faces," the gambler remarked. "I don't recollect the young fellow you were talking to."

"Oh, you mean Sandy—the boys call him that," she added rather hastily. "He's a friend of Mister Green."

Baudry had a black moment; the use of the cowboy's nickname did not please him, the less so since he knew it had been involuntary.

"Looks a likely lad," he said carelessly.

But the girl was on her guard. "We've a good outfit," was her reply.

"Well, the hardships of the trail seem to suit you. Never seen you look so bonny." Again there was warmth in his tone and it made her flush a little.

"I love it," she replied, and with a smile, "Dad always says I ought to have been a boy."

"I can't agree with Sam on that, and he won't find another man that will," the gambler said gallantly. "There's plenty boys but only one Carol Eden."

With a wide sweep of his hat, he hoisted himself into the saddle and rode away, leaving her pondering. She did not like the man, though she could have given no reason. He was a friend of her father, who was under a considerable obligation to him, and to her he had always been courteous and respectful, and yet…

* * *

The river next morning showed an appreciable fall, but there still was a vast volume of reddish, sand-laden water sweeping swiftly between the bluff banks, and to the group of men studying the swirling currents it was clear that the crossing would be a difficult and perilous undertaking. Danger to themselves would not deter them; they were thinking only of the herd.

"I guess we gotta take a chance, boys," the foreman decided. "What's yore opinion, Jim?"

"Me an' Sandy 'll try her out," Sudden offered.

Stripped to the waist and riding bareback they entered the stream at a point where the bank shelved. In a few moments the horses were swimming, Nigger's black head in the lead. Progress was slow, for the current was strong and the crossing had to be made in a long slant. The soupy state of the water and floating drift-wood which had to be avoided added to the task, but at length the riders emerged on the opposite bank and turned to wave to their watching comrades. A short rest and they again plunged in for the return journey.

"She's a gamble, with the odds against us," was Sudden's verdict. "But we've played in luck, so far."

The foreman had already made up his mind and presently the leaders of the herd appeared, trotting briskly, for in view of the crossing they had been kept thirsty. At the sight of the turgid flood, however, they baulked and would have turned but for the riders on both flanks, who drove them into the water. There they stood, knee-deep, snorting and bawling with fright, the force of the stream almost sweeping them from their feet. Beyond this they would not budge until Sudden splashed in, roped the foremost steer round the horns, and slipping the other end of his lariat across the broad breast of Nigger, headed for the far bank.

Willy-nilly the captive was dragged headlong into the flood and struck out lustily, seeing which—after a brief hesitation—those behind followed. In a few moments, a steady string of horned heads was moving across the river. Sudden, having pulled his victim up the far shore, removed the loop, and grinned at the disgruntled-looking brute, which seemed disposed to go "on the prod."

"G'wan," he said, and slapped it over the nose with the end of his wet rope. "What yu gotta belly-ache about? Yu had the easiest trip of any, an' yu'll be Big Chief Show-'em-how to them four-footed friends o' your'n from now on."

For a while he sat watching the curving line of black blobs in the water, shepherded by horsemen on the downstream side.

After drying himself in the warm sun, he recrossed the river. The foreman met him, his face beaming.

"Jim, that was a daddy of an idea," he said. "Yu shore know cows."

"Shucks," Sudden smiled. "The critters is like humans—give 'em a lead an' they'll go most anywheres. It warn't nothin'."

"No?" Jeff said. "Allasame, I'm damn glad we got yu in the outfit, son."

# Chapter 12

"Say, Jim, do yu figure we've razzle-dazzled Rogue?" Sandy asked.

"Mebbe, but he's a foxy fella an' now he knows we ain't workin' for him he's probably trackin' us," Sudden replied. "But I expect we've put one over on other gents watchin' the trail."

They were riding some five hundred yards ahead of the herd, for being in Indian territory, scouts were deemed necessary, and, since they were no longer following a used trail, the easiest route had to be selected. More than a week had passed since they left the Red River and during most of the time they had travelled westwards before turning north again. Not one of the outfit had more than a vague notion of their location, for save to the Indians and a few trappers and buffalo hunters, this was unknown country. Moreover, wide detours to avoid difficulties had been made, and they had only the sun and stars to guide them.

"Plenty lonesome in these parts," Sandy remarked presently. "We ain't seen a soul since the Red."

"Suits me," his friend replied. "Anybody we met would likely be hostile. What yu think o' Lasker?"

"I don't," Sandy grinned. "Not never."

"Huh! I'm forgettin' that yu got a single-track mind these days," Sudden said gravely. "Allatime it circles round a certain hatchet-faced——"

"Shurrup, yu idjut; here's Carol a-comin'."

Sudden's eyebrows lifted at the familiarity, but before he could offer any comment, the girl reined in beside them. .

"Jeff sent me for you, Sandy," she said. "I'm to take your place for a spell."

The boy's face fell. "Shore it wasn't Jim he wanted?" he asked.

Carol's eyes twinkled teasingly. "Quite sure," she told him, and when he had wheeled his mount and loped back towards the herd she murmured, "He seemed to just hate leaving you."

"Yeah," Sudden said. "Wonder if Jeff wants him bad?"

She saw the little crinkles at the corners of his eyes and laughed herself. "I'm afraid he doesn't," she confessed. "You see, I told Jeff I'd like to ride ahead for a while and he said, 'Send Sandy back; a fellow scouting needs his eyes in more than one place.' Now what did he mean by that?"

"I ain't a notion," was the mendacious reply, and then, with a sly smile, "Mebbe he figures Sandy ain't very dependable."

The girl bridled instantly. "Then I think it's too mean," she cried. "Dad said something of the sort last night. Just because

Sandy is gay and light-hearted——" She stopped, and her cheeks went red beneath their tan as she saw the quirk of amusement on his lips. Then she smiled also. "That was too bad of you," she accused.

"I'm askin' yore pardon, ma'am," Sudden said. "Yu see, Sandy is my friend; he can have anythin' I got, an' there's no limit."

"You have known him long?"

"That don't follow. Friendship is a funny thing; it ain't a matter o' time. Yu know one fella for years an' in the end he'll disappoint yu; yu know another for hours an' yu can gamble on him."

So he closed the subject. In those wild days a person's past was his or her concern and it was neither polite nor prudent to probe into it.

The foreman having agreed to call it a day, camp was made near a thicket of oak and mesquite, while the cattle were bunched on the flat top of a swell not far away. There was no water but the animals had had a sufficiency the night before, and the long-horn could travel forty-eight hours without drinking. Nevertheless, the lack of it made the herd restive and Jeff anxious. Sudden, giving the cook a hand with his team, offered a word of advice:

"I'd hobble them critters an' keep 'em handy, Peg-leg. This is Injun territory an' them red devils would ruther eat mule-meat than prime beef."

"All a matter o' taste, I reckon," the cook replied.

"More a matter o' teeth, I'd say," the cowboy grinned, as he swung into his saddle and went to help with the herd.

Some hours later Sandy came to relieve him and even

in the darkness Sudden could see that the young man was not his usual bright self; slouched in his saddle, head down, he appeared moody and depressed.

"Yu look as happy as a wet hen," was the greeting he received. "What's bitin' yu?"

"I dunno, Jim, an' that's a fact, but I got a feelin' trouble is comin'."

"Trouble allus is comin' an' worryin' won't stop it. Get such fool notions outa the thing that holds yore hat up, an' keep a close eye on them durned cows; half of 'em ain't even dozin' yet."

Riding back to the camp he heard the mournful, weird howl of a coyote and a moment later came an answering cry. He pulled up in doubt; to his trained ear they did not sound just right. Smiling sardonically at the reflection that Sandy had made him nervy, he, nevertheless circled to approach the rear of the timber behind the camp, whence the cries had seemed to come. This took some time for the thicket was larger than he had thought and it was incumbent to move cautiously. Reaching the trees, he sat listening; the indistinct mutter of a voice came to him. Slipping from his saddle, he crept into the undergrowth. It was nervous work; once he put a hand on a clammy, writhing form and heard a sharp hiss as the reptile slithered away. Sudden shivered.

"Fools for luck," he murmured. "If rattlers didn't have to coil afore they can strike...."

He did not pursue the unpleasant reflection, but pulled a gun and felt ahead with it before making a move. The voice was nearer now, only a few yards distant, but he could see nothing of the owner.

"Make a good job of it an' the two-fifty is yourn. Yu'll have a clear field when the cows start runnin'—which'll be soon now. Them hombres will have suthin' else to occupy 'em."

The eavesdropper stiffened; he knew that voice. Navajo! He could not hear the mumbled reply, but a cracking twig told him that the men were moving—away from him. As silently as speed would permit he retraced his steps, his brain busy with the problem so abruptly presented. Rogue's men were to stampede the herd and something was to be tried. It was not difficult to guess what this was. He hurried to his horse, leapt into the saddle, and raced for the camp.

The sight there drew an oath from his lips. Seated round the cook's fire were Sam Eden, Jeff, and the two women; blanketed forms at the other fire were preparing for their turn of night-riding; they were doomed to have their rest rudely interrupted. Sudden strode up to the foreman.

"Jeff, I've just got wind of a plot to run off the cows—right now," he cried. "Get busy—no time to talk." He turned to his employer. "Yu didn't oughta be here, seh," he went oh. "Yu...."

An outburst of gun-fire and wild yells from over the plain, with the drumming thunder of thudding hooves cut him short.

"God! they've done it!" he exclaimed.

Stooping swiftly, he seized the seated cattleman by the shoulder and thrust him sideways to the ground. Almost at the same instant, a jet of yellow flame punctured the gloom surrounding the camp and a bullet buried itself in the log against which the invalid had been leaning. Sudden's gun barked viciously, twice, and the reports were followed by the breaking of dead wood, as of a body falling among the bushes and then—silence. Half-crouched, his smoking weapon poised, the cowboy waited for one tense moment.

"Guess I got him," he said quietly. "Saw the glint o' the fire on his gun-barrel—just in time."

"What th' hell?" Eden began, as he struggled back to an upright position.

"Explanations'll have to wait," Sudden told him. "Yu'd be better in the wagon, seh. That whelp over there had friends."

Though the foreman was at first stunned by the abruptness of the calamity his natural sturdiness soon reasserted itself. The awakened sleepers were sent to the rope corral for mounts, the cattleman, vehemently cursing his helplessness, was lifted back into the wagon, and the women ordered to stay in it also,

"We'll have to leave yu in charge o' Peg-leg, Sam," the foreman pointed out. "Mebbe we can git back some o' the cows."

"Damn the cows," the old man exploded. "Let daylight into the dirty thieves what rustled 'em. Now, gimme a gun an' get agoin'."

Sending the others on, Jeff and Sudden turned towards the spot whence the bushwhacker had fired. Sprawling in the undergrowth was the body of a man. Sudden turned it over and struck a match.

"Lasker!" the foreman breathed. "Well, I'm damned."

Leaving the corpse in the bushes, they rode to the

bedding-ground. Jeff was puzzling over this latest development.

"Lasker, huh? Never did cotton to him, somehow," he mused. "Likely he was planted on us, an' mebbe we've bin follered right along." He looked curiously at the man beside him. "How did yu git on to it, Jim?"

Sudden told of the coyote calls and the fragment of conversation he had overheard, but did not reveal that he recognized one of the voices. He had just finished when a limping figure, carrying a saddle, loomed up out of the gloom. It proved to be Sandy.

"Yu hurt?" Sudden asked, observing that the boy staggered.

"Bullet burned my ribs—nothin' broke," was the reply.

"What happened?" This from the foreman.

"Yu can search me. First we knowed was the fireworks an' the shoutin'—they musta crept up on us. An', believe me, them steers didn't wait to ask questions none whatever. I tried to head 'em off an' some jasper started slingin' lead—got my hoss too, blast his soul."

"Which way was the herd travellin'?" Jeff asked.

"West—must be damn near the Pacific Slope by now," was the bitter retort. "Gawd, what a mess!"

"How many of 'em?"

"Couldn't say. It was as dark as the inside of a cow. I on'y saw the fella who creased me. Fancy I nicked him—heard him cuss."

Sandy having assured them he could make the camp unaided the other two rode on. Mile after mile was covered without a trace of the missing herd save the hoofprints which showed that they were following at least a portion of it. At length, in the dim, grey light of the dawn, they saw two riders, driving a bunch of about a hundred steers. They were less than half a mile distant and not hurrying, apparently deeming themselves safe from pursuit. Sudden pulled his rifle from the sheath.

"Hold on, Jim, they may be our fellas," Jeff warned.

"They wouldn't be headed west," Sudden pointed out.

"That's so," the foreman admitted, "but I'd ruther be shore than sorry. I'll give 'em a hail our boys would reckernize. They can't outrun us with the cows."

His voice rang out in a shrill cowboy call, familiar on many ranges, but with variations Sudden had not heard before. The result dispelled their doubt effectively. The riders' heads jerked round and then their right arms rose and fell as they vigorously plied the quirt. Sudden's face was grim as he levelled his weapon.

"Steady, boy," he said to his horse, and pulled the trigger.

They saw the pony on the right stumble and fall, throwing its rider headlong. The other man, with no more than a glance at his companion, spurred his mount furiously and soon left the herd behind. Sudden sent an unavailing shot which only served to hurry his movements. A few moments brought them to the fallen man and one look at the oddly-twisted, huddled form told them what had happened.

"Bruk his neck" Jeff said. "Yu got the hoss. Damn good shootin' too, at that range an' from the saddle. Yu don't know the gent, I s'pose, Jim?"

The reply in the negative was not all the truth, for Sudden had seen the fellow during his sojourn with Rogue.

"Well, let's git after them cows," the foreman said, adding harshly, "This ain't my day for buryin' cattlethieves."

The stolen steers had not run far and the S E men soon had them rounded up and pointed east again. The foreman's expression as he regarded the recovered remnant of his charge was savagely morose. Sudden too was feeling the same. To have the patient endeavour and strenuous labour of many weeks so wantonly wrecked was a bitter bullet to bite on. So they rode in silence for an hour, and then, from the mouth of a shallow arroyo—a mere crack in the face of the plain—a horseman emerged and hailed them joyfully:

" 'Lo, Jeff. So yu got some too?" It was Dumpy, and as he spoke, his sweaty, dirt-laden features broke into a tired grin of welcome. "Where's the rest o' the outfit?"

The foreman raised his shoulders. "Yu alone?" he asked.

"Jed's in there"—Dumpy pointed to the arroyo—"Can't lose that fella nohow, an' say, we got near three hundred cows. She's a dandy place, plenty feed, a pond, an' the way in is the on'y way out."

"See here, Jeff, why not fetch the wagon an' camp in the arroyo?" Sudden suggested. "Two men could hold the herd in there while the rest of us comb the country."

"Yo're right, Jim," the foreman agreed. "She's our best bet."

Having driven the beasts they had brought through the narrow entrance to the gully, they again rode east, taking Dumpy with them. As they approached the spot where the stampede had taken place the sight of cattle and encircling riders brought a lighter look to Jeff's face.

"We'll make a herd yet, boy," he said.

"Shore we will," Sudden rejoined.

All the rest of the outfit were there with the exception of Truthful, of whom no one had any tidings save that he had been with the herd when it began to run. The other men, unable to stay the tide of terrified brutes, contented themselves with following bunches of them and, when the scare died out, driving them back. In this way they had salvaged over four hundred and a dozen horses.

At the camp itself they found Sandy and Peg-leg sitting by the wagon with rifles. The women were inside with the invalid, who listened silently to his foreman's report.

"We've got around eight hundred an' I guess we can search out enough others to go on," Jeff concluded.

The old man glared at him. "Yo're damn right we'll go on," he rasped. "Get this, an' get it straight: I said I'd make this drive an' I'll do it, if there's on'y one blasted cow to take into Kansas."

"That goes with me, an' with all of us, I reckon," the foreman said quietly, and went on to tell of Sudden's suggestion to move camp.

"Sounds a good idea," the cattleman agreed. He looked at the cowboy. "Young fella, I figure yu saved my life—though I shore thought yu'd gone loco. That lead pill went in just where my head had been, an' I'm thankin' yu. What had Lasker against me, Jeff?"

"We've bin framed, Sam; they just waited their chance. Jim got one of 'em."

He related the passing of the unknown rustler and the old man's eyes glowed with savage approval.

"One skulking thief less, anyways," he grated. "I'm thankin' yu again, Jim."

As they left the wagon, Peg-leg handed each of them a steaming mug and hurried away in search of his beloved mules. Jeff took a big gulp of the liquid and nodded at the retreating figure.

"Peg used to ride hisself an' he knows that 'coffee at any time' makes a cook the boys will swear *by* instead of *at,*" he remarked.

The foreman went to give some instructions to the men and Sandy strolled up.

"I'm owin' yu somethin', Jim," he began, and noting his friend's look of surprise, added, "For downin' that rat, Lasker."

"I'm beginnin' to suspect that fella warn't popular," Sudden said. "Why gratitude from yu?"

"Hell's bells, didn't he try to bump off the Ol' Man?" Sandy demanded.

"O' course, daddy-in-law to be, huh?" Sudden nodded comprehendingly. "But why ain't yu in the hospital, swappin' pains with him?"

"For the same reason yu ain't in a home for the half-witted—neither of us could qualify," came the swift retort.

"Yo're sufferin' from the wrong nurse," Sudden said shrewdly. "C'mon. What yu want is work, an' it's shorely waitin' for yu."

They reached the herd—whither Jeff had preceded them—just after the missing rider, Truthful, had arrived, proudly escorting a score of steers. Ringed in by the rest, he was telling his story:

"When the mix-up started, my hoss went loco; he's as strong as Satan's breath, that roan is, an' I couldn't hold him. Where he took me I dunno but we rode around for——"

"Days," Silent suggested.

"Weeks," corrected the Infant.

"Hours, I was goin' to say, though it seemed like days," the narrator said. "When dawn arrove I found I was in the middle o' the plain——"

"Oh, bury me out on the lone pra-i-rie," chanted the Infant, and was promptly promised that fate if he opened his face again.

"There warn't nothin' in sight but a clump o' scrub, mostly mesquite, an' while I'm lookin' at this out steps one solitary steer, an' who'd yu think it was?"

"The Bull o' Bashan," Sandy offered.

"Never heard o' the brand," the tale-teller retorted. "No, gents, it was ol' Show-'em-how, shore as I'm standin' here."

"Yu ain't standin'—yo're lyin', Truthful," sniggered Dumpy.

Even Jeff laughed at this, and then commanded silence. "Go ahead, boy," he said. "I wanta hear how yu rounded up them cows."

"I didn't," Truthful replied. "When ol' Show-'em pops out I remarks aloud. 'What's th' use o' one damn cow anyways?' Well, that moss-head looks at me solemn for 'bout a minit an' then stalks back into the brush. I figure I've shortly hurt his feelin's, but presently, out he comes again with eleven more along, sorta lines 'em up, an' cocks an eye at me. I points to the scrub.

"'Good for yu, ol-timer,' I sez. 'Fly at it—fetch 'em all out. Sic 'em.'

"Shore enough he heads in again; the steers start to foller but he lets out one beller an' they stops, mighty abrupt. It's mebbe half an hour before he shows up again with eight cows.

"'Ain't there no more?" I asks, an' I wish I may die if he didn't shake his head. Then he trots off across the plain, the rest tailin' after, an' here we are."

One by one the audience stepped forward, grasped the narrator's right hand, shook it vigorously and retreated without a word. Truthful endured it with widening eyes until all but the foreman had taken part, and then:

"Jeff, they think I'm stringin' 'em," he cried.

"Don't yu care, son," was the reply. "I'm believin' yu, but"—there was a grin on the leathery face—"not until frawgs grows feathers."

# Chapter 13

With the cattle and camp safely hidden in the arroyo, which two men could guard, the remainder of the outfit were free to scour the surrounding country in search of the scattered long-horns. This meant a repetition of the work done when the herd was got together, many hours of hard riding, the routing of beasts out of brush-choked gullies and thorny chaparral. Despite the difficulties, additions to the herd dribbled in and with each one the foreman's face grew less sombre. On the fifth day, however, some of the searchers returned empty-handed, though still nearly half the cattle were missing.

"They musta got away with over a thousand head, reckonin' they'd lose some we ain't found," Jeff said. "We might as well push on; we won't find many more."

"Hold on for another day," Sudden advised, "an' let me an' Sandy have Jed an' Dumpy to-morrow."

The foreman agreed without question; he was beginning

to realize that this cool, capable young cowboy usually had a reason for anything he said or did.

On the following morning the four men set out. Jed, as ever, had his grumble: "Waste o' time. Betcha we don't git a cow a-piece."

Sandy grinned at his friend. "Don't tell 'em," he whispered.

"Shore not," Sudden said. "Besides, the nest may be empty; the joke would be on us then."

It had been on the first day that the pair of them, returning after a fruitless foray through a broken patch of country some twelve miles from camp, halted abruptly on the edge of a wide swathe of cattle-tracks. The fact that the beasts had been bunched together, and the prints of shod horses alongside, told that they had been driven. The S E men followed the trail to a small, hidden valley, rocked-rimmed the narrow entrance to which was masked by a great boulder and further defended by a rude fence of poles lashed together with rawhide, two of which could be moved to permit passage. Riding through, they found a grass-covered basin in which some hundreds of cows were feeling. There appeared to be no one in charge, and they had no difficulty in getting near enough to read the brand on the nearest beast.

"S E," Sandy cried exultantly. "Jim, our luck has shorely changed; here's a sight that'll make Jeff's eyes stick out like they was on stalks. Do we round 'em up?"

Sudden shook his head. "Here's how I figure it," he explained. "Rogue's men couldn't hold the herd no more'n we could. They're combin' the country too an' bringin' 'em here as they gather 'em. I'm bettin' that if we call again in a few days' time we'll find twice as many."

Sandy let out a whoop. "Jim, yo're a great man," he said. "The notion o' lettin' them skunks collect cows for us hits me where I live."

So they had left the valley undisturbed and for the ensuing days had ridden in other directions. It had been a gamble, and they were now on their way to learn if they had lost or won. If the rustlers had removed their plunder....

They reached the spot, and leaving Sandy on guard outside, the others rode into the valley. One glance told Sudden that he had guessed correctly; the herd had more than doubled; roughly he estimated it at nearly a thousand head, with a sprinkling of horses. His companions yelped gleefully.

"Seems we might git a cow a-piece arter all, Jed," the fat man remarked. "Wish I'd took that bet. Why didn't yu take him up, Jim?"

"They might not 'a' been here," Sudden smiled. "We'll have one fine job handlin' 'em; I didn't expect so many."

"What about sendin' to Jeff for help?" Jed asked.

"Too risky—the rustlers may be showin' up any moment. We'll go while the goin's good."

For the next few hours all four riders were far too busy to think of anything but the work in hand. It was a big bunch for so small a crew, and the cattle—loth to leave the peaceful, sheltered valley, made frequent efforts to break back. By the time the arroyo was reached the men were limp, drenched with perspiration, and utterly profane.

They found the foreman and Carol at the entrance to the arroyo, and the little man's slitted eyes widened when he saw the cattle pouring through.

"Christopher Columbus!" he ejaculated, remembering just in time that his employer's daughter was present. "Whose ranch yu bin raidin', Jim?"

But the girl had seen the brand. "They are our own cows, Jeff," she cried. "Won't Dad be pleased!"

"I'll say he will," the foreman grinned. "This'll do him more good than all the nussin'. How come, Jim?"

Sudden told the tale, while Jeff swore delightedly to himself as he listened.

"Yu shore got nerve, boy," he commented. "Lettin' them thieves collect our cows for us was one great scheme."

"Seemed fair to me," Sudden smiled. "They scattered 'em."

Jeff's eyes had been busy and as the last of the herd trotted by he slapped his thigh joyously. "Damn near a thousand head," he said. "Why, we won't be more'n three-four hundred shy after all, an' we owe it to yu, Jim."

"Shucks," Sudden said lightly, and jerked a thumb at his friend. "There's the fella yu gotta thank."

"I was meanin' both," the foreman replied. "It was shorely a good day for the S E that brought yu boys along."

Sandy cared nothing for the little man's praise; the look of gratitude the girl gave him as she rode away to tell her father the news was all the reward he wanted.

"We'll be all fixed to take the trail in the mornin'," Jeff went on. Sudden's eyebrows rose and he shot a whimsical glance at the sun overhead. The foreman read it. "Yo're figurin' we oughta start now?" he asked.

"Think it over," the cowboy replied. "We don't know how soon them hombres will discover their loss, but yu can bet they won't waste no time high-tailin' it after us—follerin' the cattle won't be no trick a-tall, we couldn't blind our tracks. Any lead we can get will be all to the good."

"Yo're damn right," Jeff agreed. "We want to be plenty absent when they arrive. Sandy, go tell the boys we'll be settin' out pronto."

In less than an hour the herd was again on the move, heading away from where they conjectured the rustlers to be encamped. Despite the disaster, cheerfulness reigned. The loss had proved far less than had seemed likely, and the riders, with the optimism born of their hardy natures, had already transformed the incident into a victory; they had "put one over" the cattle-thieves. Pebbles expressed his satisfaction in song:

"Roll yore tails an' roll 'em high,
We'll all be angels by an' by."

The foreman's face creased in a smile. "Hark to him," he said. "He's wore to a frazzle—as we all are—his clothes is sca'cely decent, an' he ain't got a dollar to his name, but he's happy. Yu can't beat them fellas."

# Chapter 14

Sudden reined in his horse on the top of a broken-backed ridge and surveyed the surrounding country; the indentation between his level brows denoted that he was not entirely pleased with what he saw. Since the stampede and the events which followed it, day after day had passed in wearying but satisfactory monotony.

For the last day or so Sudden had been wondering whether, in their search for easy going, they had veered too much to the west. Now, it was clear that the surface of the prairie was changing, the grass was becoming sparse and sand was taking its place. Ahead of him, a giant cactus, its candelabra-like arms curving upwards, stood like a warning sentinel. Far away, almost on the horizon, a swarm of black dots moved slowly nearer. He rode back to the herd.

"Desert ahead," he said briefly. "Ain't drifted on to the Staked Plain, have we?"

The question put a perturbed expression on the foreman's lined features.

"Hell, Jim, I can't say," Jeff confessed. "That cussed stampede throwed us right out, an' I dunno nothin' about this blame' country. Mebbe we're on'y on the fringe of it."

"Better swing to the east anyways," Sudden advised.

Jeff gave the necessary instruction to the point men and then rode ahead with Sudden after the herd. When they sighted it, Jeff bit on an oath; the cattle were floundering through a sea of sand, hummocks, ridges; and long rolling swells stretched out unendingly until they merged with the pale blue of the cloudless sky. As they were about to pass the wagon, Peg-leg jerked a thumb backwards.

"The Ol' Man has been askin' for yu, Jeff," he grunted. "Wanted to know what we was doin' in this fry-pan? I done told him it was better'n bein' in the fire, but he on'y cussed me."

Sam Eden, propped up inside the conveyance, greeted them peevishly; with returning strength, he was beginning to chafe at inaction, as a sick man will. The foreman set out the situation.

"At least we've dodged the redskins an' mebbe this sand ain't but a strip," he finished. "Yu got the best of it in here, Sam; the air outside would choke a wooden image."

The cattleman's reply was a wholesale condemnation of the Indians, the desert, the wagon, and the man who was responsible for his being confined to it. Though he spoke in a low voice, one of the women sitting beside the driver heard and promptly parted the curtains which screened the front of the vehicle.

"Make tracks," Judy ordered. "How'n hell am I to git

that fella fit if yu come around upsettin' him? Take yore damn troubles somewhere else."

"He's here 'cause I wanted to see him," the invalid said.

"Then yu got no more sense than he has," the lady retorted. "Did I hear yu cough?"

"No," Eden replied quickly, and clutched his cherished pipe. He knew the threat behind the question. With a feeble grin at his foreman, he added, "Better fade, Jeff; she's the doc, yu know, bless her."

Mile upon mile under the pitiless sun they crawled, both men and beasts choking in the clouds of dust churned up by thousands of tramping feet. On all sides lay the arid waste of bleached sand, the powdery particles of which covered them with a coating of dirty white, invaded eyes, mouth, and nostrils, and getting between the skin and clothing, caused intolerable discomfort. Progress was painfully slow, for the cattle sank knee-deep in the soft surface and riders had to tie their ropes to the wagon in order to pull it up the slopes. Here and there a bare shoulder of rock, a stunted mesquite, or a cactus, its spines gleaming frostily, broke the soul-sickening sameness of the scene. The sand flung the sun's rays back in their faces and they seemed to be wading through a lake of shimmering heat.

The cool night air brought some slight mitigation of their sufferings but instead of being baked they were nearly frozen. Some o the cook's cherished fuel and a few dead mesquite branches supplied a poor fire, round which those not watching the herd huddled in humorous discontent. The two barrels of water slung to the wagon were all of the precious liquid they possessed; the horses were given a bare swallow apiece but the cattle had to go thirsty. One mug of coffee was the allowance for each man.

"D'j'ever see such a durned country?" Jed complained, as he ruefully finished his drink. "Fella told me once that more'n two-thirds o' the earth is covered with water an' we gotta come to a bit, where there ain't enough to rust a nail."

At the first glimmer of grey in the east they arose, shivering, swallowed a scanty breakfast, and set out; the foreman was anxious to get as far as possible ere the sun's rays attained their full force. The day proved to be a repetition of the preceding, the discomfort intensified by the fact that even the miserable ration of water they had then enjoyed was no longer available; a quart or so, reserved for the invalid and the women, was all that remained.

By mid-day it was evident the cows could not go much farther. Already a few had fallen and had, perforce, to be abandoned; the rest still staggered weakly on, tongues protruding, sullenly lowing, and many of them nearly blind. The foreman ranged up beside Sudden, who was leading the herd. His voice was little more than a whisper:

"Jim, if we don't git outa this Devil's oven mighty soon it's our finish. That black o' yores 'pears to be in better shape than any o the hosses; ride on an' take a look-see."

Sudden nodded and forged ahead, quickly leaving the labouring herd behind, though his own pace was no more than a walk. He had covered about a mile when a flat hummock of rock attracted his attention and he rode to the top of it. From there he had a more extended view. Wiping the bitter alkali dust from his smarting eyes he stared unbelievingly. Was it a mirage, that maddening mockery of the desert, or did he really see a dark, irregular line between the sky and the sand? He gazed again, intently, but the vision persisted. He tried to utter a whoop but his swollen tongue and parched throat produced only a hoarse cackle. When the herd came in sight, a straggling string of grey ghosts he waved an arm and Jeff joined him. The foreman's squinting eyes followed the pointing finger, and he managed to articulate:

"If them's trees, it means runnin' water. Ride on, Jim, there may be Injuns about."

Sudden departed, taking his own and Jeff's empty canteens. Gradually, as he approached it, the dark line thickened and presently took the form of foliage. The trees were but half a mile distant now, a long wall of them, pine, oak, cottonwood, with a close undergrowth of thorny bushes. The nearness of them put new life into both horse and rider. In a few moments they saw the river, a sluggish stream less than a hundred yards across, passing between wide sloping banks. Sudden drank sparingly, dipped his head in the water, and then dragged his unwilling mount away from it.

"Yu've had enough, for now, yu old soak," he admonished. "Wanta give yoreself a colic or somethin'?"

The black rubbed its wet, silken nostrils against his shoulder and gave in. At the top of the bank, Sudden mounted and rode back to carry the good news. The foreman's face brightened, and when he had moistened his aching throat and sent the canteens back down the line, he looked at the stumbling beasts beside him, and said:

"They'll just about make it—we'll lose some, mebbe, but that can't be helped. They's perkin' up a'ready. See ol' Show-'em-how there; he can smell that damn water."

At the head of the herd the big long-horn was striding gallantly along, nose up, nostrils distended, and from time to time he gave vent to a feeble bellow, as of a leader encouraging his followers.

"We'll have to rest 'em up for a day or so," the foreman continued. "She ain't much of a river, yu say?"

"That's so, but I'd rest 'em the other side," Sudden advised. "She's low now, but come a storm, she'd be a rip-roarin' devil. Get 'em over, pronto, ol-timer."

"Any special reason for sayin' that, Jim?" Jeff inquired. "Them steers is plenty tuckered out for swimmin'."

"There ain't much o' that an' they'll feel different after a swill,"

Sudden told him. "See here, Jeff; the water is risin'—on'y by inches yet—but that means more to come."

The other nodded agreement; he knew how quickly a stream showing a mere trickle of water could become a raging torrent. They had almost reached the river when Sudden's restless eyes lighted on the remains of a fire, almost hidden behind a big cactus. They rode to the spot.

"Injuns?" the foreman inquired, indicating a moccasin track.

Sudden shook his head. "The sticks is laid criss-cross an' burned in the middle, white man fashion; a redskin lays 'em all pointin' to the centre an' burns the ends." He searched the surrounding ground. "Ain't no hoofprints. What's a white man on foot doin' in these parts?"

"I got riddles enough a'ready," Jeff said dryly. "Best git that cussed wagon an' hosses over first, I s'pose."

So the herd was held back till this was done. Fortunately

the bed of the stream was firm, and—as Sudden had guessed—there was not, as yet, much deep water, so the unwieldy vehicle was transported without undue difficulty. The remuda followed, and then came the cattle. Tumbling pell-mell down the bank the parched brutes staggered into the water and stood there as though rooted. It was Sudden who saw the solution.

"Keep on pilin' 'em in, Jeff," he cried.

The plan worked. The pressure of the thirsty ones behind forced the leaders into deep water and soon they were swimming for the other bank. The foreman breathed again, but his troubles were not yet at an end. The crossing was only nearing completion when a warning came from Sandy:

"Hurry 'em up, Jeff; she's risin' rapid."

It was true; the span of the river was twice what it had been, and the outfit, recognizing the danger, made desperate efforts to hustle over the rest of the herd. Sluggishly, as it seemed, the jaded longhorns fought their way through the deepening water and climbed the opposing slope, reluctant to leave the liquid they had for fortyeight hours been without.

"We'll make it," Jeff said, relief in his tone.

He spoke too soon. The last of the "drag"—consisting of the weaker animals—in charge of Jed, was little more than half-way across when a dull booming sound which grew louder every moment sent all eyes up-stream. There, at a narrow bend where the banks rose steeply, they saw a sight to make the bravest quail. Piled up between the bluffs was a great wall of water twenty feet high, the foaming crested lip of which bristled with driftwood, great branches and even whole trees, torn up bodily by the torrent.

The cowboy saw the danger, and leaving his charges to fend for themselves, spurred his mount in an endeavour to reach the bank. But the peril was advancing too swiftly. With a thunderous crash the avalanche of water broke upon the struggling forms and swept them from sight. Cursing in their helplessness, the rest of the outfit watched their comrade go to his doom. All save Sudden, who, at the first glimpse of the threatening deluge, had raced his horse to a jutting point in the bank and, at the risk of being swept away himself, had swung his rope. The loop dropped over Jed's shoulders just as the limb of a tree struck him from his saddle and buried him in a seething welter of tormented water.

Feeling that the rope, already tied to the horn, was taut, Sudden backed his horse slowly away from the river. A cheer greeted him when it was seen that the limp figure of the cowboy was at the end of the lariat. Willing hands carried him to a dry spot and sought for injuries; beyond a scratch or two, there was none. Dumpy, who, with a strangely pale face, had been feeling anxiously for broken bones, gasped with relief when the rescued man opened his eyes and sat up.

"So yu ain't drowned?" he said fatuously.

"Course I am, yu chump," Jed retorted. "My insides is, anyway. Damn this country, there ain't no reasonableness in it; yu either gits too much or none a-tall o' most things. Yu needn't look so glad I ain't gone neither."

Dumpy, fearing he had shown too much solicitude, promptly went to the other extreme.

"I mighta knowed yu couldn't drown'd a fella born to have his neck stretched," he retorted.

"Well, yo're safe thataway, seein' yu ain't got no neck," his friend grinned. He stood up and held out a hand to Sudden. "Jim, I'm rememberin' it," he said. "When yu pitched yore rope I was wonderin' if playin' a harp was difficult."

"Huh!" Dumpy grunted. "Shovellin' coal is what yu wanta practise."

This restored the normal atmosphere of a cow-camp and made them all feel more comfortable. The foreman answered Jed's question:

"Yeah, we lost the cows an' yore bronc an' got off light at that. Wonder if this cussed country has any more surprises for us?"

The "cussed country" had, as they were to discover ere long.

# Chapter 15

The days that followed seemed like a dream after the rude experience of the desert. The character of the country had changed; there were still stretches of grass-covered prairie but they were not so extensive, and varied by hills and dales, some of them thickly wooded. Creeks were frequent, and with abundant feed and water, the cattle quickly recovered, and, being thoroughly "trail-broke," gave little trouble. Beyond the certainty that they were still in Indian territory and were heading north, they had no knowledge of their position. This did not trouble them; in their own phrase, "Time to ford a river is when yu come to it." Sandy shared in the general optimism.

"That little ol' desert done us a good turn after all," he remarked, as he paused for a moment beside his friend. They were rounding up the herd for the day's drive. The slanting rays of the rising sun were dispersin the haze over the bedding-ground, a little savannah of rich grass entirely shut in by timber and brush. The camp was at the far end, some half-mile distant. "We've shook off Mister Rogue."

"Someone's been smilin' at yu," Sudden replied, with gentle sarcasm, and then, "Rogue knows where we're makin' for—he don't have to follow us. What's worryin' me is not seein' any Injuns."

"Well, that's a misfortune I can bear easy," the boy returned lightly. "Mebbe we've just been lucky."

Sudden declined to accept this view. "I've a hunch we're bein' watched," he said.

"Yu've been rubbin' noses with Jed," Sandy chaffed. "The war-whoops is all busy chasin' the festive buffalo."

Sudden started to grin, changed his mind, and gripped a gun instead. "Here's some that ain't," he said quietly.

Out of the brush a line of horsemen had silently emerged, pulling up in the form of a half-circle about two hundred yards from the herd. They were Indians, big, well-built fellows, sitting their mettlesome little ponies like bronze statues. Each brave carried a long lance, bow and arrows, and on the left arm a round shield of buffalo hide, hair inwards, stretched on hickory, with pictures of the moon, stars, serpents, and other symbolic devices painted on the front. Their fierce faces, and their chests, were daubed with colour.

At the sight of them the cowboys pulled out their rifles, but the Indians showed no hostility. Only one advanced, a tall oldish man, gaily bedecked with eagle plumes, and bearing on his shield the presentment of a black bear. His right hand was raised, palm outwards, in token that he came on a peaceful mission. Despite the cruel, crafty expression on his face he was an imposing figure. He rode straight to the foreman—having doubtless observed him giving orders—uttered a guttural "How!" and began to speak. Jeff listened for a moment and shook his head.

"No savvy," he said, and beckoned to Sudden. "Mebbe yu can find out what he's after."

The redskin repeated his statement and the cowboy was able to gather the gist of it.

"He says he is Black Bear, a great chief, that this is Comanche country, an' we got no right to take cattle through it," he translated. "He wants tribute in cows."

The foreman's face grew bleak. "How many?" he asked.

Sudden put the question and the Indian, resting his lance across his knees, pointed first to himself, then to Sudden, and raised both hands. The cowboy explained:

"Redskins reckon thisaway: one is a finger, five a hand, ten, two hands, twenty, a man. Yu can figure it yoreself."

Jeff, who had been watching the chief's movements closely, did so, and swore. "Give him fifty steers?" he snarled. "Tell him to go to hell."

"Don't know enough o' the lingo," Sudden said. "I'll offer him five—Injuns is like Jews, allus ask more'n they expect to get."

Black Bear listened gravely to the white man's explanation, haltingly told in a mixture of Indian tongues, and ending with the raising of one hand only. Then he drew himself up haughtily, flashed a meaning glance at his followers, and fixed his savage eyes on this paleface who had insulted him with so paltry an offer. Sudden met the stare with one equally steady. For one long moment the black eyes battled with the blue and then the redskin wrenched his pony round and trotted back to his band. The cowboys, who had allowed the herd to drift towards the other end of the valley, waited, rifles ready, for the expected charge. They saw Black Bear rejoin his men and face about but he gave no signal.

"What's the game, Jim?" the foreman asked, anxiously scanning the line of silent savages.

"Damned if I know," Sudden replied. "Looks like they're waitin' for somethin'."

The crash of a gun, followed by the fainter report of a pistol, came from where the camp lay and instantly a rider whirled his mount and spurred in that direction; it was Sandy. The Indians were gesticulating, waving their weapons, and reining in their eager ponies. Sudden turned to the foreman.

"They're attackin' the camp—that's why these devils were holdin' back. I'll follow Sandy; yu can handle this bunch."

A pressure of his knees and he was off, threading his way through the scared cattle. He had covered but a short distance when a bursting of yells, mingled with the spiteful crack of exploding powder, told him that the enemy had charged.

Sandy reached the camping-ground just in time to see a tall, lithe warrior, with a limp form draped over his shoulder, disappear in the brush, and oblivious to everything else, dashed in pursuit. He knew that his friend was just behind him, for he had seen the big black pounding down the valley. The trees hampered him and he arrived in the open only to see the abductor sling his burden like a sack of meal across the back of a waiting pony, spring up behind it, and dart away. The cowboy dared not risk a shot lest he hit the girl; he could but try to run the redskin down.

Sudden arrived on the heels of Sandy, saw him vanish, and turned his attention to what was happening. A dead Indian—his head half blown away—sprawled in his path, and another lay huddled by the wagon, from which a steady string of curses issued. Near the fire, Peg-leg was outstretched, a smudge of blood on his face, and over his body Aunt Judy was struggling desperately with a squat, bow-legged savage, whose paint-smeared features she had further decorated with several vivid red streaks. Fighting like a wildcat, and spitting oaths of which a cowboy might well have been proud, she was giving the Comanche brave plenty to think about. Try as he might, he could not clutch those long bony arms with their fearsome claws.

"Knock my man over, huh, ye Gawd-damned, misbegotten, copper-coloured heathen," she yelled, and with a quick stoop, snatched a skillet from the fire and whanged him across the face.

Driven back by the blow, the redskin, evidently despairing of capturing a white squaw for himself, drew his knife. His hand swung up and then a bullet from Sudden's gun toppled him to the ground. Aunt Judy staggered weakly to her husband, flinging herself on her knees beside him. As she wiped away the blood, the cook opened his eyes and sat up.

"I'm awright," he said. "One o' these bastards got me with the butt of his lance an' I took the count." His eyes roamed round the little clearing. "There were four of 'em. Where's the other?"

"Got away, takin' Miss Carol," Aunt Judy told him, adding a venomous hope concerning the redskin's future state.

"Shucks, cussin' don't help," Peg-leg said, and his better-half stared at him; Satan reproving sin would have astonished her less.

"Yu just found that out?" she asked acidly.

Sudden interrupted the squabble by putting a question. It appeared the raiders had approached the camp on foot. Peg-leg had seen one stepping to the wagon and laid him out with a shotgun. Then he had been struck down from behind. His wife took up the tale. The women had been in the tent and when Peg-leg fired, the girl ran out, to be immediately seized, overpowered, and tied. Aunt Judy following, was attacked by a third savage, while a fourth attempted to climb into the wagon.

"Sam blowed his light out an' he's liable to do the same to us if he ain't attended to," she finished.

They found the cattleman propped up on one elbow, a six shooter gripped in his right hand. The fury in his rugged face gave way to fear when he heard of Carol's capture, and he cursed anew the man whose bullet had laid him low. Sudden tried to soothe him by pointing out that Sandy was in pursuit, but the effort failed.

"They'll get him too—damn the crooked luck," he dejectedly replied. "How's Jeff makin' it?"

Hammering hoofs brought the answer and the Infant pulled his panting pony to a sliding stop by the wagon.

"We druv 'em off," he announced triumphantly. "Got

six at the first rattle. That discouraged 'em some, an' they started circlin'. It didn't help 'em none for we got two-three more. Then the ol' chief lets out a whoop an' they scoops up their dead an' vanishes—complete. Jeff said for to tell yu the herd ain't scattered much an' we'll be ready to start in 'bout an hour."

Sudden explained why this would not be possible and the youth's face lengthened.

"Hell, that's bad," he said. "Sandy went after her?"

"Yeah, an' as he ain't back, it's possible they got him too."

The rancher's querulous voice came from the wagon: "Get Jeff an' the boys an' go after these damned women-stealers."

Sudden shook his head. "Listen to me, seh," he said earnestly. "That Black Bear is a wise hombre an' he'll figure on us doin' that very thing, which is why he didn't stay an' fight it out; Comanches ain't cowards, yu savvy. If they can trap the outfit they get the herd easy."

"To hell with the herd," Eden snapped. "I'd sooner lose every hoof than harm should happen to Carol."

"Shore, but that ain't the way to go about it," the cowboy urged. "We gotta walk in the water some."

"He's right, boss," Peg-leg put in. "Let Jim trail 'em an' see how things is. No sense in runnin' our heads into a yeller-jackets nest."

The old man gave a grudging assent; he knew they were advising him wisely but his fiery disposition, and the contempt of the frontier men for the redskin called for something more aggressive; the thought of his girl at the mercy of those painted devils filled him with fury.

Sudden's preparations were soon made. He decided to take the black, for if he could liberate the captives, speed would be essential. He was mounting when Jeff rode in; Sudden explained his errand.

"O' course, it's on the cards they'll gather me in too," he said. "Then it'll be up to yu an' the boys. I'll leave a plain trail."

The foreman's face was sombre. "It looks bad, Jim," he said. "Why should they be so sot on gittin' a white woman, huh?"

Sudden did not reply to the question. He could have offered a reason, but he feared the foreman would deem it fantastic. But his knowledge of redskin nature, relentless and untiring in its pursuit of vengeance, told him that it was possible.

Following Sandy's trail, his mind was busy with the idea he had forborne to mention to the foreman. It had suggested itself when he learned the girl had been carried off. The braves from whom he had rescued her on the day he had first ridden to the S E had been Comanches, and there was a chance that they belonged to Black Bear's tribe. Had the one who escaped remained in the neighbourhood, watching the preparations for the drive, following it day by day, waiting for the opportunity to avenge his comrade? Sudden's thoughts reverted to the moccasin prints he had found when Eden was stricken down. No Indian had fired that shot, but one might have been spying on the camp and driven away by the advent of the assassin. The cowboy's lips set grimly. If this theory was correct, the girl's peril was indeed dire.

He experienced no difficulty in following the trail since neither pursuer nor pursued had any other thought than speed. The deeper indentations of the animal carrying the double burden could be distinguished. The tracks led him towards a forest of pines, the plumed heads of which shut out the sun. He paused for a moment and pulled out a pistol before plunging into the shadowy depths. The ghostly, bared trunks of the trees, rank after rank, were most of them large enough to conceal a lurking enemy. An ideal spot, the cowboy decided, for an ambush.

He had not gone far when his intuition appeared to be justified. At a point where the foliage overhead made the wood almost dark, he came upon evidence that a struggle had taken place; the carpet of pine-needles had been violently disturbed, and on the bole of a tree was a blotch of blood. Had Sandy caught his man? Sudden did not think so—the indications suggested that it was the other way about. A careful examination of the nearby tree-trunks showed that the ground behind several was slightly flattened. Moreover, the trail of the two horses continued on through the wood.

"That hombre had it all planned out," the cowboy muttered. "They were waitin' here for a pursuin' party. Well, Sandy ain't dead, seemin'ly, or they'd 'a' scalped an' left him."

Somewhat cheered by this reflection, he rode on, noting that the bloodstains recurred at intervals. Presently he emerged from the timber and at once pulled up; an increase in the hoof-prints showed that other riders had joined the pair he was following.

"The ambushin' braves picked up their hosses 'bout here," he surmised. "Must be near a dozen of 'em. Nig. Have gotta watch out."

He went on cautiously, keeping well away from any spot which offered a likely hiding-place. But he had to take some risks, for the day was advancing and it would be hopeless to follow the trail in the dark. A little later he came to a narrow ravine littered with boulders, debris wrested by the weather from the rock walls. Pacing slowly along, eyes alert for any sound or movement, he saw something which brought an oath to his lips: lying face downwards at the side of the gully was a bound and gagged man. Sudden slid from his saddle and turned him over; it was Sandy. As he stooped to remove the gag a rope swished, he was flung violently backwards, and a savage war-cry pealed out. Realizing that he too had been tricked he grabbed at a gun but a crashing blow from behind robbed him of reason.

# Chapter 16

When Sudden regained his senses his first impression was that someone was kicking him on the head, but he soon realized that the throbbing jars he felt were the result of the blow he had received. Lying on his back, his hands tied, he was unable to find out the extent of the injury. In the semi-darkness he could see that he was inside a kind of inverted funnel and knew it for an Indian tepee. Outside, the weird wail of a woman rose above the barking of dogs and guttural voices of men.

"So they got me," he said aloud. "If my head didn't hurt so much I'd say it was solid bone. Wonder where Sandy is?"

" 'Lo, Jim," a low voice answered. "Yu come to life again?"

"No, I'm dead from the neck up," was the disgusted reply. "Of all the fools..."

"It was neat, allasame," Sandy consoled. "They knowed yu'd hop off to tend to me—any fella would. All they had to do was squat behind the rocks an' rope yu. First time I ever figured as the bait in a trap."

"Where's Miss Carol?"

"Right here, wore out an' sleepin'. What d'yu reckon they'll do to us, Jim?"

Sudden was still sore in both body and mind. "Cuff our ears an' tell us to be good boys in future, don't yu reckon?" was his sarcastic reply, and then, "Shucks, we'll find a way out." After a pause, "There was blood on the trail; yu hurt?"

"No, I winged one when they jumped me," Sandy explained.

"Jeff an' the boys'll search us out," Sudden said.

"Don't bet on it. Soon after they collected yu the main bunch branched off, taking yore hoss an' mine. One brave reckoned on ridin' the black but that pet o' yores just planted both hind hoofs on his chest an' if he ain't stopped breathin' altogether, I'll lay he's findin' it a painful process. After that, they elected to lead him."

"Nigger don't like Injuns."

"I'm believin' yu. Well, the rest of us struck a stream, waded down it for near half a mile, an' then went along a stony gulch where a herd o' buffalo wouldn't leave a trace."

Sudden was silent; this put a different complexion on matters. The rescue party would follow the prints of the shod horses and probably blunder into a trap just as he and Sandy had done. The commotion outside increased in volume and other wailing voices joined the first.

"Black Bear's band has got back an' some more squaws have learned they are widders," Sudden surmised.

There was a slight movement in the gloom on the far side of the tepee; the noise had awakened the third prisoner.

"Sandy," the girl whispered. "Did I hear Mister Green's voice?"

"Shore, I'm here, Miss Carol," Sudden replied.

"Thank heaven," she said. "I feared you were—killed." He smiled grimly into the darkness; she did not realize that death might yet be a boon to crave for. Still speaking in a low voice, she went on, "Mister Green, the Indian who brought me here is the other—the one who got away."

It gave Sudden no pleasure to find that his conjecture had proved correct. Affecting a jocularity he did not feel, he said:

"Persevering beggar; we'll have to discourage him some."

"I'm—scared," she confessed.

"Don't yu be," he urged, and then lied nobly, "the boys'll be along any time now an' snake us outa this mess."

His confident tone was comforting and she uttered a sigh of relief; somehow she felt that with these two men beside her, tied though they were, the situation was not quite hopeless.

The flap of the tent was flung aside and a savage, carrying a lighted pine-knot, stalked in. Of medium height, his headdress of eagle-plumes and erect bearing made him appear taller. He was young, less than thirty, Sudden estimated, and moved with the agile sinuosity of a snake. On his bare breast the mask of a fox was crudely pictured in red, and the streaks of paint on his face intensified its sinister expression of cruelty. He shot one triumphant glance at the girl, strode across to Sudden and stooped, thrusting the torch almost into the cowboy's face. For an instant he gazed and then a flash of ferocious joy illumined the dark eyes.

"Damnation, he remembers me," the captive reflected. "Trust an Injun for that."

Spitting out a few rapid sentences in his own tongue, the Indian, after testing the bonds of all three, glided away.

"What did he say?" Sandy thoughtlessly inquired.

Sudden, though he could not have given a literal translation gathered sufficient to know that he had been promised a slow and very agonizing end. Not wishing to further alarm the girl, his reply was evasive:

"He's goin' to have a pow-wow with me in the mornin'."

Sandy's tone was incredulous. "A pow——" he began, and stopped. "Shore, he'll want to talk things over," he went on.

"Mebbe he'll dicker with us for beeves."

Long into the night the shrieks of the women mourning their dead endured. Sudden could vision them, kneeling on the bare earth, their bodies streaming with blood from the gashes they inflicted upon themselves. The spectacle would rouse resentment against the hated paleface prisoners to the highest pitch, and unless a miracle happened ... In a gust of revolt, he strained at his bonds, but the man who had tied them knew his business. He tried to sleep, well aware that he would need all his nerve for the coming ordeal.

Daylight brought them visitors, an armed brave and a squaw bearing platters of food, pieces of cooked flesh and cakes of meal, with which they had to deal as best they could with bound hands. One unacquainted with Indians might have argued from this that they were not yet to die, but Sudden knew it was but a refinement of cruelty; a man weak from want of food would succumb to torture sooner.

When they had eaten, the redskin removed the bonds from Sudden's ankles and pointed to the entrance of the tent. The cowboy saw the alarm in the girl's eyes and forced a grin on his set lips.

"Goin' to have a word with Foxy," he said. "Back soon."

"What does it really mean?" Carol's white lips whispered, as the pair went out.

Sandy was cursing softly but vividly. "It means—hell," he groaned.

They heard a fierce yell of execration as the captive appeared, and in an agony of fear, dragged themselves to the opening of the tepee. The sight they saw did not reassure them.

The camp was of fair size, consisting of more than a score of lodges, set in a rude circle and hedged in by trees and brush. Round the open space in the centre the whole tribe was gathered, men, women, and children, shrieking and yelling in savage exultation. The hubbub increased as the white man was conducted to a large tree on the edge of the clearing. Two more warriors now joined the first. Releasing his, hands, they gripped a wrist apiece, forced his arms back and again secured them behind the tree-trunk. The position was intensely painful and rendered the sufferer as helpless as a tied steer.

No sooner was this done than the onlookers surged forward, broke into an eerie chant, and began to circle the tree in a wild dance. The oblique rays of the mounting sun, flickering through the foliage, shadowed the fantastic capers on the ground. Though they shook their weapons in his face, no one of the dancers attempted to touch the prisoner. Interminably, as it seemed to the object of it, the monotonous dirge went on. All the tribe were not taking part; on the far side of the clearing stood a group of Indians whose plumed heads showed that they were chiefs; among them was Black Bear.

Wooden-faced, the bound man stared stolidly at the dancing devils who mocked as they passed him. His head still throbbed from the rough treatment of yesterday and his arm-muscles ached under the unnatural strain to which they were being subjected, but he knew he must show no sign of weakness; that was what these fiends were hoping for. To avoid thinking of what was to come he sent his mind back into the past, recalling the dark hours in Fourways, where he had also awaited death; it was a grim thought that If the outlaw's rescue might yet prove something to be regretted. It would be Sandy's turn next, and then the girl; the eyes of Red Fox had plainly told her fate.

A raucous command rang out and the droning ring broke and swept back, forming in a half-circle on the far side of the clearing. From among the chiefs Red Fox strode, his feathers fluttering in the faint breeze, to pause a few paces from the prisoner. His dark face was alight with savage triumph.

"For the slaying of Running Deer, my brother, you shall die many times. On your knees you shall beg for death and it shall not come."

Sudden's expression was contemptuous. "Red Fox has a big mouth," he said. "He might frighten a papoose."

He knew that the shaft had gone home, though only a tremor of rage betrayed the fact; the redskin was crafty.

"Red Fox has sharp teeth but will not bite too soon," he countered. "Yet if the white dog desires a speedy death, he shall have his chance."

He stepped back, drew a short, heavy-hafted knife from his belt, and glanced pridefully round at his audience. Then his right arm swung up, down, and like a streak of silver the blade flashed through the sunlight and embedded itself in the tree-trunk. Sudden felt a trickle of warm blood and realized that the keen edge, missing his head by a hair's-breadth, had nicked his ear. The thrower, bent slightly forward, watched the result of his effort with evil enjoyment.

"Move, and earn the death you will presently pray for," he called out.

A medley of mocking yells came from the spectators and a score of voices repeated the taunt; both they and the cunning devil who had uttered it knew that the invitation would not be accepted. However desperate his situation, a sane, healthy man will hold on to life as long as possible, and though Sudden could see no chance of escape, he cherished a hope that he might somehow get free and go down fighting. So he schooled his aching muscles and became as motionless as the tree against which he stood.

With steady, unwinking eyes, he saw the fling of the brown arm again, the gleam of the twinkling steel, and felt the wind of the blade on his cheek. The second knife missed him by less than an inch. Amid the shouts of admiration for the prowess of their chief, were jeers for the man who had declined to die. Sudden was concerned with someone else; from behind had come a hoarse whisper:

"Yore han's is free. When that varmint comes to git his stickers, grab one an' let him have it. Then jump for the tepee, git yore guns, and gimme a chance to start the gal an' yore friend off. There'll be a hoss waitin' for yu."

Like a dazed man, the cowboy listened. The voice was one he had heard before but in the stress of the moment he could not place it. He could feel that his wrists had been loosed and lowered his arms slightly to relieve the numbing ache. He looked at Red Fox; the chief was strutting to and fro, enjoying his triumph, and seemed to be in no hurry to fetch his weapons. Sudden wanted him nearer.

"Red Fox is clumsy," he announced loudly. "An Apache or Kiowa boy could throw the knife better."

Like a stung man the savage whirled, his dusky features aflame with fury.

"White spawn!" he cried, "I will cut off your ears with the knives; I will pin your fingers one by one to the tree."

Haughtily he stepped forward and that was the moment the victim had been waiting for. Snatching one of the knives, he balanced it on his palm for an instant, and then hurled it at the advancing savage. With a strangled cry Red Fox crumpled up, the steel buried to the haft in his throat.

For one staggering moment there was silence and then the petrified onlookers saw the man they had believed to be securely tied leap across the open space and vanish into one of the tepees. The sight restored their power to move and with a ferocious threatening howl, they rushed in pursuit.

Sudden found the tepee empty. Buckling on his belt,

he drew both guns and sprang to the entrance. A surging wave of maddened redskins was sweeping down upon him, and a cloud of arrows greeted his appearance, piercing the buffalo-hide walls of the tepee, and whistling past his ears. His Colts spouted flame and before that continuous hail of hurtling lead the charge withered and broke, the Indians scattering in all directions. But he knew the respite was but momentary; they would surround him, and then.... Reloading his weapons, he became aware that someone had entered, and swung about. He saw a brown, paint-lined face, feathered scalp-lock, and his thumb was on the point of releasing the hammer when the intruder spoke:

"Hold on thar, friend; I ain't no war-whoop."

It was the voice of the man who had freed him, and now he remembered it as that of the "still-hunter" who had come into their camp on the Colorado. Tyson gave him no time for questions.

"The gal is away on yore black an' yore friend with her, though he balked some at leavin' yu," he said. "There's a hoss waitin' an' yu ain't got but a minit—them devils is closin' in, which is why they've stopped yappin'." He pointed to the back of the tepee, where a long slit in the hide covering provided an exit, adding, "It'll be nip an' tuck as it is."

"What about yu?" the cowboy asked.

"I'm stayin'," was the jaunty reply. "I c'n pass as one of 'em an'"—he chuckled with sinister glee—"I'll make me some converts."

Sudden did not attempt to dissuade him; Tyson evidently knew what he was about. He held out a hand.

"This puts me deep in yore debt," he said.

"Nary a bit—I ain't forgot that grub an' smokin'," was the reply. "Head due west an' hump yoreself."

Sudden slid through the opening and found the horse. Being Indian property there was no saddle, but the hackamore bridle was all the cowboy needed and in a trice he was on the beast's back and spurring for the open. A shout of rage and a few spasmodic arrows greeted his appearance and a redskin rose out of the long grass and sprang at him, only to go down with a shriek under the plunging feet. A score of leaping strides and the fugitive knew that he was safe for the time. He would be pursued, but the Indians had first to secure their ponies and this would give him a fair start. Nevertheless, he pressed on at full speed, casting an occasional glance at the trail, where the prints of shod horses seemed to indicate that he was following his friends.

Unfortunately, the nature of the country did not favour him, for though undulating, it was open, offering little opportunity of keeping out of sight. Sudden had covered but a few miles when, from the crest of a long slope, he saw the pair he was in search of, and uttered a man-sized curse when he realized that they were waiting for him. With a violent gesture he signed them to go on and let his own mount feel the spurs. His greeting, when he ranged alongside, was hardly one of gratitude.

"Have ya lost yore wits?" he asked Sandy. "Yu oughta be a coupla miles farther away right now."

"We were anxious about you," the girl explained. "I insisted on waiting."

Sudden looked around disgustedly. "There ain't a hole we could hide in," he said.

As they surmounted another incline a faint whoop was borne to them on the breeze, and back on the trail was a billowing cloud of dust in which tiny dark forms could be dimly distinguished. Sudden's lips clamped together as he studied the animal he bestrode. Sandy was riding his own horse, which was a good one.

"Friend Tyson don't savvy ponies, or mebbe this is all he could lay his paws on," he commented. He reached over and removed his rifle from the saddle of the black, and said to Sandy, "Yu an' Miss Carol go ahead; my hoss is fast for a mile or two, but ain't got no bottom."

"Like hell we will," the boy retorted hotly. "What yu goin' to do?"

"Stay an' argue with these copper-coloured gents. That'll give yu time to get the girl away—mebbe."

Ere Sandy could voice his objection to this proposal a fierce yell apprised them of another factor to be considered, and effectually closed the argument. Less than half a mile distant, and coming towards them, was another band of redskins who, at the sight of the whites, quirted their ponies into a run. The fugitives were between two fires. Sudden swung his horse to the right.

"Follow me," he cried. "We gotta find a better place than this to stand 'em off."

"Mebbe they'll scrap with each other an' give us a chance to sneak off," Sandy said hopefully, as they raced at top speed across the plain.

"The second lot are Comanches too," Sudden told him, and shot a hasty glance over his shoulder. "Hell, they're gainin'. Head for that bluff; it looks a likely spot."

He pointed to a small plateau, the approaching slope of which was, at one spot, broken away, leaving a vertical wall. At the foot of this were several boulders. With the girl and the horses sheltered behind the largest of these, the two men gripped their weapons and waited.

"They may get us, boy, but we'll make 'em pay," Sudden grated.

# Chapter 17

The onslaught did not come at, once. The white men saw the two bands meet and fraternize, with much shouting, gesticulation, and brandishing of weapons. Probably the position their prey had taken did not please them; it meant a frontal attack, and most Indians had a healthy fear of the "guns that fired for ever." Sandy was counting.

"Thirty of 'em," he said in a low voice. "If they wait till dark we ain't got a hope."

"They won't—Injuns don't like night-work—too many bad spirits about," Sudden reminded him. "They may decide to sit down an' starve us out."

Sandy's face lengthened; they had neither food nor water. Lying each behind a sheltering rock they awaited the outcome of the argument taking place amongst the enemy.

"Odd that fella Tyson showin' up," Sandy remarked. "Must 'a' changed his mind about searchin' out a settlement."

"Mebbe, but he'd have time to do that an' then catch us up," Sudden pointed out. "He could easy make three miles to our one."

"Well, I ain't carin' how it was but I'm hopin' he'll play another hand. He busted in on us just as yu hid the knife in that skunk's gullet, an' believe me, he was welcome. Hell! they're agoin'."

The savages, strung out in a long line, had turned tail and were trotting slowly away.

"No such luck," Sudden said. "They're a-comin'. Don't shoot till yo're shore an' aim low; if yu miss the man yu'll get the hoss."

He was right; with a whoop the warriors whirled their ponies and raced at the men they had hoped to catch unprepared. In the sunlight the bared bodies shone like polished bronze and the levelled lances were silver-bladed. Feathered head-dresses streamed in the wind as the galloping ponies gathered speed. The muffled thunder of their thudding feet mingled with the threatening cries of the riders. Sudden waited until they were some fifty paces distant, and then:

"Let 'em have it," he said.

The reports of the repeating rifles rang out and gaps showed in the advancing line as men and horses went down. Not waiting to reload, the defenders drew their pistols—which at the short range were as effective—and continued the fusillade. The deadly stream of lead was too much for the attackers; the line broke in the middle, the two halves sweeping round, to retreat at full speed. A grin spread over Sandy's perspiring features.

"Reckon they won't come that caper again," he said, busy recharging his weapons. "Funny they didn't use their bows."

"Want us alive," Sudden explained. "I'm bettin' they didn't savvy we'd got our guns."

"Well, they know now," Sandy said, "though there's some it won't interest no more."

He nodded grimly at the plain before them, where the bodies of seven men and as many horses could be seen. Even as they looked, one of the former rose, and crouching, ran towards his friends. Sandy's rifle cracked and the runner reeled and fell.

"Been watchin' that jasper," the marksman said callously. "Had a notion I on'y got his bronc."

The incident evoked howls of rage from the Comanches, with threatening gestures, but the warriors kept their distance. They had been taught a sharp lesson and had no wish for another. Carol, crouching tiredly behind a boulder, called a question, and Sandy cursed the country, the Indians, and lastly, himself.

"Wouldn't yu fancy a fella might have brains enough to hop off an' fill a canteen at the first stream, huh?" he queried savagely.

"Why, no, when two minutes' delay could mean life or death," his friend consoled.

He went over to the girl and explained the position, concluding with the droll little smile which, even in the direst danger, he was able to summon. "Yu see, we left in just a suspicion o' haste: Still, Sandy might have ..."

She would not have that. "He had enough to think of,

and I ought not to have said anything. Do you think the redskins will attack again?"

Sandy's voice answered the question. "Hi, Jim, they're linin' up; looks like they aim to have another try."

In fact, the long line was moving forward again but this time it extended farther—yards separating the riders. Also, they were moving slowly, the ponies gradually gathering pace for the final dash. This made the task of the defenders more difficult, for instead of firing into a mass, they had to place every shot.

"No use waitin' till they're near," Sudden said. "Pick yore man an' let fly soon as he's in range."

"I'm takin' that jigger on the pinto," Sandy said, and pulled the trigger. "Cuss the luck," he added, as the horse went down, and its rider, after rolling on the ground, arose and shook a vengeful fist.

Sudden toppled a tall warrior from his seat and then an amazing change came over the scene. From somewhere behind the attacking line rang out a volley of rifle-fire which sent half a dozen ponies careering across the plain masterless. The Comanches, taken utterly by surprise, scattered and fled, hotly pursued by the newcomers, who wore the garb of white men. Sandy swung his hat and whooped.

"It'll be the boys, Jim; they've found us at last," he cried. "Why for yu lookin' as if yu'd lost a dollar?"

"If that's the outfit, the S E has been takin' on hands—there was a dozen of 'em," Sudden replied. "Ever hear o' the steak that fell outa the frying-pan?"

Before the boy could reply, the rescuers came racing back, and their leader, reining in, pushed up the brim of his battered sombrero and disclosed the malevolent face of Navajo. He grinned evilly as he recognized the men to whose aid he had come.

"Well, well, see who's here," he drawled. "Sandy, his side-kick, an'"—his triumphant eyes travelled to the girl—"that must be Eden's gal. Shore was lucky for yu-all that we took a fancy to see what mischief this red scum was up to."

"We're obliged to yu," Sudden said shortly.

"Oh, yeah," the ruffian sneered. "But seein' we're Rogue's men yu'll have to thank him in person. I'm bettin' he'll be main pleased to see yu."

The covert intimation that they were prisoners was no more than Sudden expected. For a moment he did not reply; he was studying their new captors. Two of them he had seen at the outlaw hide-out, though he did not know their names; the rest were strangers.

"I was wantin' a word with Rogue anyway," Sudden said.

"Good, then we'll be movin'—I reckon them 'paints has got their needin's," Navajo returned. His eyes narrowed. "There's on'y one point: yu boys must be tired; guess we'll carry yore guns for yu."

Sudden laughed scornfully. "Yu don't guess very good," he retorted. "If yu want our weapons yu'll have to buy 'em an' the price will be high. Sabe?"

Navajo did. The cowboy had rested his rifle against a rock and now stood with hands hovering over the butts of his revolvers, his slitted eyes boring into those of the other. The half-breed hesitated; he had seen those long, nervous fingers at work before. It was twelve men against two, but...

His glance went to the plain, still dotted with brown bodies. His shoulders shrugged submission.

"Yu an' yore men lead the way—we'll follow," Sudden said. "At the first sign of funny business, yu'll take a header into hell, Navajo."

The man scowled, but made no reply. He realized that the prisoners would be of no use dead, and he was not sure of his leader's attitude towards them; Rogue did not confide in him. So, when they set out, he and his ruffians went first, followed by Sudden and Sandy with the girl riding between them. Carol, who had not heard all that passed, was curious.

"Who are these men?" she asked.

"Some of Rogue's Riders an' they are takin' us to their chief," Sudden told her. "We ain't out o' the wood yet."

"Rogue?" she cried in amazement. "But he's a Texan outlaw. What is he doing so far north?"

"He followed us—it was his gang stampeded the herd."

"Well, at least they are white—not savages."

Luckily she did not see the look her companions exchanged; it would not have added to her comfort.

Two hours of slow but arduous riding, owing to the difficult nature of the trail, brought them to the outlaws' camp pitched in a glade on the bank of a stream and shadowed by tall pines. A small fire, near which lay cooking utensils, a little heap of stores covered by a slicker, saddles carelessly thrown down, picketed ponies, and the absence of any shelter, denoted the temporary nature of the halting-place. Around a spread blanket four men were playing cards, while another paced slowly to and fro. He looked up as Navajo rode in.

"Get any buffalo?" he asked.

"Never seed hide nor hair o' one," the half-breed replied. "The boys'll have to pull their belts in to-night. Allasame, we had good huntin'."

Rogue's eyes widened when he saw the last three of the party. "How come?" he asked sharply.

Sullenly the man recounted the circumstances. His coup was not being received with the enthusiasm he had looked for. His chief heard him with an expressionless face until he came to the weapon incident, and then he said:

"So Jim didn't wanta part with his guns, huh?"

The jeer in his voice stung the half-breed. "It would have meant a battle; I reckon I played it right," he retorted angrily.

"Yu played it safe, anyway," came the sneer. "Awright, I'll talk to Jim now—alone."

"Yu ain't overlookin' what this means, Rogue?" the other urged. "That's Carol Eden there, an' her dad'll turn over the whole herd to git her back. Why, it's a pat hand. But mebbe this is what yu bin plannin'? Mebbe Jim an' Sandy was fetchin' her in when the Injuns——"

His leader's cold gaze stopped him. "Mebbe yu'll mind yore own business, Navajo," he said. "When I want yore advice I'll shorely ask for it. Tell Jim I'm waitin'."

The scowling half-breed slouched to where the girl and her companions were standing, and gave the message. His leering eyes swept over Carol and brought the hot blood to her cheeks. Sudden saw the look and said sternly:

"If any guy gets fresh, Sandy, shoot him."

When he had gone, the girl turned to her companion and said quietly, "What is going to happen?"

"I dunno," the young man told her. "Jim'll get us out; he's a wizard, that fella."

"You seem to think a great deal of him," she said.

"I think more of him than anyone else in the world—but two," he added hastily.

"Your father and mother?" she suggested.

Sandy shook his head. "Dad, yes, but I can scarcely remember my mother."

She did not pursue the inquiry. There was a warmth in his eyes which stirred her pulses despite the danger which threatened them.

Sudden found the outlaw sitting on a fallen tree at the edge of the camp. He greeted the young man with a hard smile. He seemed to have aged, the lines in his face were deeper, and he looked haggard. Sudden sat down and rolled a cigarette.

"Howdy, Jim," the outlaw greeted. "Navajo said yu wanted to see me."

"Well, I wasn't goin' to let him fancy he fetched me in," Sudden explained.

Rogue nodded in comprehension. "Allasame, yu've lost out, Jim, an' I've won," he stated.

Sudden's eyebrows went up. "That so?" he queried. "The game ain't finished yet."

"Talk sense, boy," Rogue retorted. "Sam Eden thinks the world an' all o' that girl; I can make my own terms. She's the winnin' card an' I hold it."

"But yu won't play it," Sudden said quietly.

The elder man glowered at him. 'Th' hell I won't? Who'll stop me?"

"Yu will," came the cool response. "Listen to me, Rogue. Yo're one tough hombre—I never met a tougher—but at bottom yo're a white man an' yu can't forget that once yu had women-folk yu thought a lot of, an' that there was a time when yu'd 'a' shot a man just for speakin' disrespectful of a girl like Miss Eden. She's in yore han's by accident; yu can't use her to rob her father, *and yu know it*".

For a moment he thought the man he had spoken to so boldly was about to spring upon him. The cold eyes had grown hot and the big fists were bunched into knots. But the outlaw held himself in, only his voice betraying the tearing passion which possessed him.

"What's past is past an' no damn business o' yores," he said thickly. "Why should I care how she comes to be here? To Sam Eden I'm a road-agent an' cattle-thief an' if I fell into his han's, even by accident"—with a heavy sneer—", he'd stretch my neck. All right, I ain't blamin' him, but this time it happens to be my turn. I'd be loco to pass up such a chance as this, an' what d'yu s'pose my men would say, huh?"

Under his hat-brim, the younger man's eyes gleamed slyly. "Hadn't thought o' that," he admitted. "Yeah, I reckon yu'd find it middlin' hard to persuade 'em."

He saw the other's jaw tighten and his own face remained wooden under the sharp scrutiny it received. Rogue pondered heavily for a while, his brows knitted, and then stood up, motioning the cowboy to follow. The card-game had ceased and the men were gathered in a group listening to the half-breed. They opened; out when their leader approached.

"Well, Navajo, yu got it figured out to yore satisfaction?" Rogue asked.

The man shrugged his shoulders. "Don't need any figurin'," he, replied. "Eden hands over the herd an' gits his gal back; that's all there is to it."

The outlaw leader folded his arms, his eyes flinty.

"The girl goes back to her father, now, an' without conditions," he said deliberately. "I don't war with women."

The decision stunned them to silence for a moment and then babel broke out. Above the protesting voices that of Navajo made itself heard:

"See here, Rogue, we all got a say in this," he cried. "Yu ain't the on'y one."

"I've said it," the outlaw told him. "As long as I'm boss o' this band I run things my own way." His baleful, bloodshot eyes travelled to the half-breed. "Navajo, yu got ambitions to fill my shoes. Step out an' pull yore gun; we'll settle it here an' now."

The other men watched the half-breed curiously. Any one of them might have shot down the challenger but it would have meant a battle, for not all of them were disloyal to Rogue. Also, there was that lean-limbed cowboy, of whose ability to use his gun there was no doubt. Navajo was not the stuff to stand an acid test.

"Yu got me all wrong, Rogue," he protested. "I ain't makin' trouble, an' I reckon the boys don't want none neither. Gittin' the herd is all that matters. It seemed an easy way, but if yu got it fixed different, we ain't carin'."

Having gained his end, Rogue was too astute to overplay his hand. He knew the men, understood that self-interest was the only factor which governed their crude natures. Once satisfied that they would not lose, they would be tractable enough.

"I want them cattle as bad as yu do—got to have 'em, in fact," he said quickly. "So yu needn't to worry 'bout that."

Boldly turning his back on them, he walked to the tree-trunk. Sudden stepped after him. The tempest of emotion which had raged through him seemed to have weakened the outlaw physically; he looked tired and his face was drawn.

"Rogue, yu acted like a white man an' I'm rememberin' it," Sudden told him.

"I acted like a damn fool an' I'm forgettin' it," came the sardonic reply. He was silent awhile, pondering. "How in hell am I to get that gal back to her ol man? It's most of ten mile. Can't use any o' the boys, an' I dursn't leave 'em just now."

"Send Sandy, an' yu can have my word, an' his, that he'll come back—alone," Sudden suggested. "Yu can tell him that my life depends on his doin' that, though there's no need."

"Yu trust him that much?" the outlaw asked, almost a wistful note in his voice, and when Sudden nodded, "Well, it 'pears to be the on'y trail out."

He walked over to where the girl and her companion were waiting, anxiously. Carol, born of fighting stock, faced the famous desperado fearlessly. With scarcely a glance at her, Rogue said roughly:

"I don't want yu here. This fella"—he gestured to Sandy—"will take yu back to yore camp; it ain't so far."

"Thank you," the girl said. "I am sure my father——"

"Don't get any fool notions," he interrupted harshly. "Tell Eden I can win without usin' women." He beckoned Sandy aside. "The herd lies due west—yu can't miss it. Now, I want yore word that yu'll come back—alone. If yu don't show up, or bring company, it will go hard with Jim. Yu sabe?"

"I'll be back—if the war-whoops don't get me," the young man promised. "An' Rogue, I wanta say this is a mighty han'some act——"

"Aw, go to hell," the outlaw retorted. "She interferes, an' that's all there is to it. Get agoin'."

Furtive glances followed the pair as they rode away, but there was no protest, and the inevitable ribald remarks were uttered in undertones. Sudden had waved a cheerful paw but purposely did not go near them; he had no desire to invent explanations. When they had gone, Rogue came to him.

"What about them guns o' yores, Jim?"

"I've pledged myself to stay here till Sandy returns. Don't yu reckon it would be wiser to let me wear 'em till then?"

The other considered the proposition; in the event of more trouble with the men, the prisoner would necessarily be on his side.

"Mebbe yo're right," he decided.

Meanwhile the girl and her escort were slowly making their way in the direction they believed the S E camp to lie, slowly because, there being no trail, they had to pick a path for themselves in the wilderness.

Despite the necessity for constant caution. Sandy stole

an occasional glance at the girl riding beside him. She had courage, and if the slim, straight figure now drooped slightly in the saddle, it was only to be expected after nerve-wracking ordeal of the last forty-eight hours. Her first words, after they had ridden a mile in silence, took him by surprise:

"Some of those men seemed to know you."

"We'd met 'em," Sandy admitted. "Yu run up against all sorts when yo're driftin round."

She did not speak for some moments, and then, "Why did that man let me go? He could have made his own terms with my father."

"It's got me guessin'," the boy told her, truthfully enough.

"Mebbe Jim struck some sort o' bargain, seein' he stayed behind."

Carol shook her head. "He could have kept all of us," she pointed out. "He was disputing with his men when the shooting occurred. Was anyone hurt?"

"I expect so," Sandy replied. "That's a tough team an' it takes a hard man to handle 'em. Rogue's all o' that."

"Somehow I wasn't afraid of him," Carol said reflectively. "Though I believe he had just killed or maimed a fellow-creature."

# Chapter 18

In the S E Camp, anxiety at the absence of their young mistress deepened when neither Sandy nor Sudden put in an appearance. A search-party was sent out but owing to the redskins' ruse of dividing their forces, was led astray and lost the trail completely on a wide strip of stony ground. Its return without Carol reduced the invalid to a state of blasphemous despair; he cursed everything and everybody, including himself for exposing her to such a peril. Aunt Judy, who had spent all her life among rough-tongued men, fled before the torrent of vituperation, and her husband, nursing a sore head, listened with awe. As he afterwards confessed to the outfit:

"For comprehensive cussin' I never heard the beat of it; the Ol' Man shorely covered the ground. I reckon he musta bin a muleskinner one time."

But bad language, however "good" it may be, gets one nowhere and morning broke upon a helpless, and wellnigh hopeless community. The cattleman, propped up by the fire, looked at his foreman in sullen misery.

"Never oughta let her come," he burst out presently. "Jeff, yu gotta find that damn trail. Take all the boys ——"

"The herd ——" the foreman began, and stopped when the lightning commenced to flicker in his employer's eyes.

"Hey, Jeff, there's a coupla riders a-comin'," Pebbles yelled.

The foreman ran to the speaker's side. Two horsemen were entering the valley at the far end. Jeff studied them for a moment and shook his head in disappointment.

"That ain't Jim's black," he said.

"They might 'a' swapped hosses," Pebbles said hopefully.

"It ain't neither of 'em," Jeff replied, and, as the visitors drew nearer, added, "Why, if it ain't Mister Baudry."

The gambler it was, and with him was a middle-aged, bentshouldered fellow, with a long horse-face and deep-set sly eyes.

With a word of greeting to the cowboys, the pair rode to where Eden was sitting, and dismounted.

Baudry shook hands with Eden and presented his companion:

"Meet Davy Dutt; he's in a deal with me."

The cattleman received the stranger without undue enthusiasm —Mister Dutt's exterior was not impressive. Then, in reply to an inquiry for Carol, he told the story of their predicament, and was surprised at the effect it produced; the gambler's full, faintly tanned face took on a yellowish tinge and his voice betrayed real concern.

"My God!" he cried. "Miss Carol in the hands of savages? That's terrible, Sam. What are you doing about it?"

Eden told him and Baudry swore in perplexity. "You

can't do a thing till you locate those damned heathens. Got any ideas, Davy?"

"Nope," the stranger confessed. "Yu seen the kind o' country we come through; yu could hide Noo York in it."

The gambler explained that they had been travelling northwest from Fort Worth, and finding a cattle-trail some way back, had followed it on the chance of it proving to be the S E.

The day passed monotonously enough for the little group left in the camp, and when, as the sun sank in the west, the searchers again reported failure to discover the trail of the red raiders, a blanket of gloom descended upon the whole company. For the cattleman, weakened by illness, the blow was a crushing one, and, strange to say, Baudry was little less affected. Of them all, Judy was obstinately optimistic.

"That Green fella's got savvy," she announced. "He'll fetch her back."

The prophecy proved nearly correct, for as the dusk was deepening into dark, Sandy and his charge rode wearily into camp and were instantly surrounded by whooping cowboys. The rancher's eyes bulged when he found the girl he feared was lost for ever, kneeling beside him. One arm hugging her close, the other hand went to Sandy.

"By heavens, boy, yu've put me deeper in yore debt than I can say," he cried.

Sandy fidgeted. "I ain't done nothin'," he said. "Yu gotta thank Jim."

Naturally Carol was the centre of attraction; everyone was avid to hear what had happened to her. The story of

Sudden's slaying of Red Fox brought ejaculations of "Bravo Jim" and "Good old Texas" from the cowboys, but when she related how they had been rescued from the redskins by some of Rogue's riders, it was Baudry who spoke:

"What's brought that road-agent to these parts?" he asked. Think he's been trailing you, Sam?"

"It would be a safe bet he stampeded our cows," the foreman volunteered.

"But if he's after my herd why did he let yu an' Sandy go?" Eden asked the girl. "He must 'a' knowed he had me cinched."

"I was to tell you that he could win without women," she replied.

"Huh! there's two words to that," her father said grimly. With the girl safe by his side he was becoming his own dour self again. He looked at Sandy. "Can yu explain it?"

"No, but I'm guessin' Jim fixed somethin', an' that's why he stayed an' I've to go back."

"Like hell yu have," the cattleman exploded.

"I've promised."

"A promise to a prowlin' thief don't hold."

Sandy looked at the girl; in the firelight her cheeks appeared pale; her lips were silent, but her eyes spoke.

"Rogue's word to me was that if I didn't show up it would go hard with Jim," Sandy added.

"Did he call him by his name?" Baudry put in.

"No, he said 'yore friend,'" was the quick reply. "An' because he's that, I'm goin' back—alone."

The rancher was about to make another angry protest, but Carol anticipated him: "Daddy, he has to go," she said, and the young man's heart leapt at the regret in her voice. "Yu would do the same yourself."

The old man snorted, but his hard face softened as he looked at Sandy. "She's right, boy, o' course," he admitted. "Yu have it to do, but yu can tell Rogue that if he harms either yu or Jim I'll hound him down an' hang him, if it takes the rest o' my days."

Sandy grinned. "I'll pass on the message, but he don't strike me as a man to scare easy."

An hour later, having fed, Sandy transferred his saddle to a fresh horse and started for the outlaws' camp. He had seen Carol for one moment before he left, had grasped a slim brown hand, had heard a whispered, "Good luck, Sandy." The kindness in her eyes went with him as he rode into the gloom.

Eden and the gambler were alone at the fire. The women had retired to their tent and Dutt had expressed a desire to view the sleeping herd. Baudry, biting on a black cigar, was the first to speak.

"Damned if I can fathom Rogue's game, Sam," he said reflectively. "He has you cold and throws the hand in. Why?"

"Yu can search me," the rancher replied. "Carol figures he has a soft spot, but gals get romantic notions 'bout fellas like him. He's reckoned the most ruthless ruffian in Texas, an' that's sayin' a lot."

"Those two men joined you for the drive, dropping in from nowhere," Jethro proceeded. "And one of them—Green—answers pretty well to the printed description of Sudden."

"Whose last job was pulled off while Green was at the S E."

"True, but it would be a safe play for one of Rogue's men to put the blame on a fellow he knew could prove an alibi."

"Yu suggestin' that Green an' Sandy are in cahoots with Rogue?" Eden asked, and there was a rasp in his voice.

"I'm saying it's possible, that's all," was the reply. "Your daughter said some of the outlaws knew them."

"Then why did them two boys fetch back near a thousand head after the stampede?"

Baudry chuckled. "You have to admit they knew where to find them," he pointed out. "See here, Sam. Mightn't it be that Rogue realized that the stampede was a mistake, that it would pay him better to let you drive the cattle north for him to steal within reach of a market where they'd fetch four or five times as much. Why, that may be the reason he ain't forcing your hand now."

The rancher's brows drew together. Put like this the plan seemed all too probable, and the idea that he was being played with was far from pleasant. Little devils of doubt began to trouble him, but his obstinate disposition drove him to argue.

"Tryin' to bump me off don't seem to fit in."

"Why not, if his first scheme was to grab the herd as soon as he could? I'm supposing it was later he got the notion of aiming for the bigger prize, an' I'd wager something it was Green gave it him; he ain't a fool, that fellow, believe me."

"I don't think yo're right, Jethro," Eden said stubbornly.

Baudry smiled. "Well, perhaps not," he said easily. "But I'm telling you, those two men will be back before long; they're more use to Rogue here."

"I'll be glad to see 'em," the cattleman said stoutly, but the seeds of suspicion had been sown. "Aimin' to travel with us, Jethro?"

"Maybe we can be of some use," was the reply.

"Pleased to have yu," the rancher said heartily.

The visitor was silent for a time, and then, with the air of one who has come to a decision, he flung the butt of his cigar into the glowing ashes, and looked across at his host.

"Sam, you know what I do for a living," he began. "Well, I'm planning to give myself a fresh deal and drop the cards. With the coin I get when you cash in on your herd I'm starting a ranch—I've got options on land not far from the S E; with the railways coming west and the northern ranches needing stock, there's going to be money in cattle. But more than that, I want to settle down, with a home of my own—and a wife."

"Why, that's good hearin', Jethro," the rancher said. "Mebbe yo're on the way to fetch the lady, huh?"

The gambler's teeth gleamed as his thick lips parted in a half-smile. "Not exactly," he said. "The lady is travelling north too; in fact, she's less than fifty yards away at this moment."

Eden straightened up, his eyes wide. "Yu—mean—Carol?" he cried incredulously.

"Sickness hasn't dulled your wits, Sam," the other replied with a heavy attempt at jocularity. "And why not?"

"I never dreamt of it," the old man evaded.

This was true; though Baudry had been a frequent visitor at the S E, the possibility that the girl was the attraction had not once occurred to its owner. Now, faced with the fact, he suddenly realized that he knew very little about the man, save his profession. A chance meeting over a card game in San Antonio had been the beginning of their friendship, and later, Baudry helped him in his plan of purchasing land. Still on the right side of forty, suave, well-dressed and apparently wealthy, the gambler did not lack attraction for the other sex, but…Sam Eden shook his head, as though in answer to his own query, and Baudry's narrowed, watching eyes grew cold.

"Any objections, Sam?"

"Have yu spoken to her?"

"No, I reckoned the square thing was to ask you first."

Eden breathed his relief; it gave him a way out. Sandy's devotion to the girl was patent, and once or twice he had seen her looking at the boy; women were queer, but he could not conceive that she would prefer the older, sophisticated man for her mate. So he replied with more confidence:

"It's entirely her affair, Jethro. Even if I could claim her as my own girl, I wouldn't attempt to influence her. Whatever she says, goes, with me."

The gambler lit another cigar. "Fair enough," he said evenly. "I'm not asking you to do my courting, Sam. When do you expect to pull out from here?"

Can't say; must give them boys a chance to come in."

"They'll do it—with a fine tale of how they hoodwinked Rogue and got away," Baudry sneered.

Long after, when he had been lifted back into his bed in the wagon, the words recurred to the rancher. He fought against the fear that they might be the truth but could not completely convince himself; Baudry's arguments had seemed all too plausible. Moreover, the outlaw's impudent warning that he intended to have the herd was disturbing; Eden was well aware that his outfit was numerically weak and if two members of it could not be depended upon...

# Chapter 19

Sandy experienced little difficulty in finding the outlaws' camp again. A bright moon enabled him to recognize the landmarks—a twisted tree, a jutting spire of rock, a wedge of chaparral, which the plainsman instinctively notes when travelling a trail by which he must return. As he rode in, a man with a levelled gun stepped from the shadow of a tree and ordered him to halt. A glance satisfied him.

"So yu come back?" Sligh said, for he it was. "Damned if I thought yu'd be such a fool."

"It warn't folly, Sligh, just pure affection—for yu," was the flippant reply. "What's the next move?"

"Yu pass yore gun to me."

Sandy pulled out his revolver but instead of handing it over, he pointed the muzzle at Sligh. "Now yu can blaze away an' we'll go to hell together," he said pleasantly.

"Rogue's orders," the man growled.

"Then I'll take 'em from him," Sandy retorted. "Where is he?"

The outlaw pointed to a small fire apart from the larger one in the centre of the glade. Sandy grinned.

"Go ahead," he said. "I might lose my way."

"Think yo're smart, huh?" came the sneer.

"Smart's my middle name," the young man chuckled. "Do we take root here?"

With a curse the sentinel slouched off. Two men were sitting by the fire and when Sandy reached it, Sligh had already voiced his complaint.

"Pulled his gun on me," he growled. "If it hadn't bin for yore orders, I'd 'a' blowed him apart."

Rogue looked up as the boy slid from his saddle. " 'Lo, Sandy, I'm wantin' that weapon," he said quietly.

Sandy's eyes were on the other figure at the fire. "What's the word, Jim?" he asked.

"Yu got Miss Eden back?" Sudden queried, and when his friend nodded, he drew his own guns handing them, butts first, to the outlaw leader. "Ante up, Sandy," he went on. "Rogue has kept his part o' the bargain an' we gotta keep our'n." He smiled sardonically across the flames. "We're yore prisoners, Rogue, but I'm givin' yu warnin' that we'll light out if we get a chance."

"Then I'll have to tie yu," Rogue rapped.

"I don't blame yu," Sudden smiled, and at a nod from him, Sandy relinquished his revolver.

Later, three shapeless, blanket-covered forms lay round the smaller fire. The only difference between them was that two of them were tied hand and foot and appeared to be fast asleep. The third was wide awake, wrestling with the problem of what to do with his prisoners. The disarming and binding had been merely a bluff, for he did not want them; they could only be a burden. The girl had been a different proposition—a weapon—but he could not credit the rancher with great solicitude for two of his hands. Their detention would mean two less to defend the herd, but he dismissed this aspect; his own force was strong enough. A gleam of steel in the flickering firelight caught his eye; it was a knife, used in the binding and forgotten. It helped him to a decision.

He glanced at the sky, where clouds had now blotted out the moon, flinging a pall of darkness over the camp. Soundlessly he edged over until he was close to Sudden, and able to reach the knife. The cowboy was breathing stertorously. Carefully raising the blanket, Rogue severed the bonds which confined the sleeper's wrists, and dropping the blade, rolled back to his former position. For a time nothing happened and then he saw Sudden stretch and lie still again. Rogue knew he had discovered that his arms were free.

Presently the dark blotch of the cowboy's blanket stirred as he slowly sat up. He saw the knife, reached for it, and freed his ankles. With a whispered warning, he did the same for his fellow-prisoner. Then, on hands and knees, Sudden crept to the outlaw, whose heavy breathing suggested deep slumber. The confiscated '. weapons were beside him. Leaving their blankets rolled in some semblance of human forms, the captives crawled away from the fire, and reached the edge of the glade.

"The hosses are on the far side," Sudden whispered. "We'll have to pass Sligh. While I deal with him, yu slip around an' get the broncs."

Skirting the edge of the encampment, they moved swiftly and silently over the floor of matted pine-needles and presently saw the sentinel leaning against a pine, his rifle beside him. Like a shadow Sudden darted from tree to tree, and then, dropping on his belly, wormed his way forward. All that the unsuspecting watcher knew was that out of the murk a figure rose at his very feet and fingers of steel clutched his throat, prisoning any sound he might have uttered. Savagely he fought back, twisting, striking, kicking, but the relentless pressure of that vice-like grip was paralysing; he could not breathe, his throat throbbed with pain, and the world went black before his bulging eyes. A few moments and the man was a limp and senseless weight. Sudden let him fall and hurried after Sandy. That young man had not been idle; he had found the horses, and saddles. Soon the outlaw camp was behind them. For a while they rode in silence and then Sandy could restrain his curiosity no longer.

"How in hell did you manage it, Jim?" he asked.

"I didn't," Sudden smiled. "Some kind gent cut my paws loose an' left the knife handy."

"Cripes, I'll bet it wasn't Sligh."

"Yu'd win. It was another fella, an' when he came creepin' up on me with that sticker in his fist, well, I've knowed happier moments. I played I was asleep—snored real hearty."

"Yu can too," Sandy complimented. "Did you recognize him?"

"It was Rogue hisself."

"Oh, yeah," came the sarcastic reply. "Havin' tied us up he would turn us loose, wouldn't he?"

"Them bonds was just eyewash for the gang. Rogue didn't want us—we gotta be watched allatime, an' he knows Eden ain't goin' to part with a single steer on our account, so he gets rid of us—his own way. That was Sligh's knife—I saw him drop it; he'll get the blame an' we'll get the credit. Rogue is one smart hombre."

A smudge of grey in the eastern sky had turned to a golden glow and the red rim of the sun was pushing above the horizon when they rode down the valley and sighted the S E wagon. Peg-leg, busy preparing the morning meal, let out a yell which brought men leaping from their blankets and grabbing for guns. When they saw that it was not an Indian raid they laughed and swore at the cook. The foreman, his wrinkled face one smile, surveyed the pair delightedly.

"Nice damn couple, ain't yu?" he said. "Holdin' the drive up thisaway. The ol' Man oughta give yu yore time."

"An' yore chin would hit yore toes if he did, yu holy fraud," Sudden retorted. "Now, Sandy an' me ain't had no sleep for 'bout a year. Who's got spare blankets? We had to leave our'n behind."

For a couple of hours they slept like dead men and then Jeff aroused them. "Sam's askin' for yu," he said.

They found the cattleman sitting at the end of the wagon. He was recovering rapidly; the tonic air of the prairies, aided by his tough constitution, had worked wonders. Baudry and Carol were with him, and several of the outfit lingered near.

"Here's the truants, boss," the foreman grinned. "I was tellin' Jim yu oughta give 'em their time."

Eden had smothered his doubts and his rugged face softened as he surveyed the men to whom he owed so much. "I reckon they oughta have anythin' they ask for, but I'm hopin' it won't be that," he said. "Green, Sandy tells me I gotta thank yu for gettin' my girl back."

"Sandy's modesty'll be the ruin of him," Sudden smiled.

"I ain't forgettin' his part," Eden replied. "I'm curious to learn how yu persuaded that ruffian to let her go; he had me thrown an' tied."

"Yeah, he knowed that," the cowboy agreed. "I gambled on two cards—his past an' his pride. I figured that, sunk as he is, some respect for a good woman might remain, an' I was right. For the rest, his message to yu explains it—just the natural vanity o' the man. These were his weak spots, an' I hit 'em good an' hard."

"Then we'll hear more of him?"

"Shorely. He'll strike when he's ready, but I'm guessin' that won't be till we're nearer a market. He's got nigh a score o' men."

Baudry looked at the cattleman and nodded; he had expressed the same view of the rustler's intentions. With a half-sneer he turned to Sudden.

"Yu seem pretty well acquainted with this cattle-thief," he said. "Perhaps he turned you loose too?"

"Now I wonder who told yu?" Sudden debated. "He did that very thing."

Sam Eden's keen eyes widened at this and there was suspicion in them.

"D'yu mean that, Green?" the rancher asked sharply, and when the other nodded, "Why should he do that?"

The cowboy related the manner of their escape.

Sudden sensed the hostility in the tone. "His men had none of his finer feelin's."

"Fine feelings—in an outlaw?" gibed the gambler savagely. "That's more than I can swallow."

"He let her go," the cowboy reminded.

"Yes, at your request," came the sneer. "Were you ever one of his gang?"

"No were yu?" Sudden asked.

Pebbles, who was one of the listening riders, chuckled audibly, and the visitor's face flushed with anger.

"Damn your impudence," he shouted. "What do you mean by that?"

Sudden bent forward, his eyes bleak. "Just what I said," he replied. "Listen to me, Mister Man. On'y two fellas here can talk down to me with safety—my boss an' his foreman. Yo're speakin' outa turn."

For a moment the gambler's narrow eyes clashed with those of the speaker and then turned in mute appeal to his host. Sam Eden was nonplussed. Torn between gratitude and friendship, he did not know how to deal with the tiny tempest which had so swiftly arisen. Carol came to his aid.

"Mister Baudry appears to be forgetting that these two men risked their lives to save me, first from Indians, and then from outlaws," she said. "To my mind, that alone matters."

Like a dash of cold water the words brought Baudry to his senses; his ill-humour vanished and he achieved some sort of a smile.

"You're right, Miss Eden," he said heartily. "Nothing else

counts. I'm sorry, Sam, but I let my ideas run away with me. If that rogue fellow happened to be here, I'd thank him, whatever his motive may have been."

This ended the discussion, but as Sudden and the foreman went to get their horses, the cowboy asked casually:

"Yu known friend Baudry long?"

"Nope, an' yu needn't name him my friend neither," Jeff said bluntly. "Don't fancy that fella nohow, an' I'll bet if he had a tail there'd be rattles on it."

"Sandy an' me ain't popular in that quarter." Sudden reflected aloud.

"Aw, yu should worry," Jeff told him. "So yu don't think Rogue will try again yet?"

"I ain't worryin', not that yu'd notice," was the reply, and then, "No, barrin' Injuns, flooded rivers, stampedes, storms an' dry stretches, I figure we'll have an easy trip for a while."

Jeff's expression was one of mock disgust. "Yo're a cheerful cuss, I don't believe," he said.

Later, Sudden had a word with Sandy. That young man was still puzzling over the outlaw's complicity in their escape, and said so.

"Shake yore head an' start that stuff yu think with workin'," was the smiling advice he received. "Without us, the S E would be short-handed an' Rogue wants the herd to go through yet a while."

"Then why did he stampede it?"

"I figure his idea then was to sell the cows to the jasper who was payin' him to break the drive. Now, he's aimin' to handle 'em himself an' clean up a packet."

"Then he's double-crossin' the other man."

"It don't follow. Rogue is a pretty ornery proposition, but he's got points. He told me that this fella was willin' to take the S E cows, but he didn't say he's promised to let him have 'em."

"Glad yu put brother Baudry back a bit. What yu think of him?"

"I don't," Sudden grinned. "But—I'm goin' to."

# Chapter 20

The cattle, rested by the stay in the valley, made good progress, and the tally of the miles covered grew as the peaceful days passed. The members of the outfit, living in their saddles through the long, lazy hours, became jubilant at the thought that their tremendous task might soon be accomplished. Jed, true to his nature, was pessimistic.

"It's too easy," he complained. "Like slidin' down a steep hill, yu gotta watch out for the bump at the bottom."

Sandy too was not of the cheerful ones, but for a different reason. Baudry's monopoly of Carol was so complete that the young man rarely had an opportunity of riding with her. Moreover, the gambler, as a guest, ate with the women and Eden, a circumstance which did not lessen Sandy's resentment.

"Cuss it, he's got all the chances," he grumbled.

"Too bad," Sudden commiserated. "Now if yu could show her that red head o' yores..."

The boy had to laugh. "Yu misbegotten son o' misfortune. Some day I'll tell her all about yu," he threatened.

Sudden's hands went up. "Keno!" he cried. "Wait till I'm outa the country."

Sandy's soreness over the situation would have been diminished had he known that Carol was beginning to find the constant company of the visitor irksome. Hitherto it had never occurred to her to regard him as a possible suitor, but his attentions and rather fulsome compliments were forcing her to face the fact. She had never liked him; but Baudry, with all his astuteness, had not discovered this.

Like most of his type, he held a poor opinion of the other sex; they were all alike, save that some were more desirable than others. The budding beauty and dewy freshness of this prairie flower had aroused in him a physical intoxication which he called love, but was little more than lust. He wanted, and would have her, and if marriage was the price he would pay it, but...

In the cowboy, Sandy, he recognized an obstacle to his hopes, just as in the fellow's friend, Green, he saw a menace to his other plans. Bitterly he cursed Rogue for releasing them. Somehow, they must be got out of the way.

Camp was pitched on the tree-fringed bank of a widish river, but the fact that it had to be negotiated on the morrow gave them no uneasiness. They had crossed several streams of varying size during the past weeks and had come to regard the operation as of no more than ordinary moment.

The herd was bedded down and the crooning voices of the watching riders came faintly to the rest of the outfit loafing and smoking round the fire.

To Sudden, as they went to take their trick of night-riding.

Jeff addressed a query: "Can yu make any sort o' guess where we're at?"

"Never been north," Sudden told him. "This river might be the Wichita, but that don't mean we're clear o' the redskins; they hunt all over."

"I ain't worryin' much about the war-whoops—it's that lousy outlaw loses me sleep—not knowin' when he's goin' to strike."

"I'm allowin' it won't be yet," the cowboy assured him.

Pacing slowly around the slumbering herd, under a star-specked sky, he found himself thinking of Rogue. An odd mixture, this miscreant who robbed and killed without compunction, yet retained a respect for women. An outcast, leader of a band recruited from the scum of the settlement, afraid to show his face in any decent community, that, for such a man as Rogue must once have been could only mean hell on earth. It was easy to understand how, whipped by his degradation, in savage disdain, he plunged more deeply into the mire. Sudden knew the feeling, had experienced and almost yielded to it. But for this drive to a new country where he might start afresh....A wise Providence veils the future; Sudden could not know that events were even then shaping to hurl him back into the quicksands of shame and danger. Two men, seated out of hearing of the camp, were discussing him.

"Those cowboys have to be got rid of, Davy," the gambler said.

"They're liable to make things difficult. Why in hell Rogue let them go I can't guess. What's his game?"

"I'd say he's tryin' to double-cross us," was the reply.

"If he does, I'll kill him," Baudry said. "No man ever did that to me and got away with it."

There was no anger, no boastfulness in the low, even voice, and well aware that it might be a warning to himself, Dutt, toughened as he was, was conscious of a slight shiver which was not due to the night air. He had no illusions regarding Jethro Baudry, knowing that he would slay his best friend if it suited his purpose.

"I've got the glimmerings of a scheme," the gambler resumed. "Let me know when it's worked out. In the meantime, keep a close eye on those fellows."

At dawn they crossed the river without mishap and resumed the long trek northwards across a plain which spread out before them as far as the eye could reach; there were no trees, no hills, and the foreman—fearing the next stream might be far away—took care that the beasts were well watered before a start was made. The air was cool yet, but the sun, thrusting up into a clear sky, promised plenty of heat presently.

Baudry, as usual, had loped his horse to Carol's side. The gambler's greedy eyes gloated over the girl's slim, supple form as it swayed easily to the paces of her pony. Schooled as he was by his profession to conceal all emotion, and cold-blooded as a fish, her beauty and desirableness turned the ice in his veins to fire. He bent low over his horse's neck lest his look should betray him. "You get more charming every day," he murmured. "This nomad life seems to suit you."

"I love it," she smiled.

"The West is wonderful," he said, "but don't you ever

have a hankering to see the real big cities of the world, New York, London, Paris, Rome, with their fine streets, famous picture-galleries, palaces, cathedrals, theatres, and to join in the whirl of pleasure they offer?"

"Why, certainly, that would be great, and I expect every girl has such dreams," Carol confessed. "But after a while I would want to come home to Texas."

"Just to go on raising cows," the gambler said, a suspicion of contempt in his tone.

It brought a faint flush to the girl's lightly tanned cheeks. "Just to go on raising—a new Empire," she said quietly.

Her shining eyes and low voice proclaimed her earnestness. This was a phase of her he had not suspected, but—though he might inwardly sneer at her vision—he was quick to take his cue.

"You're entirely right, Miss Carol, though I'll admit I hadn't looked at it quite that way," he responded. "And I'm proposing to do my share by starting a ranch not very far away from the S E—just to raise cows." He smiled, hesitated a moment, and then, "But first, I'm taking a holiday, to see all the places I mentioned, and others." He leant across and laid a hand on one of hers. "Will you come with me—Carol?"

Completely taken by surprise, she could only stare at him. He did not wait for a reply.

"I want you for my wife, girl," he said hoarsely. "I'm mad about you—have been since we first met. I'll give you everything you ask for. We'll see all the world can show us and then come back—to Texas. I'm planning big, my dear, but I can swing it; the West is going to hear of Jethro

Baudry, believe me." Carol's eyes opened wide and she shrank from him, dragging her hand from his hot clasp. His gaze enveloped her avidly, yet she could scarcely credit she had heard aright. To her youthful mind the idea of a husband nearly twice her own age seemed preposterous.

"But I've no intention of marrying yet, Mister Baudry, and I don't like you—in that way," she stammered at last.

The gambler's face showed his chagrin. Women were usually kind to him and he had flattered himself that the dazzling prospect he had held out, combined with his own power of attraction, would be more than sufficient to win this unsophisticated girl of the wilds.

"Perhaps I've spoken too soon. Will you try to care for me, Carol?" he urged. "There isn't anyone else, is there?"

He saw the warm colour steal into her cheeks again at that and his lips bunched in an ugly pout.

"No, of course not," she protested.

"You haven't got notions about any of these scarecrow riders, have you?" he asked keenly, and instantly saw that he had made a slip.

The impertinence angered her. "These men may be poor and ragged, Mister Baudry," she retorted, "but there is not one of them who would do or say anything to hurt me, or who would not risk his life for mine."

"I know it—I'm all wrong," he said contritely. "It's pure jealousy, girl; you've got into my blood. Promise me you'll think it over."

"I would much rather forget it," she replied. "We can be friends."

"No," he cried passionately. "It's all or nothing with me.

I'm not taking your answer yet. I'll make you care. Do you know what they say of me in the settlements? 'Jethro Baudry always wins—sooner or later.' That's my reputation, and by the Lord, it shan't fail me now."

Wounded pride, desire, and disappointment transformed his usually immobile face into that of a savage beast, but in a moment the smiling mask was back.

"I'll not bother you any more now, Carol," he said. "I fancy Dutt is in front; I have a word to say to him."

He rode off, raking his mount ruthlessly with the spurs, a fact which did him no good with his lady-love; Carol loved horses, and distrusted those who ill-treated them.

Scarcely had he gone when his place was taken by Sandy—one of the "scarecrows"—and the girl could not but mentally compare them. Certainly the boy's attire was shabby and worn, but the lithe body, poised so easily in the saddle, and the deeply-tanned, youthful face, with impudent eyes which always dropped before her own, more than swung the balance in his favour.

"Don't often get this chance nowadays," he greeted. "How come the guardian angel ain't ridin' herd on yu?"

"You ought not to speak so of my father's friend," she reproved, but there was a demure twinkle accompanying the words. "Mister Baudry wanted to find Mister Dutt. I expect he thought there was no danger of Indians stealing me again just now."

"Sometimes I 'most wish they would," Sandy told her.

Not daring to ask the obvious question, she changed the subject. "Are we nearing the end of the drive?"

"I dunno, but I'm hopin' there's quite a ways to go yet."

Once more she felt she was on dangerous ground, but her eyebrows rose. Sandy's explanation was glib enough:

"When the herd is sold, I figure we won't be wanted, an' I'll be out of a job."

Her face was turned away; truth to tell, she was afraid to look at him lest he should see her fear. For his words had brought a sudden realization of what parting with him would mean, and with it all thought of Baudry vanished like smoke before a puff of wind. Her voice shook a little when at length she spoke:

"Dad will need you all at the ranch. He won't let any of you go—unless you want to."

"Then here's one he can't lose—I'll stick closer to him than his own skin," the young man replied gaily.

"And Mister Baudry is starting a ranch near the S E."

Sandy whistled softly. "Is that so?" he said, and then, "I wouldn't ride for him."

There was no rancour in the remark and she knew that she herself had nothing to do with his decision; the gambler—as a man—had been weighed and found wanting, in the cowboy's estimation.

# Chapter 21

The man was sitting, his back against a tree, his eyes closed. By his side lay a rifle and a saddle, while round his middle was slung a heavy revolver. His thin, harsh face, from which jutted a beak of a nose, gave him a predatory expression, and a straggling, uncared for beard lent an appearance of age which his wiry frame belied. It was Jed, riding point, who discovered him.

"Hey, stranger, yu have shorely picked a pore place for a nap," he called.

The man opened his eyes. "Hell!" he said weakly, "I was beginnin' to think I was the last fella left in the world. Ain't got a shot of licker, I s'pose? I'm about all in."

"Friend," the cowboy grinned, "I've helped hustle these yere long-horns from near San Antonio. If yu think a Texan would carry painkiller all that way yu don't know the breed. I figure yu lost yore bronc?" The stranger nodded. "The chuck-wagon an' remuda'll be along presently; they'll fix yu up."

In camp that night the stranger told his story. His name he said, was "Rollitt," and he was horse-wrangler to the trail outfit they had followed. One morning he had missed several horses, set out to track them, and had been surprised and chased by Indians.

"Kiowas, they were, I guessed, but I didn't wait to make shore," he said. "I've got used to my hair bein' where it is an' didn't nohow fancy it as a decoration for a brave's bridle, so I scratched gravel plenty eager. By bad luck they was between me an' the camp, so I had to run west. Well, I lost them war-whoops, but I killed my hoss doin' it—just dropped under me—an' then I discovered I'd lost myself. That musta bin near a coupla weeks ago, though I lost count o' time too—I'm a good loser, yu see. Wanderin' around, totin' a saddle ain't so funny, 'specially when yo're outa grub. I was afraid to shoot, case them red devils was about, so I lived mainly on berries an' nuts. Once I knocked a sage hen over with a rock, an' I got a rattler—after he come close to getting me an' skinned an' et him."

Aunt Judy uttered a grunt of disgust. "Lawsy me, man, yu must 'a' bin hard put to it," she said.

"Shore was, ma'am," Rollitt replied. "But that rattler was good —nice white meat like a chicken; I've had wuss eatin'."

Listening to the story, Sudden had studied the man closely but could call up no recollection of him. A whispered question to Sandy brought only a shake of the head. Rollitt's explanation seemed likely enough and yet Sudden had a feeling that something was wrong. Eden, however, seemed satisfied.

"Yu've had a tough time, stranger, an' I reckon there's small hope o' joinin' yore own outfit yet awhile," he said. "We lost our wrangler back on the trail; one o' the boys has been deputizin', but I guess he'd be pleased to hand over the job. What do yu say?"

"Well, I'm shorely a maverick an' I'm thankin' yu," the newcomer replied, and, as the cattleman put a question, "This country is new to me but I figure yu should be north o' the Wichita. We kept a straighter line, but we got held up an' had to hand over cash or cattle. I'd say the longer trip'll pay yu in the end."

So it was arranged. Rollitt took over the remuda and appeared to know the work. He did not mix much with the men but was frequently seen in converse with Dutt, who explained that both of them hailed from Missouri. Sudden saw little of the man, but, as he confided to Sandy, that little was enough.

"What's the poor devil done to yu?" the young man asked.

"Nothin'—yet," was the reply. "Yu didn't see all Rogue's men, did yu?"

"Less'n half, I'd say; he had a biggish crowd—scattered too. Yu ain't' thinkin' this jigger was planted there to wait for us? His tale seemed straight enough."

But Sudden was serious. "I've a hunch he's here to make trouble —mebbe for us."

"Well, ol-timer, man is born to trouble, as the sparks fly upward," Sandy quoted. "We've met the gent afore an' we're still here, ain't we?"

He was in a gay humour these days. His lady smiled

upon and permitted him to ride with her again, for Baudry—though he accompanied her now and then—deliberately absented himself in the hope that she might miss him.

It was nearly a week later that Sudden's forebodings were justified. The foreman, distress signals flying in his face, strode over to where the men were breakfasting and called Sudden aside.

"The Ol' Man wants yu an' Sandy, pronto," he said.

The cattleman was sitting with his back to a wagon wheel. Carol, Baudry, and Dutt were seated near, and standing by was the new hand, Rollitt. Eden's brows bent in a heavy frown when he saw the men he had sent for. He wasted no time.

"Green, how long yu been one o' Rogue's riders?" he rasped.

"I ain't," the cowboy said coolly.

"Don't lie," the old man roared. "Rollitt here saw yu in Rogue's hide-out just before yu come to the S E."

Sudden looked at the wrangler. "So yu are one o' his men?"

"Nope, I happened to drift in," the fellow said sullenly. "He made me an offer an' I refused it."

"My own case exactly," Sudden said dryly.

"Yu were seen workin' with the outlaws, brandin' stolen cattle," Eden went on.

"Those men were feedin' me; I gave a hand," Sudden explained. "I was told the cows were mavericks."

"Yu were mighty friendly with Rogue, an' after yu'd gone he gave out that yu were on an errand for him."

Sudden's eyes sought the informer again. "For a casual stranger yu seem to have been pretty deep in Rogue's confidence," he said acidly.

Eden ignored the comment. "An' yore 'errand' was to get into my outfit an' help wreck the drive," he said bitterly.

"I' pear to have failed down on that," the accused replied.

"Yeah, for yore own reasons," Eden sneered. "No wonder yu could round up them stampeded steers. Easy, warn't it, when yore boss—gettin' a better idea—told yu to do it. An' then, for some devil's purpose, he lets yu fetch my daughter back."

"Make a job of it," Sudden urged with savage sarcasm. "Say I was in cahoots with the Comanches too."

"Yu went after yore fellow-thief—I'll give yu that much credit," the cattleman snapped.

"I'm obliged," the cowboy countered.

Baudry drew a paper from his pocket, unfolded, and held it up. "Isn't this your description?" he asked.

Sudden did not need to read it—every word had been branded on his brain as by a hot iron. Nevertheless, he leant forward and scanned it leisurely.

"Them particulars might apply to a hundred others," he evaded. "An' my hoss ain't got a white face."

"Hasn't it?" the gambler rapped out. "I'd like to be sure of that. Rollitt, fetch that black."

Sudden's face hardened to stone. "Don't yu—unless yu want to die," he warned. "Sometime, when he was a colt, I reckon, that hoss had an adventure with a skunk, an' he hates 'em."

"Never seen the bronc I couldn't handle," Rollitt growled.

"Go ahead," Sudden said. "I'm givin' yu permission, but I won't promise to bury yu; I don't like skunks neither."

The wrangler hesitated, and was obviously relieved when the cattleman broke in angrily: "To hell with the hoss. Where's the need o' that when Rollitt heard yu referred to as 'Sudden' by the outlaws? Yu denyin' it?"

"I'm not denyin' anythin'," Sudden said tersely. "An' now—what?"

"I oughta tell my men to string the pair o' yu up to the nearest tree."

The unjust threat stirred the cowboy to anger. "Come alive, Eden," he said roughly. "What sort of an outfit would yu have left?"

"Showin' your true colours now—gunman stuff, eh?" Baudry said scornfully.

"Lettin' myself be hanged wouldn't prove my innocence," the other retorted. He looked at the rancher. "Eden, yo're followin' a false trail," he said quietly. "One o' these days yu'll find that out. For now—I'm goin'."

The old man did not reply at once; doubts were disturbing him. He could not forget that Sudden had saved Carol from the Indians, but—as Baudry had been at pains to point out—the worst outlaw in the wilds would have done no less in like circumstances. His troubled gaze travelled to Sandy. The youth forestalled him.

"Jim's my friend; if he goes, I do," he said.

The defiant tone roused the rancher's quick temper again. "Yo're damn right there," he rasped. "But first yu'll answer a question. What took yu outa camp the night I got this?" He tapped his wounded chest.

The boy's face flamed at the accusation—for it amounted to that. "Yu think I creased yu?" he cried indignantly, and then, "Hell! what's the good ...?"

"I don't think—I know," came the passionate assertion. "Yore boss, Rogue, put yu up to bump me off, an' when yu failed, Lasker had to try."

"He'd have got yu too, with a second shot, if Jim here hadn't stopped him," Sandy savagely reminded. "Yu explainin' that?"

"Simple," Eden sneered. "Laskar had bungled it an' might 'a' talked. It was a safe play to silence him an' get solid with me."

Sandy had no more to say. His world had come crashing about his ears and he could see nothing but the set, pale face of a girl, who, with downcast eyes, had been a witness of his degradation. Baudry, seated next to her, was watching him with an expression of contemptuous amusement. Little did the gambler suspect how near he was to death at that moment. Eden made a violent gesture.

"Punch the breeze, the pair o' yu," he said hoarsely. "Jeff, yu go along an' see they don't take nothin' but what belongs to 'em."

At this gratuitous insult, Sudden, his thumbs hooked in his belt, shot a scornful look at the speaker. "Don't overplay yore hand, Eden," he warned. "As for yore threats, there ain't a man in yore outfit would pull a gun on me, 'cept that cardsharp an' his two friends, an' they haven't the guts." His cold, appraising gaze travelled from Baudry to Dutt and Rollitt. "Like I said," he added, as they made no move. "Three—yaller—dawgs. Adios!"

As he turned away, the gambler's hand went to his pistol, but the rancher spoke sharply: "None o' that, Jethro. Call him back if yu want, but yu should 'a' took him up when he offered."

The other shrugged his shoulders indifferently, but there was a frozen fury in his voice as he replied, "You're too squeamish, Sam; you don't give a rattler an even break—if you're wise."

In the rope corral which held the night-horses Sudden and Sandy found their mounts. The foreman watched in silence as they rolled their blankets, and then burst out:

"Jim, I just can't believe it—the Ol' Man must be loco. It warn't no use sayin' a word—on'y 'a' made him wuss."

"I know, ol'-timer," Sudden said, with a hard smile. "It's a queer yarn—too long to tell now—truth an' lies all snarled up. I ain't blamin' the boss—much; he's sick, an' with Rogue hangin' on his heels, it ain't surprisin' he's suspicious. Things look bad, but yu can take it Sandy didn't fire that shot an' I'm not as black as Nigger here."

"Is it true yo're the fella they call 'Sudden', Jim?"

"Yeah, but there's an explanation to that too. Keep a-smilin', Jeff; there was never a rope so badly tangled it couldn't be straightened out."

At this moment Peg-leg stumped up, carrying a small package. "Here's a bit o' grub an' a skillet my ol' gal has sent," he began. "Said she didn't care what yu'd done but she'd be teetotally damned if she let yu be turned loose without the means o' makin' a mouthful o' coffee. She's agoin' to give Sam hark from the tomb when she gits him alone."

"She's a lady, Peg-leg," Sudden replied, tying the parcel to the cantle of his saddle, "This will shorely be welcome."

From the back of the big black he smiled wryly down at the two men. "We'll be seein' yu—mebbe," he said.

For upwards of two miles neither of the outcasts spoke and then Sandy's bitterness overflowed: "Damnation, even she believes I shot the Ol' Man."

"Yu ain't no right to say that. Yu weren't lookin' but I fancy I saw a hand wave from the tent as we left camp."

Sandy's doleful face changed magically. "Yu did, Jim?" he asked eagerly.

His companion grinned.

"He's just as happy as if she had waved," he reflected. "An' anyways, he'd do more'n tell a lie for me."

"Where do we head for, Jim?" the subject of his thoughts asked. "We got plenty choice."

"We have to find Rogue," was the unexpected reply.

Sandy stared at him. "Hell, Jim, yu ain't goin' to throw down the Ol' Man, are yu?" There was real concern in his voice. "I'm admittin' he's treated us pretty mean, but he's been misled, an' the boys are our friends..."

"Findin' don't mean joinin'," Sudden pointed out. "The S E is finished with us—or fancies so—but I ain't finished with them. I don't figure on lettin' Rogue beat me, an' I'm mighty interested in Mister Baudry."

"Me too, in fact, I was so interested that I damn near beefed him where he sat."

"I guessed that an' was all set to knock yore gun up."

"Whatever for?" Sandy inquired.

"It would 'a' turned that camp into a slaughter-pen.

Now, we gotta keep cases on Rogue an' the herd, an' be ready to sit in the game."

"Yo're right, Jim," the boy agreed. "I'm a durned fool."

"Yu said it," his friend smiled. "There's time when yore brain wouldn't keep a flea outa trouble."

"Awright, Solomon the Second," Sandy grinned. "Mebbe yu can tell me who pulled the floor from under us."

"Rollitt is my guess, but who put him up to it?" Sudden debated. "Was it Rogue, tryin' to get rid of us, or that tin-horn cardcheat? An' what's he after, anyways? Hell's flames, it's one fine tangle to unravel an' we got on'y loose ends."

"Here's another," Sandy contributed. "Baudry is goin' in for cattle—startin' a range somewhere near the S E."

Sudden whistled and relapsed into a long silence. At dusk they camped in a dense thicket of scrub and dwarf-oak little more than a mile to the right of the herd, with which they had been keeping pace. They were building a small fire when a low voice called, "Howdy, friends!" and a man slid from the shadows. The flickering flame showed that it was Tyson.

"Didn't hear me a-comin', did ye?" he asked, and chuckled at his own cleverness.

"We're glad to see yu," Sudden said heartily.

When the business of eating was concluded, the little man filled his pipe and looked quizzically at his hosts. "So the S E has give yu the air?" he remarked.

"They told yu?" Sandy queried.

"Ain't talked with 'em," Tyson said. "Here's the how of it. When yu busted away an' the Injuns took after yu, I follered. Bein' on the hoof, I didn't arrive till the fandango was finished. I collects them scalps yu left lyin' around, for which I'm thankin' yu; worth ten wheels apiece, them top-knots is, if yu know where to take 'em. Then I trails yu, figurin' yo're still in dutch an' that mebbe I can turn the trick, but I'm too late, yu've went. I points for the S E."

"So yu know all about it?"

Tyson shook his head. "I ain't clost enough to hear much, but my eyesight is fair an' I'm a good guesser," he said. "When I see Monte Jack in the company I knowed dirty work was afoot."

"Monte Jack?" both his hearers repeated.

"Yeah, fella sittin' next the gal."

"He calls hisself 'Baudry' now."

"Like enough, but he was knowed as Monte Jack in Kansas City less'n two year ago, an' bad medicine. Catched cheatin' at poker an' shot the fella under the table—gun on his knees, yu know. It warn't the first time an' he had to flit plenty rapid. A close call for Monte, that was."

"An' Eden believes in him," Sandy said.

"Well, yu don't have to worry," Tyson laughed. "He fired yu, didn't he?"

"Yeah, he fired us, shore enough," the boy agreed. "But there's Miss Carol, that toad's got his poisonous eye on her, an' the outfit —decent fellas—are dependin' on puttin' that drive through.

They're our friends—still."

"An' not likin' Mister Monte Jack nothin' to notice we're kind o' hankerin' to pile him up," Sudden added. He went on to tell of the decision he and Sandy had come to, and the "still-hunter" listened, his bright little eyes darting from one to the other, his jaw working on a plug of tobacco, alert as, and very like, a squirrel.

"Well, I took a fancy to yu boys," he said, when their plans had been made plain. "If yo're willin', me an' Betsy"—he patted the rifle beside him—"will take a hand. Three pairs o' peepers is better nor two, an' I savvy Injuns."

The cowboys were glad to have him, and said so. Apart from his bloodthirsty occupation, there was a great deal that was attractive in this odd little man. Moreover, they were already deeply in his debt, and neither of them was of the type to forget that.

# Chapter 22

Early on the following morning Tyson left them. "Hang on to the herd an' I'll be with yu come dark, or sooner," he said. Then he plunged into the thicket and was lost to sight and sound in a few seconds.

They spent a lazy day, their only concern being to keep under cover. Several times, lying flat on a ridge, they got a sight of the herd, a long, twisted string of dots, dipping into hollows, plodding up slopes, inexorably pushing northwards. And though the distance was too great for him to recognize the rider, Sandy cursed when he saw that Carol had a companion.

The shadows were gathering when Tyson joined them in the dry arroyo where they had decided to spend the night. He had the hump ribs of a buffalo calf, wraped in part of the skin, and a bow and arrows, for which, he grimly explained, the late owner had no further use.

"I can use her pretty good—lived with 'Paches onct. She'll fill the pot an' save powder."

But this was not what the cowboys were thinking of. A brave with a bullet in his brain might well bring his tribesmen on the trail. The little man divined their thoughts and grinned as he pushed a gory hank of black hair into his pack.

"Nothin' to go grey over, boys," he said lightly. "I used steel an' blinded my tracks. 'Sides, I'm wearin' 'Pache moccasins, so them devils will git the blame. Allasame, I could 'a' shot him, so Betsy gits her tally."

Calmly he cut a nick in the stock of the gun, one more in that terrible register, using the knife which had let the life out of the red man, and, as they knew, must later have skinned and cut up the flesh they were about to eat. Life in the wilds, however, knocked the fastidiousness out of one, and the broiled ribs tasted none the worse.

Tyson had, they learned, located the outlaw band a few miles east, creeping along on the heels of the herd like a mountain cat, ready to pounce on its prey at the propitious moment. He had counted a dozen men, and gathered that others were away hunting.

"They ain't too well fixed for grub an' is grumblin'," he said. "A mighty hard lot. Eden will need all the help he can git, an' then some."

A week passed and save that all parties were nearer their destination, the position remained unchanged. Then, with the suddenness of a summer storm, danger loomed up, dire and overwhelming.

Tyson had, as usual, after the morning meal, gone to discover possible signs of activity in the outlaw's camp, and his companions were riding leisurely in the wake of the herd. It was Sandy who saw the "still-hunter" first.

"Tyson is a-comin' an' ain't losin' no time neither," he said.

In fact, the little man—abandoning his customary Indian-like stride—was running, and when, spurring their mounts, they met him, he dropped, gasping, on a nearby mound. His usually mild features were hard and fierce.

"Trouble ahead, boys," he panted.

"Rogue going' to strike?" Sudden asked.

"Naw, Injuns," the other replied. 'Two score, mebbe even more —they was hidden—waitin' to jump the herd."

"No chance o' dodgin' 'em?"

"Not a hope—the cattle has to go that way. Them war-whoops has picked the right place. For miles now the plain is narrow, with rough country both sides. There's one spot where they might hold the herd an' make a fight of it."

He described it, and Sudden listened carefully. Sandy's face was haggard with anxiety.

"My God! Jim, what can we do?" he asked.

Sudden turned to Tyson. "Climb Sandy's bronc an' fetch Rogue," he said. "Don't let on about us; yu just happened on the redskins, saw the herd, an' figured that, as a white man, he'd help his own kind."

"Shore, but I'll git there quicker afoot—it's rough goin'," Tyson replied, and was gone.

Sandy stared at his companion in amazement. "Yu sendin' for Rogue?" he gasped. Then comprehension came to him and he chortled with delight. "Yu wily devil," he complimented. "That shore is great medicine. Do we warn the S E?"

"I do; yu cross the trail an' follow on the other side, keepin' outa sight. I'll join yu later an' mebbe the war-whoops'll get a surprise."

Sandy was disappointed—he might have seen Carol—but he did not demur; the situation was desperate, but he trusted this hard-faced friend of his and was prepared to obey blindly. So he too went on his appointed errand, while Sudden spurred after the herd. The latter passed the remuda in a cloud of dust and heard Rollitt's curse of astonishment. Sam Eden, sitting at the back-end of the wagon, greeted the visitor with a glare as he reached for his gun. The young man's cold voice interrupted:

"Don't be a fool, Eden. If I'd come for that yu'd be half-way to hell by now. I'm here to tell yu that a big bunch o' redskins is layin' for yu."

The rancher laughed jeeringly. "Yu don't expect me to believe that yarn, do yu?" he asked.

"No, but I had to warn yu," Sudden retorted. "Walk into the trap if yu must; I'll do what I can to get yu out. I've sent for aid."

The cattleman's frowning brows went up at this. "Now I know yo're lyin'—I'd say there ain't a settlement within a hundred mile. Where'd yu send—San Antonio?" he sneered.

"I passed word to Rogue," was the calm reply.

With the force of a blow, the statement took the rancher's breath away. For a moment he was speechless, and then, with a furious oath, he cried, "So that's yore scheme, huh? Rogue's to come an help himself an' I'm to let him. Now listen. I ain't swallerin' yore Injuns, but I'd sooner they had the cows than that bastard roadagent leader o' yores. Get that."

"Yu seem damned anxious to make yore daughter a squaw."

The biting reminder only whipped the rancher's rage to a white heat. "Curse yu, I can fight my own battles," he roared "I don't want yore help nor his."

"Allasame, yu gotta have 'em. I ain't goin' to see men I have worked with an' liked sacrificed to yore bull-headed obstinacy. Can't yu savvy that just because Rogue aims to steal yore herd later, he's gotta protect it now? Hell, I must put Jeff wise."

The black horse shot ahead of the wagon and with its disappearance the old man's fury evaporated, and the ability to reason returned. Scowling darkly he went over the conversation again.

"Damnation, he's right," he muttered aloud.

"O' course he's right, an' allus has been," said a sharp voice. Aunt Judy, from the driving-seat of the vehicle shook a minatory finger at him. "That young fella has a brain where yu on'y got bone, Sam Eden."

"Put a bridle on that tongue," the cattleman snapped. "If yore husband had any sense he'd 'a' taken a whip to yu years back."

"An' if yu had any yu'd 'a' listened to Green 'stead o' that mealymouthed, fat-faced card-sharp yo're so fond of," she countered.

"The fat-faced card-sharp is obliged for your opinion, ma'am."

Baudry had just ridden up. Though his voice was studiously polite, his eyes were venomous. The lady was not abashed.

"Yo're welcome," she retorted, and vanished behind the canvas flaps.

"You take a lot from your hired folk, Eden," the guest said.

"Shucks, women must chatter, an' she'd give her life for Carol," the old man excused.

"Well, that alone lets her off with me. What brought Green?"

The other told him, and the gambler's face grew grave. "Seems to be nothing else to do, but it's like setting the fox to guard the chickens," was his comment.

Meanwhile, Sudden had reached the head of the herd and told his news to the astounded foreman.

"A piece along is a steep-walled gully with a'most no outlet," he, explained. "Throw the cows, wagon, an' remuda in there, take cover at the entrance, an' wait. When yu don't show up, the Injuns'll come a-lookin' for yu. If yu can stand 'em off for a while there's help on the way."

"Help?" ejaculated Jeff. "Where in blazes from?"

"I've sent for Rogue," Sudden replied. "Yu see, he's figurin' to lift this herd—presently, so he won't stand by an' let the redskins have it."

The foreman's troubled face broke into a grin. "Gosh! that's one bright idea, boy," he exclaimed. "We can deal with that damned outlaw later, but for the time we use him. What did the O'l Man say?"

"I ain't got time even to tell yu what he didn't say," the cowboy smiled. "Get busy, ol'-timer, an' if anybody starts shootin' from behind the Injuns yu'll know that me an' Sandy is sittin' in."

He whirled his horse and raced for the far side of the trail. The foreman's gaze followed him reflectively. "Outlaw, huh?" he muttered. "Pity the damned country ain't got a lot more like him."

Riding ahead, he soon found the spot Sudden had described and saw its suitability. The floor of the gully lay below the level of the plain, which sloped into it, and the walls on either side were wellnigh vertical. The outlet at the far end was too rough and steep even for long-horns to attempt unless badly scared. The entrance was guarded by scrub and rocks which would afford good cover for the defenders. He saw no sign of Indians and surmised, rightly, that knowing the herd must come that way, they were not troubling to watch its progress.

Jeff waited there impatiently, having already given orders for the cows to be hustled along. Soon the leaders appeared, at a lumbering, clumsy trot, bellowing a protest against the unusual exertion. Hurriedly they were hazed into the gully as they arrived and left to their own devices. This took time, and the foreman cast many anxious glances up the trail. When, at length, the wagon and remuda followed the last of the cattle, he breathed more freely, and telling the outfit to hunt cover, sought his employer. He found him fuming.

"Ain't I the owner o' this herd no more, or are yu takin' orders from Green?" was his first question.

"Shore yo're the owner, an' I'm doin' my best to keep yu that," Jeff said tartly. "Yu gotta remember this, Sam, they may be yore cows, but the boys' lives are their own."

"Yu think that fella was talkin' straight?" Eden demanded.

"Yeah, an' so would yu if yu weren't as prejudiced as hell," was the blunt reply. "Anyways, we'll know soon. The

Injuns will have heard the cattle an' be wonderin' why we ain't turnin' up."

"Bah! I don't believe ——"

The crack of a rifle cut him short and the foreman dashed to the entrance of the gully. The Infant, kneeling behind a ridge, was disgustedly reloading. He had, he claimed, seen a feathered top-knot above a bush some two hundred yards up the trail. Jeff returned to report.

"That scout'll spill the beans," he said. "They'll be along plenty soon."

"Help me outa this an' reach my gun," the old man ordered.

"Boss, yu ain't fit," the foreman protested.

"I can sit behind a rock just as well as in that blasted hell on wheels," Eden snorted. "Gimme a hand."

With Jeff's assistance he climbed out, walked weakly to the line of defence, and ensconced himself behind a boulder. The outfit cheered him lustily. As one of them put it, the Old Man might be short on temper, but he had grit enough for ten. As Jeff turned away, Judy had a last word:

"Tell that ornery man o' mine not to git hisself shot, 'cause I'm dependin' on him," she said.

But Peg-leg never got the message, for when the bearer emerged into the open, it was driven from his mind; the enemy had grown tired of waiting. Down the trail from the east came a long line of mounted savages, their paint-smeared, copper-coloured bodies gleaming in the bright light. Each warrior carried the circular shield of buffalo hide, a bow, and a sheaf of arrows. Here and there came the flash of a gun-barrel—old-fashioned muzzle-loaders, bartered for skins, or gained in a raid on some solitary settlement. Save for an occasional shrill cry, the advance was made in silence.

" 'Paches," the foreman decided. "Commanches would 'a' bin screamin' their dirty throats out." With the quick eye of one accustomed to count cattle he made a calculation. "Over fifty. Gosh! I'm hopin' Rogue don't dawdle any." He surveyed his slim line of defence anxiously. "Lie close, lads," he warned, "an' don't let loose till I give the word; we can't afford to miss."

Baudry, rifle in hand, had joined the cattleman. No one, looking at his passive, unconcerned features, would have guessed that all his carefully planned scheme depended upon the defeat of the redskins. With narrowed eyes he watched the far end of the line swing round until, with one screeching yell, the riders flogged their ponies into a dead run and charged full at the mouth of the gully. Like a wave of destruction the savages surged on and it seemed that the handful of whites must be swept away. Silent, grim-faced, with levelled weapons, they waited for the word. It did not come until the foe were less than a hundred paces distant, and then:

"Give 'em hell, boys," the foreman rasped.

The crash of the rifles was followed by exultant shouts from the marksmen as they saw bronze bodies go down before their bullets. The stream of lead disrupted the wave in the centre and the two halves curved left and right, replying to the rifles with a cloud of arrows, some of which sang past the ears of the white men. Out on the trail a half-dozen dead or wounded were stretched, and as many horses.

The redskins were soon on the move again. Strung out

in a line they headed west and then whirled and raced their ponies across the gully mouth, each horseman, as he arrived opposite the opening, vanishing from sight.

"Where in hell they got to?" the Infant queried.

"Lyin' alongside the hoss, with a foot through the belly-band," Jeff explained, and added grimly, "Down the hosses, son, an' Watch out for arrers."

The caution was needed, for from under the necks of the galloping ponies the red riders sent a succession of the deadly shafts, which whistled through the air and searched the cover. The defenders replied with their rifles, but the moving single marks were difficult to hit, and they did not meet with much success. The braves who had successfully crossed the firing-line swung up into their seats again and circled round to repeat the manoeuvre. From the far side of the trail two rifles crashed and the same number of ponies became riderless. The foreman chuckled. "Jim an' Sandy is gettin' interested," he said.

His satisfaction was short-lived. From a clump of thorn ten paces distant came a gasping gurgle and the rattle of a dropped weapon. At the risk of his life, Jeff sprang to the spot, only to find he could do nothing. Crumpled up on the ground, an arrow through his throat, lay Silent. The foreman straightened the body, placed the hat over the face, and swore savagely. As he turned away, the Infant called: "Hey, Jeff, pull this damn stick out—it hurts like blazes."

An arrow had transfixed the boy's forearm. Snapping the shaft the foreman drew out the barbed end, inspecting the edges of the wound closely. Then he nodded, and tied it up with a handkerchief.

"Mighta bin wuss," he said. "Keep down; they've got Silent."

The procession of seemingly masterless mustangs had passed and a respite from the rain of arrows ensued. The Apaches were bunched together farther down the trail. The intermittent bark of two guns from the rear of the attackers indicated that Jim and Sandy were still interested. At the other end of the firing-line Jed was wrinkling his brow.

"Say, Dumpy, how many d'yu figure we've knocked over?" he asked.

"Well, yu ain't got any, but the rest of us has downed 'bout ten," was the answer.

For once his friend ignored an insult. "There's more'n twice that number layin' out there an' some of 'em is movin'," Jed asserted.

"Creased an' tryin' to crawl clear," Dumpy suggested.

"They wouldn't come this way," Jed objected. "No, sir, dropped off'n their broncs an' playin' dead so's they can sneak in an' rush us that's what. The jigger with the eagle feather in his top-knot is five yards nearer than when I spotted him. I'm savin' him the trouble o' pretending'."

Raising his rifle he pulled the trigger and they saw the brown body jerk convulsively, struggle, and flop back.

"Who fired?" Jeff asked sharply. "Wanta kill 'em twice over?"

Ere Jed could explain, the supposed corpses did it for him, seven or eight of the nearest scrambling to their feet and sprinting for their lives, zigzagging to escape the bullets the cowboys sent after them. Several were bowled over but the others regained their comrades.

"Good for yu, Jed," Eden called out. "I'm rememberin' it. I reckon they won't try that trick again."

As though they had been awaiting the result of this ruse, the Apaches began to show signs of fresh activity, massing together in readiness for another charge. Two rifles spoke from the opposing side of the trail and a brave toppled to the ground, while another jumped clear of his staggering pony.

"Well done, Jim an' Sandy," the foreman cried.

"Yu figure it's them?" the cattleman asked.

"I'm damn shore," Jeff said stoutly. "If we git clear o' this it's them yu gotta thank, like it or not."

The savages were hesitating, the attack from the rear seemed to be bothering them. They were now galloping to and fro, jabbering, gesturing, apparently discussing what action they should take. The matter was to be decided for them. From behind a hillock up the trail a band of more than a dozen riders emerged, spurring their mounts madly, and firing as they came.

At the sight of this reinforcement, the Indians, already discouraged by the resistance of the cowboys and the toll the two hidden marksmen were taking, broke and fled. With shouts and wild oaths the new-comers followed, ruthlessly shooting down the runaways. Their leader only did not join in the pursuit. Wheeling his horse, he rode to where the rancher was standing, and got down.

"Well, Eden, I reckon we didn't come any too soon," he said.

"I'd liefer yu hadn't come a-tall—we could 'a' beat 'em off without yu," the old man ungraciously retorted. "If yo're lookin' for thanks yo're liable to be disappointed."

"I ain't," Rogue returned dryly. "But if yu warn't needin' me, why send?"

"I never did. If Sands came to yu ——"

"It warn't Sands," the outlaw interposed. "A little runt of a fella, dressed in deerskin an' wearin' moccasins; looked like a forest-runner."

"Ain't seen him," the rancher snapped. "I naturally figured Green would use his side-kick."

"So it was his idea, huh?" Rogue said reflectively, and chuckled. "It would be, o' course. Where is he?"

"I dunno, an' I care less," Eden told him. "I set 'em adrift when I learned they belong to yu."

"They don't—I wish they did," Rogue admitted. "I could use 'em, but it looks like they're still workin' for the S E."

"Waitin' for a chance to carry out yore orders an' drill me again, I s'pose?" the cattleman sneered.

"I'd no hand in that, Eden; it's not my way," the outlaw said sternly. His face hardened. "I could take yore herd right now if I wanted." "Yu could take a slug through the gizzard now if I wanted," the old man growled, gripping his rifle suggestively.

Rogue looked at him in grim amusement. "An' what would that buy yu? My men, mebbe, ain't got my respect for youth an' beauty."

He removed his hat and bowed, either in real or pretended politeness, as Carol—anxious about her father—appeared. Baudry, who had apparently been to fetch her, was just behind. His eyes met those of the bandit leader for one brief instant but his face was devoid of expression.

In twos and threes the rescuers were returning, whopping triumphantly, some of them waving ghastly trophies from which the blood dripped redly. They grouped themselves behind Rogue, their cruel, reckless faces alight with the lust of slaughter. The cowboys too rallied round their boss; they did not like the attitude of these men who had come to their aid. Rogue alone seemed unconscious of any tension.

"We seem fated to meet in unpleasant circumstances, Miss Eden," he said easily, aware that by speaking to her he was rubbing the rancher on a raw place.

"My daughter don't wanta talk to a rustler," Eden said.

The girl gazed reproachfully at her angry parent. "He came to our assistance," she reminded. Her eyes widened as she saw that Rogue's wrist was torn. "You are hurt," she went on. "I've some bandages here—I got them ready, in case ...."

"It's on'y a graze—not worth fussin' over," the outlaw muttered.

But Carol insisted, and Rogue's eyes regarded her curiously as she deftly bound up the wound.

"I'm obliged," he said gruffly.

"I got a scratch too," Navajo put in, his evil, leering gaze on the girl.

Rogue spun round. "Get to hell outa this," he hissed and before the deadly menace in tone and look the half-breed fell back.

The outlaw leader stepped into his saddle. "Well, so long, Eden," be said. "We'll be seein' yu. If yu bump into any more trouble, send, an' we'll come a-runnin'. This time we couldn't help ourselves; next time, mebbe we'll be able to."

With this meaning jest he signed to his men and rode away, indifferent to the threatening growls which greeted it.

# Chapter 23

The herd went on, leaving behind one of the oblong heaps of rock which were only too frequent on the western trails. The rancher was hard to live with during the ensuing days. The loss of one of his men had depressed him; he became moody, savage. The very thought that he had been placed under an obligation to one he despised as an outlaw, who made no secret of his intention to rob him, filled the old frontiersman with fury. He was troubled too with odd doubts in the matter of Green and Sandy.

Baudry also was far from happy, for Carol avoided him as much as possible, and was coldly courteous when she could not. But this, though it put a raw edge on his vanity, was not what most concerned him. It was several days after the Indian attack that he made an opportunity to speak with Dutt alone.

"Well, Monte, yu ain't lookin' too peart," was the greeting he received. "What's disturbin' yore rosy dreams?"

"I've told you not to use that name," the gambler growled. "So you are satisfied with the situation, eh?"

"Shore I am. Rogue has got this outfit where we want it, an' with those two cowboys in the discard, it looks like pie to me."

"Unless Rogue keeps the cows and sells them himself."

"At that, we're on velvet. Eden's busted an' we get the S E."

"And that damned outlaw picks up fifty thousand dollars or more. No, Davy, I'm not standing for that. I offered to take those cows at five a head and I'm going to have them. There's another danger, the damn fool is turning soft. Did you see his face when Carol tied his wrist up?"

"He certainly didn't seem to enjoy it as much as—yu might—for instance."

"Enjoy it? That was torture for him, it fetched back his past and showed him where he had dropped to. I don't suppose a good woman has stretched out a hand to him for years. She played a big card then, though she didn't know it. I was watching him and I tell you I wouldn't be surprised if he let Eden keep his cows for her sake."

Dutt was plainly incredulous. "Rogue's too tough to fall for a skirt," he said. "An' his men wouldn't let him; we can see to it that they don't."

The gambler nodded. "Tell Rollitt to find Navajo and warn him. Rogue must steal the herd. Afterwards—we shall see. My share of that fifty thousand would pay for the wedding trip I have in mind, Davy."

"First catch yore bride," the other parodied.

"She'll come to heel, when her father is faced with finding a job," Baudry said.

"Yo're probably right, but don't forget the fella they call Sandy is interested in that quarter."

The gambler shrugged his shoulders. "That cowboy? He's easy."

"Mebbe, but I wouldn't think it," Dutt replied. "An' he's got a friend—who ain't."

"Sudden, no, but if he shows his face in Abilene he'll be strung up and we'll split the reward two ways," Baudry smiled, tapping the pocket containing a certain printed notice.

"Suits me," Dutt agreed. "I'll search out Rollitt."

* * *

Camp was being struck and preparations made for the day's trek when Sudden and his two companions made their appeara'nce, greatly to the astonishment of such of the S E outfit as were present.

For days since the encounter with the redskins they had trailed the herd, watched the crossing of a river which Tyson opined must be the Cimarron, a stream with an evil reputation but which they fortunately found not in flood.

The two cowboys had found the "still-hunter" more than useful. Not only had he kept them well supplied with game, but his knowledge of woodcraft made him an ideal spy on the outlaws. But he had not yet learned when they intended to make the final move. Sudden, however, guessed that the blow could not now be long delayed, and that was why he had ridden in. The rancher received him with a scowl.

"Eden, I want a word with yu," the cowboy said. "I'm goin' to put my cards on the table, an' yu'd better look at 'em."

Without waiting for assent, he dismounted and trailed the reins. The S E men silently ranged themselves by their employer. When Carol appeared, the cattleman would have sent her away, but Sudden intervened:

"I'd like Miss Eden to hear what I gotta say."

"We're going to listen to some more lies, eh?" Baudry sneered.

"Not unless yu say somethin'," came the acid retort. "This'll be the truth, though I misdoubt yu'll recognize it." He turned to Eden. "First, I gotta talk about myself."

Very briefly he told the tale of his adventures to the time he joined the S E outfit and the supercilious smile on the gambler's lips became more pronounced. When Sudden paused he laughed outright.

"Damned good," he jeered. "You ought to be writing dime novels. Why didn't you come out with this fine story then?"

"I couldn't prove it," the cowboy said simply. "An' I wanted to get outa the country."

"I'll bet you did," came the gibe. "Besides, you were working for Rogue."

Sudden raised his shoulders. "This fella claims he's goin' to ranch near yu," he said to Eden. "Did he mention his brand?" The old man shook his head. "Well, it don't signify—he told yore daughter. See here."

He picked up a half-burnt stick from the fire and in the sand at his feet traced the letters, S E. Then he joined up the ends of both, turning them into 8 B."

"That's his iron," he said quietly. "Convenient, ain't it?"

Baudry's expression of amused indifference vanished. "By heaven, Sam, I never thought of that," he cried. "Comes of not being a cattleman."

It was well done, but his laugh met with no response; brand-blotting was not a subject of mirth in that company.

"Yeah," Sudden said ironically. "While I was stayin' with Rogue, his men brought in a bunch o' cattle to brand. As I told yu, they were feedin' me, so I did my share. They were supposed to be mavericks, but most of 'em was S E when they was thrown an' 8 B when they got up."

"Which only proves that Rogue was taking advantage of my ignorance to sell me stolen steers," Baudry pointed out. "Till the other day I'd never seen the fellow. I let it be known I wanted stock and took it for granted they would be unmarked strays."

"Rogue told me a man was payin' him to bust this drive an' was willin' to take all or any o' the herd," the cowboy went on. "Who gets yore ranch, Eden, if yu fail to put yore cattle through?"

The rancher started, and looked suspiciously at his guest. Baudry reached out a cigar, lit it, and laughed.

"Dime novel stuff," he said. "Prove it."

"Right," the other rejoined. "Eden, I want yore hoss-wrangler, Rollitt."

The gambler's eyes flickered. "Fetch him, Davy," he said.

"No," Sudden said sharply, and motioned to Jeff.

The foreman returned with the wrangler, whose shifty eyes widened when he saw the visitors. "Yu wantin' me?" he asked his employer.

"I'm wantin' yu," Sudden told him. "How long yu been in with Rogue?"

The abruptness of the question caught the fellow off his

guard, but he recovered quickly, his look of alarm giving place to one of sullen obstinacy.

"Ain't never," he growled. "What yu gittin' at?"

"The truth," Sudden retorted. A gun seemed to leap into his hand. "Rollitt, I'm givin' yu a chance to come clean. If yu don't, I'll kill yu." The cold, merciless tone drove the threat home. The wrangler's gaze travelled round the circle of faces. "Nobody can help yu," the icy voice went on. "Whatever happens to me, yu'll be as dead as Moses."

Rollitt looked at the levelled gun; if the thumb moved and let fall the hammer.... He was not the stuff of which heroes are made.

"Mebbe it's a year," he said huskily. "I broke away ——"

The gun roared and a line of red on the man's cheek-bone showed where the bullet had grazed him.

"The next lie will be yore last," the marksman warned. "Yu've been watched, yu fool. What was the word yu took from that man"—he pointed to Dutt—"to Navajo?"

The nearness of death had shattered the ruffian's nerves. With trembling lips he mumbled the message: "Rogue is sellin' yu; get busy with the boys an' strike quickly."

"That's a ——" Dutt began, and promptly subsided when he saw Sudden's eye upon him; he did not relish the cowboy's method of dealing with liars.

"Well, Sam, are you taking the word of this gunman with a price on his head against me, Jethro Baudry, a respected citizen, and your friend?" the gambler asked coolly.

Before the rancher could reply another voice chimed in, and the little Indian-hunter thrust himself forward.

"Jethro Baudry, huh?" he piped. "When I see yu in Kansas City not so far back yu was Monte Jack, a card-cheat who skipped outa town two-three jumps ahead o' the Vigilantes, wanted for killin' a sucker yu'd trimmed—shot him under the table, didn't yu?"

Save that it was a shade more pallid, the gambler's face did not alter. "You are mistaken, my friend," he said.

"No friend o' your'n—never did cotton to coyotes, nohow," Tyson said bluntly. "Monte had a scar runnin' up his right arm from wrist to elbow, where a Mexican had tried to slip a knife into him. All red an' puckered it was, like the edges had been sewed up clumsy."

"Roll up yore right sleeve."

It was Sudden who gave the order, and his gun was again out. Baudry's face was livid; he knew the game was up—for the moment.

"No need—the scar's there," he admitted, and turned to Eden.

"You win—for now, but don't forget I hold your paper."

The rancher, whose rage had been steadily rising as the revelation of how he had been duped proceeded, boiled over at this.

"Yu dirty thief," he cried, and gripped his gun.

The threatened man jeered, "It would be a good way of paying your debt, wouldn't it?"

Eden's fingers released the weapon as though it had been redhot. He glared at the scoundrel who had gauged him so correctly.

"Yu'll get yore money—every cent of it—when I sell the herd," he promised. "Yu needn't worry."

Baudry's lips curled in a wolfish snarl. "I don't propose to," he replied. "I'll have the money, the S E, and—anything else I want of yours." His eyes went to Carol as he made the insolent boast and the contempt with which she received the look swept away the barrier of his self-control. "You damned old fool," he gritted. "I'll make you curse the hour you quarrelled with me. I'll break you and grind your face in the dust. When Rogue has done with you ——"

"Rogue can speak for himself, Mister," came a quiet voice.

The outlaw was standing there. So absorbed had everyone been in what was taking place that they had not seen him ride in and dismount. He addressed the cattleman:

"Far as I'm concerned, Eden, yore herd is safe," he began. "I can't speak for my men; that toad there has poisoned 'em an' they've named a new leader."

"So you sneaked off here to save your hide?" Baudry sneered.

The outlaw's eyes flashed. "Best take care o' yore own," he said. "I don't owe yu money." He looked at Eden. "Jim has given yu the straight of it," he went on. "What yu aimin' to do with these rats?"

The cattleman gestured angrily to his foreman. "clear 'em out," he ordered, and to Sudden, "Green, I'm takin' yore word, but yu ain't told who drilled me."

Sudden looked at Rogue, who shook his head. "I don't know, seh," he replied. "But it warn't Sandy."

The rancher turned his hard eyes on that young man. "I ain't convinced," he said stubbornly, "but I'm willin' to be."

And with this grudging admission Sandy had to be

content, but there was a welcome elsewhere which more than compensated; Carol's eyes were friendly.

A word from the foreman sent the other men about their tasks, leaving the boss and the outlaw alone. An awkward silence ensued, broken at length by the visitor:

"Studying why I'm here, Eden?" he asked. "If yu think it's because o' that scum over there yu got another guess comin'. I'd 'a' stayed an' shot it out with 'em, but I thought I could undo some o' the harm I done yu."

The rancher's expression was frankly sceptical.

"Don't believe me?" the outlaw went on. "Dunno as I blame yu, but it's a fact. Ain't yu wondered why I let yu get so far after that fandango with the 'Paches? Well, I've been tryin' to persuade the boys that it would be a better play to let yu sell the cows an' then lift the dollars, trustin' yu could find a safe place for 'em. That cardsharp put a crimp in that an' here I am. What yu gotta say?"

The rancher hesitated; he was not in the frame of mind to trust anyone, and this man had threatened to steal his cattle.

"Yu can stay, but my men'll have orders to shoot yu at the first sign o' crooked work," he decided.

"That's on'y fair," Rogue said, and walked away.

# Chapter 24

The country stretched before them, flat, brown, uninteresting, but the trail-drivers found it satisfactory, since no danger could approach unseen. The herd, spread out fan-wise, moved slowly forward and Sam Eden—able to sit in a saddle again—pulling up his pony to watch the beasts pass, exulted as he noted their fine condition. Then he frowned as he remembered that catastrophe might yet overtake them. Behind the drag, Rogue was riding alone. The rancher joined him.

"What d'yu figure them coyotes will do?" he asked bluntly.

"We talked it over," the outlaw replied. "To attack on the march would shorely mean stampeding the steers; we'd have to gather 'em again an' might lose quite a number—not all my men knows cattle. The other way was to wait till the herd was bedded down an' rush yore camp after dark; the night-riders could be easy dealt with later. I'd say that's what they'll try, an' it'll be soon, mebbe to-night."

The rancher was silent for a while, furtively studying the hard face of this desperado who had striven for his ruin and was now, apparently, eager to help him. He could not understand it, and still suspected double-dealing.

"What yu know o' that fella Sands?" he asked.

"Mighty little," was the reply. "He drifted in one day, a piece before I met up with Green, and hung around. Didn't mix well with the rest—too clean, I reckon." He smiled and shook his head. "No harm to him; just a boy gone a bit wild."

The cattleman grunted, his eyes travelling ahead to where the subject of their conversation was riding gaily by the side of the girl. Whatever his thoughts were he did not express them.

Hour after hour under the scorching sun the herd drifted on but evening brought them good fortune in the shape of a disrupted strip of plain, with a camp site which could be defended. The bare wall of a small bluff protected the rear, thick scrub shadowed by pines and cottonwoods, the two sides, leaving only the front open. Across this, after the wagon had been driven in, they dragged a couple of tall trees, felled for the purpose, the branches of which formed a leafy screen. Just past the bluff was a pool of water, residue of the last rain, and when the herd had satisfied its thirst, it was driven to a plateau nearby and bedded down, two men only being left in charge. A few horses, ready for instant use, were in a rope corral by the pond; the others were turned loose.

Supper was eaten almost in silence, and hurriedly, each man with his rifle beside him; at any moment he might have to jump up and fight for his life. Then the women were sent to lie down in the wagon and Eden posted his men, with a grim word of warning:

"Don't shoot till yo're shore," he said. "Then—get 'em."

Sandy, squatting beside his friend, voiced a complaint:

"Hell! Don' yu want a smoke, Jim?" he asked.

"Didn't till yu mentioned it, damn yu," was the disgusted reply.

"I hope they show up—we won't find such a good place in a hundred miles."

"I'm bettin' they do—it's pretty near their last chance, an' with no moon, they'll figure on a surprise."

"They'll get it too," Sandy chuckled. "Where's Tyson?"

"Saw him siftin' into the brush," Sudden replied. "Gone to smell 'em out for us; he's a four-eyed wonder in the woods."

The cowboy's guess was a good one. As soon as he had eaten, the forest-runner, with a word to Eden, had faded into the shadows, leaving his beloved Betsy behind. Now, prostrate on his belly, he wriggled a way through the brush, ears attentive to the slightest sound. For an hour or more he heard nothing but the scuttling of some disturbed denizen of the undergrowth, the hoot of an owl, and an occasional faint bellow from the herd.

Then came a new noise, one he had been expecting—the crack of a snapped dry twig, directly in front. Rising to his knees he drew the long, keen blade from his belt and waited. The bush beside him shook and a man on all fours appeared, pushing his rifle ahead of him. Swiftly, silently as a striking snake, the knife flashed and the victim, without even a groan, flattened out like a pricked bladder. Rollitt would rob no more.

The slayer callously jerked his weapon from the throat, wiped it on the dead man's shirt-sleeve, and thrust it into his belt. A muffled curse away to his left and another cracking of dried wood on his right told him that the marauders were getting close; he must warn the camp. With infinite caution he retraced his path; no one of the watching outfit saw him return, but the word was passed along.

Tense moments ticked by and from behind a cactus a shadowy, indistinct form appeared to gradually grow out of the ground. It saw what it expected—the glow of a fire, and round it, dark shapes of sleeping men. A low whistle brought other shadows, and then a dozen guns shattered the silence of the night, driving bullets into the artfully arranged blankets. To the attackers' surprise, no reply came.

"We must 'a' got most of 'em—there'd be several with th' herd," Navajo reasoned. "Come on, fellas."

Confident of success the outlaws emerged from concealment and dashed forward. This was the moment for which Eden had been waiting. "Now," he called sharply.

From behind the-barricade guns spat in a spiteful chorus and in the advancing line men dropped silently, or stumbled and cursed as they fell. Their leader, realizing that they had walked into a trap, turned and raced for cover again, calling to his men to do the same. A number succeeded, but motionless black blotches on the ground told that the attacking force had suffered. Silence again ensued, broken only by an occasional shot when a cowboy fancied he detected a movement in the scrub. Navajo was cursing.

"They was waitin' for us, burn their souls," he grated. "Somebody musta tipped 'em off—them fallen trees wasn't no accident. I'm bettin' it was Rogue, the...." A stream of obscenities followed, cut short by a glance at the sky. "Hell! th' moon'll be up in less'n half an hour an' they'll be able to pick us off like cottontails. We gotta rush 'em before then—it's our on'y chanct."

The charge was made, and met—as before—with a leaden shower, but this time the attackers were desperate. Though several dropped, the rest came on, climbed the barricade, and leapt down upon its defenders. Most of the combatants having emptied their weapons and reloading being an operation which required time, the battle became one of single-handed encounters in which guns and pistols served the purpose of clubs. Grunts, curses, and the thud of blows replaced the crash of exploding powder.

Sudden, having fired his last shot, bringing a man down, slipped aside just in time to get his head out of the path of a swinging riflebutt. Ere the wielder of the weapon could recover his balance, the cowboy stepped in and drove a venomous fist to his jaw. The fellow collapsed limply, dropping like a sack of meal, and at the same instant, claw-like talons encircled Sudden's neck from behind, sinking into the flesh and shutting off his breath.

"Got yu, yu damned spy," came a sibilant hiss.

It was Navajo. With all his weight on the cowboy's back he was striving to fling him to the ground. Sudden knew that would be the end and fought desperately to keep his feet. But the strangling clutch on his wind-pipe was sapping his strength, his lungs ached for air, sharp pains pierced his eyeballs and sight seemed to be leaving him. With groping fingers he tried to loosen the half-breed's hold but it was of no use; the relentless fingers might have been hooks of steel. Then, in despair, he savagely jabbed an elbow backwards into the body behind him. The result was magical; caught fairly in the solar plexus, Navajo's hands fell away, and he tottered back, gasping, helpless.

For some seconds the cowboy could do no more than suck air into his starved lungs, and then, seeing that his enemy was recovering, he ripped across a blow which sent the outlaw reeling to earth. Snarling curses, he sprang up, and as Sudden ran in, flung a handful of sand in his face, and bolted. For the moon was up and a quick glance had shown him that his men were scuttling like rabbits. Completely blinded by the stinging particles of grit, Sudden could do no more than express himself, stamping about, dabbing his smarting eyes with his neckerchief. So Sandy found him, listened awestruck for a moment, and then, with a mischievous grin, remarked:

"Don't yu take no notice, Miss Carol; I reckon he's loco."

The irate cowboy whirled round, only to find he had been caught. The relief of the discovery restored his good-humour. Somewhat ashamed of himself, he explained the reason for the outburst.

"Tough luck," the boy commiserated. "What yu goin' to do?"

"Search out that pond," Sudden replied "I got half the Staked Plains in my eyes an' the other half down my neck."

"Hi, yu wait till we've fed," Sandy cried in affected alarm.

"We gotta drink that water." He paused. "Not that I wanta stop yu from washin', Gawd knows."

Sudden chuckled. "Talkin' o' washin', I wonder how yu' look, with half yore head scrubbed?" he queried.

"Yu go to blazes," Sandy retorted. "Poison the whole damn herd if yu gotta."

The foreman arrived, bringing the news that save for sundry slight wounds and bruises, the outfit had come out of the ordeal unscathed. "I reckon we've discouraged them cattle-thieves a whole lot," he concluded grimly.

They had; the struggling light of the dawn revealed the twisted, contorted bodies of seven men between the brush and the barricade. Two prisoners had been taken and now sat, with bound limbs, in a far corner of the camp. Rugged, ill-favoured rogues, both of them, stolidly refusing to answer questions. Yet not without a certain courage. They knew what was to come and could joke about it. One of them had awakened the other.

"Take a look at yore last sunrise, Hank," he said. "Yu don't wanta oversleep—it's goin' to be a mighty short day for us."

"Shucks!" the other replied. "We'll have a long night to make up for it, hombre."

They fed and smoked, interestedly watching the preparations for breaking camp. When the wagon rolled ponderously away, the foreman and three of the outfit remained behind with two unsaddled horses. Sudden, the last to leave, saw that the prisoners were lighting fresh cigarettes. He felt no pity for them; they had gambled, lost, and must pay, but he had a swift vision of two limp forms dangling in the sunlight-shafted shade of the trees, and was aware of a chilly sensation in the region of his spine. He had come near to meeting the same fate, and would yet if the sheriff of San Antonio or of Fourways laid hands on him.

# Chapter 25

He was a long, scraggy fellow of middle-age, with a thin humorous face, and his rig-out proclaimed that he had recently visited a settlement, clothes, saddle and weapons being patently new. He came into view as they were about to bed-down the herd, and Eden rode to meet him.

"Howdy, friend," the stranger opened, and then, as his gaze ranged over the milling horde of lean-limbed, fierce-eyed beasts, with their wide-branching horns, he added, "Where in hell have yu fetched 'em from?"

Eden laughed. "On'y from Texas," he said. "We passed through the place yu mentioned."

Karson—so the stranger named himself—told the rancher that Abilene was less than a dozen miles distant.

"Mebbe we can do business. I'm in these parts to buy cattle."

"I'm here to sell 'em," Eden replied, not to eagerly. The experiences of the past few months had made him distrustful.

The cattle-buyer slept in camp, having decided to accompany them on the final day's march. He advised that the herd be halted a couple of miles short of Abilene, where there was good grazing.

"She's the toughest burg I ever see—an' I've been in a few," he said. "Yu wanta warn yore boys to stick together an' step light. Crooked men, women, an' games are as plenty as ticks on a cow."

Darkness was still distant when they sighted a haze of smoke on the horizon and realized that the end of the long trail was within reach. But no more than that, for until the herd was sold, the cowboys would lack money, and to visit town without anything to spend would be worse than not going at all. So, when the cattle were bunched and bedded on a raised stretch covered with short curly grass, it was but a small party which headed for Abilene; Karson, Eden, and the women would stay the night there, and the foreman had urged that Sudden should go also.

"Like enough Baudry an' that Navajo fella is infestin' the place," he said." 'Sides, yu may need to send me a word."

They reached the town as dusk was falling. After months in the silent wilderness the noise and bustle amazed them. The principal street, a dusty strip between two rows of flimsy buildings, was antlike in its activity, thronged with a hustling horde. Loaded freight wagons, driven by bull-voiced, blasphemous men churned up the surface, filling the air with a grey powdery deposit which covered everyone and everything; reckless riders flickered to and fro, swinging their mounts dexterously around pedestrians; at the hitch-rails stood rows of patient ponies, heads down, tails swishing in an endless battle against a myriad flies. From the windows of saloons, dance-halls, and gambling "joints" came a warm glow as the lamps within were lighted.

Karson conducted them to his hotel, where they secured rooms and dined. Then he carried the cattleman off to "take in the town." Eden, having warned his daughter to remain indoors, told Sudden he was at liberty to amuse himself. The cowboy did not like this arrangement, but could hardly protest.

Leaving the hotel, he mingled with the motley mob streaming along the street.

At the door of the Palace Saloon he hesitated a moment and then went in. Ordering a modest drink he leant against the bar, studying the ebb and flow of mixed humanity, drinking, gambling, and exulting or complaining as fortune favoured or flouted them. A bleary-eyed individual sidled up to him.

"Yo're a stranger," he accused, shooting out a grimy finger.

"Yu must be a magician," the cowboy quizzed.

"I ain't, but I savvy all the fellas in thisyer burg," the other replied. He pointed to a big, red-faced, flashily dressed man near the bar. "Know who that is? Mick Donagh, owner o' this joint. They say he's good for a hundred thousand dollars."

The corner of the cowboy's eyes crinkled up. "What of it?" he asked lazily. "I'd be good my own self for a lot less'n that."

The bleary citizen decided to take this in a friendly spirit; the nonchalant young stranger did not look too easy.

"I'm bettin' yu would," he agreed. "Me too, don't yu reckon?"

This time he got it straight from the shoulder. "Yu?" the cowboy drawled. "I'd figure yu good—for—nothin'."

The level look which accompanied the contemptuous speech apprised the bleary one that he had selected the wrong victim, and muttering something about "fresh fellas," he drifted away. His place was soon taken by a short, pot-bellied man with mean little eyes and a ludicrous air of importance.

"I'm the town marshal o' thisyer city," he began pompously.

Sudden regarded him gravely. "That so? What am I s'posed to do—throw a fit—or somethin'?" he inquired.

The marshal's bloated face got redder. "I can tell yu what yu ain't s'posed to do an' that's wear them guns," he snapped. "It's agin the law. I'll trouble yu to hand 'em to me."

Sudden's eyes narrowed. "I hate trouble," he said. His gaze swept over the room, nothing that nearly every man in it wore a weapon. "Why start on me? Clean up on them others an'—I'll think about it."

"Yo're a new-comer; I know them fellas," was the lame reply.

"Yeah, that's where the rope rubs—I don't know 'em," the cowboy said quietly. "See here, marshal, I'm attached to my guns an' they're attached to me"—he smiled—"partin' would be—difficult. Don't yu reckon yu'd better take a drink instead?"

Looking into those frosty grey-blue eyes and observing the lean, out-thrust jaw, the officer discovered that he was thirsty.

"I'm trustin' yu not to raise no ruckus," he said.

"Marshal, I'm a li'l woolly lamb long as folks treat me right," the cowboy assured him.

Having absorbed his liquor, the keeper of the peace went in search of another, and presently Sudden saw him in converse with two men whose entrance he had not noticed—Baudry and Dutt. Even as he caught sight of them they were moving towards him. The gambler opened the ball:

"Yes, marshal, that's the man," he said. "Known as 'Sudden' in Texas, and wanted for cold-blooded murder and robbery."

"An' that fella, marshal," parodied the cowboy, "is Monte Jack, a tin-horn who was run outa Kansas City for shootin' a pilgrim he had cheated."

Baudry drew himself up. "That's not true," he protested.

"This is," Sudden rasped, his open hand striking the gambler on the cheek with a crack like a pistol-shot.

Staggering back under the force of the blow, his face livid with passion, Baudry clawed at his shoulder-holster. Dutt flung his arms round him.

"Don't be a fool, Monte, he'll get yu," he cried.

At the name unwittingly used the marshal's pig-like eyes widened. He snatched out his own gun.

"If there's any shootin' here, gents, I'm doin' it," he announced. "Settle yore differences outside."

"Good enough," Sudden said, and looked at Baudry. "At eight to-morrow mornin' I'm walkin' down the street; if yu ain't lost yore nerve an' skipped by then, yu can come an' meet me."

"I'll be there," Baudry spat out.

Followed by curious glances—for the fracas had attracted attention—Sudden left the saloon. At the hotel he found Eden and told him only that the gambler was in town.

"Glad of it," the rancher said. "I can square my account with the dirty sneak an' be a free man again."

Abilene, on the following morning, presented an unwonted appearance of emptiness, save on the sidewalks of the principal street where a number of daring souls had lined up; others, whose courage did not equal their curiosity, contented themselves with the windows and doors of the buildings. For the news of the challenge had quickly spread and a crowd had come to see one man kill another, and to wager on the result.

An excited whisper ran through the throng when, on the stroke of eight, the cowboy walked from the hotel to the middle of the street. That he was a famous gunman from the south was already known to all. For an instant he stood there, his arms hanging down, fingers almost touching the butts of his guns. Silence seized the spectators as, a hundred yards away, another man was seen to be unhurriedly approaching. So the gambler had not gone. Sudden's lips tightened.

The seconds ticked on, each bringing one of the men, or both, nearer eternity. The onlookers gazed breathlessly as the gap between the combatants lessened. Then the angry bark of a pistol smashed into the silence and Sudden's hat was swept from his head. Almost without looking, the cowboy drew and fired, and a man who had stepped into view round the corner of a store reeled and went down, his smoking gun clattering on the boards. It was David Dutt, and a howl of disgust came from the nearest spectators when they realized the treachery he had attempted. Sudden himself, bareheaded and swinging the revolver loosely in his fingers, paced steadily on. He had eyes only for the man he was going to meet.

To Jethro Baudry, the failure of the plot was a crushing blow; it had seemed so sure and easy to explain: an unknown enemy, seizing the opportunity to pay a debt. Why had Dutt let himself be seen, and above all, why had he missed? Savagely he cursed the man who had died for him, and gazed with anxious, haggard eyes at the advancing figure.

Step by step the cowboy came on, relentless, inevitable as death itself. A cold sweat oozed from the gambler's forehead and his heart seemed to become a lump of ice. He had killed, and was no novice in gunfights, but they had been quick affairs, over in a moment or two, allowing no time for thought; the deliberation of this encounter called for a courage he did not possess. Forty yards —thirty— twenty—damnation, would the fellow never stop? He felt like a condemned criminal, awaiting execution, and watching the leaden hours creep by, but in his case they were moments, seconds, and at that thought he pulled up.

"Can't miss at this distance," he muttered, and wondered who had spoken.

He tried to raise the gun he was carrying but found he could not; it seemed to weigh a ton. His antagonist was now only a dozen paces away and he could see the grim, grey face and narrowed ice-cold eyes. A shiver shook him as he realized that he was nothing more than a target. Already he seemed to feel the scorching, blinding pain of lead tearing through his body. Desperately he made another effort to fire but his paralysed muscles refused to act, and in a panic of frenzied fear, he dropped the weapon, flung up his arms, and bolted. Staggering, slipping in the loose dust, expecting every instant the numbing jar of a bullet in his back, he did not hear the yell of derision which followed him as he vanished behind a convenient building.

The cowboy watched him go, a mingled expression of contempt and doubt on his face.

"I figured him right," he said to himself. "Allasame, I'd oughta got him."

Men crowded round the victor, patted him on the back, invited him to drink, and hailed him as a good fellow. Dutt, they told him, was dead, with a bullet between the eyes, and all agreed that it was less than he deserved. Sudden had hard work to get away from his admirers, but he pleaded that he had a job, and his boss was waiting for him. Which was no more than the truth, for on returning to the hotel, he found Eden and the buyer ready to ride out and inspect the herd.

"I'm glad yu didn't kill him, Jim," the rancher said. "It would 'a' looked like yu Were payin' my debt."

"It may come to that yet," Sudden told him.

"Yu don't think he's finished?" Eden asked.

"There's on'y one way to keep a rattler from bitin'," was the meaning reply.

Karson was evidently of the same opinion, for as they passed the scene of the gambler's humiliation, he said:

"Yu oughta rubbed that fella out like a dirty mark, which is what he is; it was a plain frame-up."

"I expect yo're right, seh," Sudden agreed.

When they reached the camp, Eden had the cattle lined out and driven past, he and the buyer counting independently. Their figures nearly tallied.

"Call it two thousand, two hundred," the rancher offered.

"Good enough," Karson nodded. "They're a likely lot an' in fair fettle, but I on'y want four-year-olds—twenty-five a head."

Eden's face fell; this meant taking the pick of his herd and leaving him with the less saleable residue.

"That ain't a square offer an' yu know it, Karson," he said bluntly. "Gimme an all-over price of twenty an' take the lot. With the northern ranches yelpin' for stock, yu can't lose."

The buyer took one look at the cattleman's stubborn jaw. "Yu know yore business," he smiled. "I was hopin' yu'd let 'em go for fifteen."

"I've been lookin' at cows' rumps since I was weaned," Eden grinned. "Well, what do yu say?"

"It's a deal," Karson replied, aware that he had made a good bargain. "Of course, yore boys'll hold the herd here till I can arrange for shippin'? Good."

The news that the steers they had safeguarded through so many vicissitudes were actually sold caused great jubilation among the cowboys, and the difficulties of the trail were made light of in a way which vastly amused the buyer.

"Trouble?" Jed echoed in answer to his question. "Why, nothin' to notice. O' course, cows git contrary an' thinks they knows a better road than the one yo're taken' 'em, but yu expect that."

"I heard somethin' about Indians," Karson smiled.

Jed's bony face was sardonic. "Mebbe we had to flap a blanket now an' then to scare them critters off," he confessed.

And Karson, who had been told much of the real story, grinned delightedly and distributed cigars all round.

"Yu'll do," he said. "If ever I want a herd o' real classy liars I'll come to Texas."

They saw nothing of Rogue. He had, the foreman said, ridden off the previous afternoon and had not re-appeared. The news brought a frown to the rancher's face; he still distrusted the outlaw.

When the party returned to town, Sandy—at Sudden's suggestion—went with them. Eden was to receive payment for his cattle at once, and had announced his intention of taking charge of the money himself. Banks were few and far between in Texas and he had little faith in such institutions. So he tucked the big roll of bills into an inside pocket and tapped the butt of his gun meaningly.

"Any fella who tries to lift those off'n me will shorely get a shock," he boasted.

From this resolution he could not be turned, even by his daughter, who was obviously apprehensive of the risk he was running.

In the back room of a Mexican dive at the other end of the town, Navajo, with contemptuous amusement on his thin lips, listened to the stumbling excuses of the man before him.

"Can't think what came over me, but I couldn't have raised my gun for a million dollars," Baudry said. "Never felt like it before; I must have been sick."

"Yu shore looked it, but for a sick man yu ran almighty well," the half-breed sneered.

The gambler's eyes grew malevolent. "I'm not sick now, Navajo," he warned.

"Glad to know it," was the reply. "Yu'll be better able to bear the shock o' hearin' that Eden has sold his herd an' got the mazuma. To put it plain, we're beat."

If he meant to anger his companion he did not succeed; Baudry was regaining his habitual veneer of imperturbability.

"Quite a slice of that money is mine," he said, "and, do you know, I believe the old fool would pay up."

"Better ask him, but mind Mister Sudden ain't around or yu'll be meetin' Dutt mighty soon."

"So it was Davy?" the gambler mused. "I suspected it. Well, he was always fond of me. How many would do a thing like that for you, Navajo?"

"Not one, even if I asked," the half-breed replied, with an incredulous laugh; he was not deceived. "I do my own dirty work."

"But you got Lasker to shoot his employer," came the reminder.

"I offered him a price—same as yu did me," Navajo said sullenly.

Baudry's brows went up. "You are in error, my friend," he pointed out. "I made a bet with you—quite a different thing, and you look like losing it. I shall deduct the amount from your share of the herd-money."

The outlaw straightened up. "Yu are goin' to get it?"

"What else did you think?" the gambler retorted. "Yes, I

am going to get it—the money, the ranch, the girl, trample Eden in the dirt, and kill that damned gunman."

The mask was off now, showing a face white with rage, hatred in the eyes, and the thick lips drawn back in a feral snarl.

"Why not run the herd off too, while yo're about it?" Navajo asked mockingly.

"Too risky—we'd have the whole damn place on our tails," snapped the other. "Besides, it wouldn't hurt Eden—he's been paid—and it's his scalp I'm after. If you don't care to come in, I can swing it alone."

"Oh yeah," the half-breed gibed. "Yu'll do some swingin' alone if yu show yore face in town; that frame-up ain't made yu one bit popular. Well, let's hear yore plan."

For some time Baudry talked earnestly, and when he had finished, sat back and looked triumphantly at his confederate.

Navajo nodded. "Yu can count me in," he said shortly.

His malignant gaze followed the gambler as he went out. "Yellow-bellied coyote," he muttered. "Yu'd sell yore own sister for ten cents, an' right now yo're figurin' to double-cross me. That's a game more'n one can play at, an' when I pull a gun runnin' won't save yu."

Then he too left the place, slinking along behind the buildings until he reached his destination.

# Chapter 26

Soon after dark that same evening, a Mexican lad slid into the Palace Saloon and made his way to where Eden and Sandy were watching a game of poker in which Karson was taking part. Twitching the rancher's sleeve, the boy whispered:

"Meestair Green wantin' yu, pronto—outside."

Without waiting for an answer he darted away. Telling his friend he would be back, Eden started for the door, and Sandy stepped after.

"No need to drag yu away, boy," the cattleman said.

"I'm comin'," Sandy replied. "Jim's word was to stick to yu like yore shadow."

"Shucks, I've had too much nussin' lately," Eden laughed, and as he stepped into the street and looked round, "Where in blazes is he?"

A blurred shape detached itself from the gloom, an arm snapped viciously down and the rancher dropped like a pole-axed steer. Sandy grabbed at his gun, but before he could get it out three men sprang upon him. Uttering a lusty yell for help, he flung his fists right and left, and had the satisfaction of hearing a grunt of pain follow each blow. His shout brought other citizens and these hurled themselves enthusiastically into the battle. Since they knew neither the cause nor the combatants, they were soon fighting each other and were of no use to those they had come to assist.

Standing astride his employer's body, Sandy struggled on, wrenching himself free from clutching hands and driving his fists vengefully into indistinct faces. But it could not last. From behind came a bitter oath in a voice he remembered, and ere he could turn, a sweeping blow with the barrel of a pistol sent him down.

It was at this moment that Sudden, who—deeming the rancher safe with the other two—had gone to comb the town in search of Rogue or Navajo, heard that there was trouble at the Palace and came to investigate. He found an excited group outside, many bearing marks of the conflict, gathered about two senseless men.

"What happened?" he asked a bystander, who was wiping blood from his cheek.

"Durned if I know," was the reply. "There was a shindy, so I sat in—never could keep out'n a scrap, nohow. Then three-four fellas ran away an' I found I was fightin' a friend. Do yu know them hombres?"

The light of a match confirmed the cowboy's fears. "Hell, yes, one of 'em is my boss," he said, and made a hurried examination. "They ain't cashed, anyways."

Karson was found and the injured men carried to the hotel.

"This is a bad business, Green," the cattle-buyer said. "I s'pose they got the money?"

"Reckon so—it's gone."

"He was askin' for it; yu can't keep anythin' quiet in this place It was known he'd sold his herd an' these scallywags took the chance he'd have a fat wallet. I oughta stayed with him, but poker's a fair curse with me."

Sudden did not undeceive him. His own mind was full of conflicting conjectures. Baudry, Navajo, or even Rogue might have planned this latest development, and that it was one or more of them he was convinced. Bitterly he reproached himself for allowing the gambler to escape.

At the hotel they found Aunt Judy in a state bordering on frenzy: Carol was missing. When she saw the two unconscious men, her hands went up in the air and she called down a curse on Abilene which should have wiped the town off the face of the earth. Having acquitted herself like a man in this direction, she promptly became a woman again.

"Lemme look at him." She scrutinized the rancher's injury. "Huh! Must 'a' bin a stranger; nobody as knowed him would try to kill Sam Eden by hittin him on the head."

She bathed and bandaged the hurts and was just through with Sandy when he sat up and asked weakly:

"Where's Jim?"

"Dunno," Judy snapped. "Gone to get his head busted, I reckon. 'Pears to be the on'y use yu men got for 'em."

The sarcasm was excusable, but applied to Sudden, unjust. He unearthed a grubby urchin who ran errands and did chores at the hotel, and learned that a lady had called to see Miss Eden about two hours earlier and that they had gone out together. Asked if he knew the visitor, the boy hesitated.

"She gimme a dollar not to say," he admitted.

"I'll give yu two dollars," Sudden offered, and reading the youthful mind, added, "Yu can give hers back an' say yu changed yore mind; that'll make it right."

This somewhat specious reasoning satisfied the boy. "They call her 'Lily Gold' an' she rooms with Mammy Porter, opposite the drug store," he said. "I guess she ain't much class."

Sudden returned to the sick-room. Eden was still unconscious but breathing easily. Sandy was in a fever to see his friend.

"Jim," he cried, "Navajo was there—I heard his voice. Damnation, they've got Carol. What we goin' to do?"

"Yu'll stay here," Sudden replied. "I've got a line on the girl an' I'm goin' after her, right now."

He told what he had learned and Aunt Judy snatched up her bonnet. "I'm a-comin'," she stated. "No use yu arguin', Jim Green; yu may be able to tackle a man but it takes a woman to handle a woman. I can't do nothin' more for these two saps."

With a face which might have been carved from a block of wood she followed the cowboy down the street. They found the house, a two-storied, ramshackle frame building. The door was opened by a stout, middle-aged negress.

"Mis' Gold is upstairs but she ain't seein' nobuddy," she told them.

"She'll see us," Sudden said, and slipping a coin to the woman's hand, pushed past.

They found Miss Gold smoking a cigarette and lolling

in an armchair. Not yet thirty, she still had charm of a kind, but her once pretty face had become hard, predatory, and her yellow hair was obviously dyed. The silken frock which revealed too much of her opulent figure was shabby and the high-heeled satin shoes were rubbed and worn. She greeted her unannounced guest with a stare of surprise.

"And who the hell may you be?" she asked belligerently.

"That don't matter," the cowboy said. "We wanta know what yu've done with Miss Eden?"

"Don't know the lady," the girl replied insolently, but there was a flicker of fear in her eyes.

"Lyin' won't help yu," Sudden said evenly. "We know that yu called on her an' that she left the hotel with yu."

Lily Gold studied him appraisingly. Usually she found cowboys easy to handle, but this one seemed different; her wiles would have no effect on him.

"Oh, that kid," she said. "I showed her round a bit and then she said she wanted to do some shopping. I expect she had a fellow to meet."

Her sneering laugh was rudely cut short. Aunt Judy thrust Sudden aside. Her eyes were blazing.

"Lemme talk to her," she said. "Listen, yu dance-hall drab. Do yu know how the Injuns serve women o' yore sort? They slice their noses off, an' yu can take it from me it don't improve their looks any—I've seen 'em." Her left hand shot out and fastened like a claw on a bare shoulder, digging into the soft flesh and forcing the girl back in the chair, while her right jerked an eight-inch bowie knife from the bosom of her dress and flashed it before her prisoner's frightened eyes. "Come clean, yu slut," she raged.

"or by the livin' God I'll make yore face somethin' for men to shudder at."

The harsh discordant voice, fierce angular features, and set grim lips told that it was no mere threat, and the dance-girl—who would have faced a furious man and told him to do his worst—shrank back in stark terror from this fiend in female shape. Out of the raddled, bloodless mask on which the patches of paint stood out with startling distinctness, her terrified gaze travelled to the cowboy.

"She'll do it," she whimpered. "She's mad. Call her off."

"I ain't interferin'," Sudden said sternly. "It's up to yu."

The girl was shaking. "There's men in town who'll hang you for this," she panted.

"Mebbe, but that won't put yore nose back," Judy retorted, and raised the knife.

The story came tumbling out. She had been paid to lure the victim to a certain Mexican dive, the bait being that a cowboy named Sandy had been badly hurt in a brawl. Two men had met them there, seized Miss Eden and ridden away. One of the men was Baudry; the other a stranger.

"Where have they taken her?" Sudden barked.

"How the hell do I know?" the woman snapped, and then shrieked as the steel gleamed before her eyes.

"There's an old shack out on the plain, about two miles due north," she gasped. "I heard them mention it. That's all I know. Get out, damn you. Get out!"

Aunt Judy looked at her. "If yu've lied, or they've harmed Carol, I'll find yu an' cut yore rotten heart out if I swing for it," she promised.

When they had gone, the woman staggered to her feet,

flung open a cupboard, and pouring out a stiff dose of spirit, gulped it eagerly.

"Christ! I wanted that," she muttered. "What a devil, and she meant it! I'll have to get away, pronto. If they've hurt that kid..."

Hurriedly she began to throw her few possessions into a bag. Miss Gold was taking no more chances; she was attached to her nose and wished to remain so.

When Sudden and Aunt Judy reached the hotel the cowboy turned to her and said meaningly:

"I'm gettin' my hoss an' follerin'. This is a man's job."

To his great relief, she uttered no protest. Her violence seemed to have evaporated; she had resumed her sex.

"Yu'll bring her, Jim, won't yu?" she pleaded. "An' yu won't say nothin' to nobody 'bout me gittin' peeved back there?"

"Why, yu done noble," Sudden replied. "I'd never 'a' got the truth outa that dame."

"Mebbe, but I misdoubt I behaved like a lady oughta."

Sudden, saddling his horse a few moments later, was moved to express his thought:

"Nig, I reckon in choosing a hoss, a friend, or a wife, looks oughta come way down in the list, ol'-timer."

* * *

In a lonely, tumble-down cabin to the north, lit by a guttering candle stuck with its own grease to the rickety table, two people were facing one another. Carol Eden, her hands bound, leaned against the wall, contemptuous, defiant.

Baudry, seated upon an up-ended box, regarded her

with a fiendish smile of exultation. As the fitful light set the shadows dancing about the room, now revealing and then half concealing her disdainful form, his sense of satisfaction grew. He had sworn to have her and here she was. Soon they would be away—headed for civilization, and by the time they reached it…Affairs had not gone quite as he had planned, but with the girl, the herd-money, and the mortgage on the S E in his possession, he would take most of the tricks. But first he must deal with the half-breed, the man who had jeered at and taunted him.

"Sit down," he ordered, pointing to a second box on the other side of the table.

"I prefer to stand," Carol replied. "I can keep farther away from you."

The man smiled tolerantly. "When you're my wife, you'll know me better," he said.

"Impossible!" she cried. "What else are you besides liar, cheat, and coward?"

This time the scorn in her low vibrant voice seared him. He stood up and stepped towards her, slowly, like some wild beast about to pounce on its helpless prey. Staring at him with fear-wide eyes, she backed away until she could retreat no more. The gambler's gaze dwelt gloatingly on the lissome, rounded form.

"I'm a man who can tame women and make them do as I wish," he said softly. "In a little while you'll come creeping to me for a kind word and be happy if you get it, though now you dislike me."

"Dislike?" the girl echoed passionately. "I hate and despise you."

The nearness of her intoxicated him and he laughed evilly as his hands darted out, prisoning her arms. The feel of the firm flesh beneath his fingers fired his blood and sent his hot lips questing for hers. Mad with terror and loathing, she fought to avoid them, but bound, and held in that grip of steel, could do little. Drunk with desire, he tore open her shirt-waist and rained kisses on her bared neck.

"I'll teach you, my beauty," he panted quickly.

And then, when she had given up hope, he flung her violently from him. A horse had whickered outside.

# Chapter 27

Dazed and weak, Carol saw her assailant fall into a half-crouch his gun drawn, death in his eyes. She tried to shout a warning but no sound issued from her dry, throbbing throat. The door was flung open, Baudry fired, and the new-comer stumbled, coughed, and slithered to the floor, a pistol dropping from nerveless fingers. After a moment's pause, the killer bent over him.

"Rogue?" he muttered. "Wonder how he got wise? Well, that's a debt I was afraid I'd have to leave unpaid. Where the hell is Navajo?"

"Right here," the half-breed replied from the doorway, and stepped noiselessly into the cabin. His mean eyes rested callously, on the supine form of his late leader. "That saves me a job but I ain't thankin' yu."

"Did you get Eden?"

"I reckon—'less his head's made o' rock," the ruffian replied "The crack I gave him would 'a' split the skull of an ox."

"Hope you haven't overdone it," Baudry said viciously. "It will hurt him more to live."

"Mebbe, but that fella Sandy came out o' the saloon with him an' fought like a wildcat. With townsfolk joinin' in we had to do the best we could," the half-breed explained, and tapped his pocket. "We corralled the cash."

Dull despair took possession of the prisoner. Her father injured, probably dying, and Sandy.... For since the woman Gold had brought that lying message, Carol had comprehended what the cheerful young cowboy had come to mean to her, and the thought that she might never see him again turned her heart to lead.

"You did well, Navajo," the gambler said. "If we'd got that devil, Sudden, it would be a clean-up."

"I'll tend to him," the other said darkly. He threw a roll of bills on the table. "We split that two ways an' then settle about the gal."

Baudry jerked round as though he had been spurred. "She goes with me," he answered harshly.

"Mebbe, after we've cut the cards for her," Navajo replied.

In the flickering light of the candle he could not see the murderous gleam in the other's eyes, but he knew it was there. At the moment he saw Rogue's body he divined that the outlaw had saved his—Navajo's—life, and that Baudry would kill him if he could. So, when his proposal was agreed to, he watched yet more warily.

"Have it your way," the gambler said quietly. He produced a pack of cards and squared them up on the table. "Help yourself. Highest wins. Sudden death."

"Yu said it," the half-breed assented.

The fingers of his left hand closed over the cards, gripping them gently. A touch told him they had been prepared—the ends and sides of some of them treated with a file, so that the man who knew what had been done could cut high or low as he desired. He knew now why Baudry had given in, but it made no difference to his plan. He hesitated only for an instant and then lifted the whole pack and hurled it in the other man's face.

"Cold-deck me, would yu?" he cried, and snatching out his gun sent two bullets into the gambler's breast.

Grimacing horribly, hands reaching blindly for support, the stricken man collapsed like a house of cards, shuddered convulsively once, and was still. Navajo's smile was that of a demon.

"Sudden death it was," he said hoarsely, and turned to the girl, only to find her unconscious upon the floor. The tragedies she had witnessed, added to the mental torture of the past few hours, had proved too much for even her Western nerves.

Stuffing the roll of money into a pocket, the half-breed stood gloating over his captive for a moment or two, his lewd eyes dwelling on the graceful curve of her neck and the rounded white shoulder which Baudry's brutality had left exposed.

"A pretty piece—an' mine—now," he exulted evilly. "Well, beautiful, we'll be on our way."

Lifting the limp form, he carried it to where the gambler's horse was hitched outside the hut, and roped it to the saddle. He was about to mount his own beast when he remembered something; both the dead men would have money. He went back and was kneeling by the side of Baudry when a word rang out like a pistol-shot:

"Navajo!"

Sudden was standing in the doorway, a gun levelled from the hip. The icy passionless voice fell on the outlaw's ears like a deathknell. Though he had bragged to Baudry, he feared this cold-eyed young cowboy who had so quickly gained a reputation as a gunman. "Sudden death!" The phrase recurred to him with a new and ominous significance. Bitterly he cursed himself for his delayed departure; but for his greed...

"Yu can stand up."

Navajo rose slowly to his feet, his devious mind searching for a way out.

"These hombres 'pear to have bumped each other off," he said. "I was just seein' if they was cashed."

Still keeping the man covered, Sudden picked up Rogue's gun; it was fully loaded; the butt of Baudry's weapon could be seen protruding from its shoulder-holster. He looked at the half-breed.

"Rogue reloaded an' Baudry put his gun back after they were killed," he said sarcastically.

"I was guessin'—on'y bin here a few minutes an' found 'em like this," the man replied sullenly.

"So it wasn't yu who carried Miss Eden out?"

"Yeah, I was meanin' to take her back."

"Tied to the saddle?"

"Couldn't do no other way—she'd fainted."

"An' the herd-money. Takin' that back too?"

"Dunno nothin' about it."

Sudden laughed scornfully. "Yo're a pore liar, Navajo," he said. "Hand over yore gun."

The ruffian stiffened. He remembered now that he had fired twice and had not replaced the charges. An examination of the weapon would produce apparently conclusive evidence and...During the conversation he had been edging backwards an inch at a time. Now, with a quick sweep of one arm, he knocked the candle from the table and dropped prone to escape the expected bullet. None came, only a taunting voice:

"Fine! Figured yu'd play it that way when I saw yu sneakin' back. Don't waste no shots, Navajo; yu on'y got four."

Sudden was surmising, but correctly, and the outlaw gritted his teeth at the reminder. He must be sure, and how could he be in that blinding darkness? For there was no light; even the tiny unglazed window could hardly be located, so dark was the night outside. Flat on his belly the half-breed lay motionless, waiting for some movement which might betray his enemy's whereabouts.

An idea came to him—Baudry's gun. If he could obtain that and fire four shots, Sudden would deem him defenceless, and...He knew the direction in which the body lay and began to make his way towards it. Hardly daring to breathe, he crawled on inch by inch, feeling cautiously for obstacles. It.was a blood-chilling task, for the slightest sound might bring first the agony of tearing hot lead, and then—death. At length his groping fingers touched a still face, travelled downwards and found a shoulder-holster—empty. He stifled the curse which rose to his lips, and edged away.

"Yu ain't a quick thinker, Navajo," the taunting voice said. "I've got Baudry's gun."

In his rage and disappointment the half-breed fired at the spot where he judged the speaker to be. An answering spit of flame stabbed the gloom and a bullet nicked his neck. The voice spoke again:

"Near thing, Navajo. A mite to the right an' yu'd be travellin' the one-way trail."

The incident shook the outlaw's confidence. Hell! if the fellow could see in the dark...And he had wasted a shot, for though the silence was profound again he knew that he had missed. The thought of what his cupidity had cost came back to torment him: wealth, possession of the girl, for whom he had hungered since first he laid his leering eyes upon her, freedom. He visioned the pair of them riding into the trackless wilderness and his lips went wide in a lecherous grin. Then he came to earth again and blasphemed at the reality; he was trapped, likely to lose all, even life itself.

Lying there in the stillness so pregnant with danger he flogged his faculties to find a device to extricate himself and, at length, hit on a plan. It would be a desperate risk but he resolved to take it. And he must act at once, for he knew that his courage was ebbing; the jeering devil waiting so patiently to kill him was his master. Rising swiftly to his knees, he fired and swayed away instantly. Sudden aimed at the flash, heard the thud of a falling body, and a deep groan. Five—ten minutes passed and no sound came. The cowboy moved a foot noisily but nothing happened.

"Looks like I may've got him," he muttered.

Groping on the floor, he found the candle and lighted it. Navajo was lying on his side, his face buried in the bend of his left arm, his right arm hidden under his body. His gun lay some feet away. In the uncertain light he appeared to be dead. Sheathing his pistol, Sudden stooped to turn the body over. Instantly it came to life, the right hand darting upwards in a vicious stab. With a lightning snatch the cowboy clutched the wrist, wrenched it aside, and springing back, pulled and fired. Navajo, his face ferociously distorted in a murderous grin, sank back. This time there was no doubt.

Chilled to the bone by the narrowness of his escape, Sudden leant against the wall. Had he delayed an instant, or missed the deadly thrusting wrist, eight inches of steel would have ripped him open. He drew a long breath and wiped the cool moisture from his forehead. Then he looked at the dead man with an odd respect.

"Didn't figure yu had the savvy for a play like that," he mused. "Yu fooled me plenty an' a'most deserved to get away with it, though I'm just as pleased yu didn't."

He searched for and secured the stolen money, and then the sound of a galloping horse straightened him up, gun in hand. It was Sandy who thrust open the door.

"Jim yu all right?" he called.

"Yeah, an' it's lucky," Sudden reproved. "If any o' these other hombres had been on their feet instead what would 'a' happened to yu, bustin' in like that? Ain't yu got nothin' but sawdust in that red head?"

"Where's Carol?" the boy asked, disregarding the aspersion.

"Outside—tied to a hoss," Sudden told him, adding grimly, "I've been too busy to turn her loose."

Sandy's eyes widened as he looked round. "Gosh, Jim, did yu get 'em all?"

"No, yu chump," Sudden replied, and told what he believed to have happened.

As they bent over Rogue, his eyelids flickered and his lips breathed a question.

"She's safe," Sudden assured him.

Sandy went out and found that Carol was conscious again. He untied and lifted her down. She asked about Rogue.

"He's badly hurt," the boy told her.

"I must go to him" she said.

"It's—pretty terrible—in there," he demurred.

"It would have been more terrible—for me—if he hadn't come," she cried, and to that Sandy could say nothing.

A spark of life shone in the dying outlaw's tired eyes when she entered the cabin. Kneeling by his side she strove to thank him, sobs choking her.

"It don't matter," he said.

"Can't I do anything?" she asked hopelessly.

A little shake of the head, and then, doubtfully, "Once I had a lass who would be about yore age ..."

With swift comprehension, she bent over and pressed her lips to the furrowed brow of the man who had killed and robbed, yet given his life for her.

"It's too good—an end—for a—rogue," he murmured.

The ghost of a smile passed over his hard mouth and that was all. Sandy led the weeping girl out of the hut, clumsily trying to comfort. In her overwrought state she could think of one thing only.

"Sandy, he died for me," she cried. "I'll never forget that.'

"If I didn't owe him so much I'd feel jealous," the boy said huskily.

Carol turned to him impulsively, thrilled by his tone. Her forth-right nature scorned evasion.

"You needn't be," she said softly. "Oh, Sandy, when that woman told me you were hurt, I—nearly—died."

Sudden unnecessarily slammed the cabin door, propped a plank against it to keep out prowling coyotes, and came towards them.

"The boys will be over in the mornin'," he said.

Through the black velvet of the night they rode back to town. Sudden led the way, his thoughts dwelling on the dead outlaw. Though his meeting with the man had meant nothing but misfortune, he had liked him, and in some way he could not understand, was conscious of a sense of loss. The pair behind were riding close together, and Sudden smiled a little bitterly at the reflection that he was soon to lose another friend. Had Rogue lived...

It was not until the morning that the rancher was sufficiently recovered to hear the full story of the previous night's happenings. Varying expressions chased each other across his rugged features as Carol told the tale, and when it was ended, he brought his fist down with a thump on the pillow beside him.

"By heaven, Jim, all the herd-money wouldn't pay what I owe yu," he said. "But yu'll be comin' back to the S E with me, an' ——"

A shake of the head interrupted him. "I'm obliged," the cowboy replied, "but yore memory ain't workin'."

"Shucks! I got friends who can pull ropes," Eden said.

Sudden's grin was sardonic. "I got enemies who can do the same an' mebbe my neck would be in the loop o' one," he pointed out. "No, seh, I'm shore fond o' Texas but I ain't honin' to end my days there—yet." His face sobered. "Besides, but for another man yu'd have nothin' to thank me for."

"I ain't allowin' that," Eden returned. Despite the amend Rogue had made, he found it difficult to think kindly of the outlaw. His gaze went to Sandy. "I'm told yu kept them rats from finishin' me off," he went on. "Yu must 'a' had a change o' heart since the Colorado."

"Hold yore hosses, seh, an' take a squint at these," Sudden interposed, producing a pair of beaded moccasins. "Found 'em in Navajo's saddle-bag; they fit those tracks I measured. An' there's this."

The rancher took the proffered slip of paper. "Baudry's fist an' signature," he muttered, and read the contents aloud:

"I have today bet Navajo one thousand dollars that my friend, Sam Eden, gets his herd through and comes safely back to the S E."

The document bore the date the drive started. With knitted braws Eden studied it; then the sinister import dawned upon him.

"Why, he's offerin' the fella a thousand cold to put me outa business," he burst out.

"Yu said it," Sudden agreed. "An' when he failed to turn the trick hisself he bribed Lasker."

The old man looked woodenly at Sandy. "That appears to let yu out," he said. "S'pose I'll have to take yore word."

This ungenerous surrender brought a reproachful

"Daddy!" from his daughter, and an expression of angry scorn on the young man's face.

"I ain't offerin' it," he retorted. "Think what yu please."

Aunt Judy flung herself into the discussion with her usual impetuosity. "Sam Eden," she said sharply, "if I was yore daughter—even by adoption—I'd box yore stubborn ears." She slanted a bony finger at Sandy. "Do I have to tell yu who that boy is?"

A slow smile softened the rancher's face. "No, that's my scamp of a son, Andrew Eden," he replied, and the harshness was gone from his voice also.

"Your son, and you treated him so—unkindly?" Carol cried. "You could even think..."

The rancher wriggled uneasily and then shook his head. "Don't reckon I ever really believed that, but I had to be shore," he excused. "An' I wanted to see if he would stand the iron. I didn't know the game, but I was willin' to play it his way, so I told Jeff an' Peg-leg to keep their traps closed—they savvied him too. How come yu to be with the Rogue, boy?"

"Got word he was rustlin' yore cattle," Sandy explained. "Later, I learned it was more serious an' when he sent Jim an' myself to join yore outfit it looked like a chance to put a crimp in his plans."

"Why pretend to be a stranger?" Eden asked.

Sandy looked embarrassed. "Yu ain't rememberin' how we parted," he said.

The old man chuckled contentedly—his boy was trying to spare him; but he was no shirker.

"I've not forgotten," he admitted. "Threatened to fill yu

with buckshot if yu showed up again, didn't I? Well, that's all past an' done—I reckon we've both learned sense since that day. Yu've made good an' I'm proud o' yu, son." His eyes twinkled as he went on, "It's a pity Carol don't like redheads—claims she's had enough trouble with me, but mebbe she ——" He looked round the room and seemed surprised to find the girl had slipped away. "Now where in mischief has she gone? Yu better go find her, boy; somebody is liable to steal her again."

Sandy's old impudent smile was back. "Somebody's goin' to," he promised.

From the crest of a ridge in the plain, a man on a big black horse watched a lumbering, canvas-topped wagon and its attendant group of riders diminish in the distance. The S E outfit was homeward bound and Sudden had ridden with them this far. Bitterness was again upon him; once more he was friendless. Even Tyson—well supplied with "smokin'," but disdaining the offer of a new rifle to replace his cherished "Betsy"—had returned to the wilderness in search of, as he had grimly put it, "copper-coloured marks to shoot at."

Sudden was sorely tempted to spur on and take his chance in Texas. Then came the memory of Bill Evesham, the man to whom he owed everything, who had passed out leaving him a legacy of hate. Somewhere on the far-flung frontiers of the west the two men who had wronged his benefactor were to be found. He had given his word and must keep it, at any cost. His young face became flint.

"I have it to do," he muttered, and whirling his mount, rode resolutely towards the town.

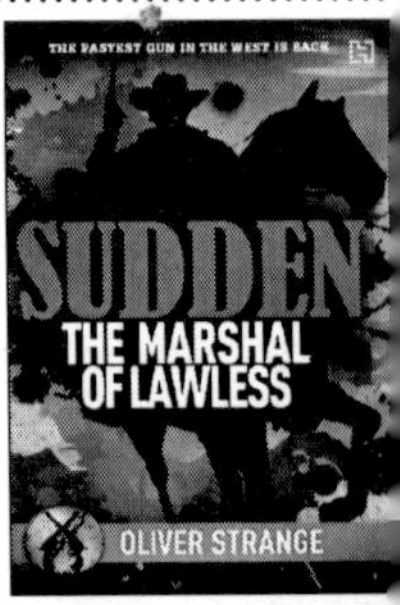

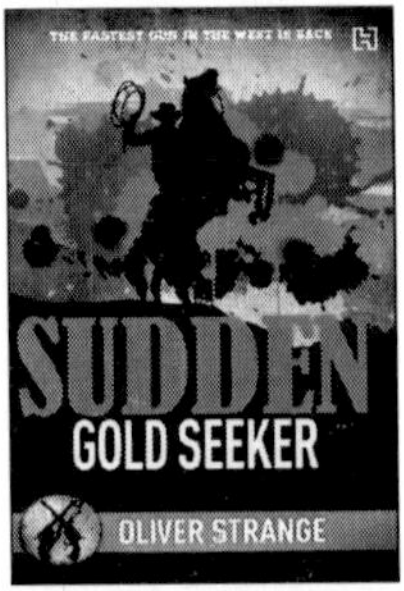

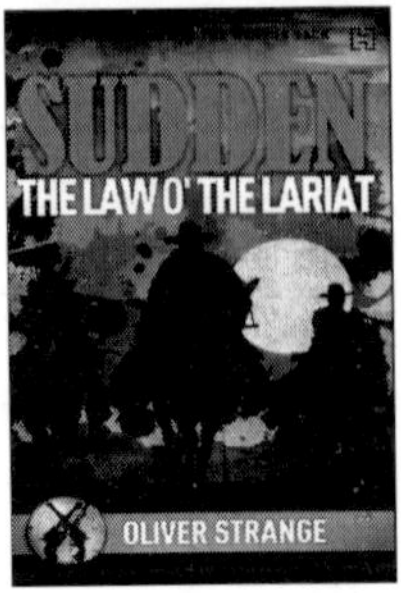


The classic Sudden series by Olive Strange is now back. Available at you bookseller or on order.